ISLAND GIRL

OTHER BONNIE INDERMILL MYSTERIES BY CAROLE BERRY

Good Night, Sweet Prince
The Year of the Monkey
The Letter of the Law

ISLAND

CAROLE · BERRY

GIRL

ST. MARTIN'S PRESS NEW YORK

Design by Judith A. Stagnitto

Library of Congress Cataloging-in-Publication Data

Berry, Carole.
    Island girl / Carole Berry.
        p.   cm.
    "A Thomas Dunne book."
    ISBN 0-312-06381-4
    I. Title.
PS3552.E743I8   1991
813'.54—dc20   91-19987
                                                   CIP

First Edition: December 1991
10 9 8 7 6 5 4 3 2 1

TO MY MOTHER

ISLAND GIRL

PROLOGUE

*The job pays next to nothing but the white sand beach is
a mile long, the water is turquoise, you work no more
than four or five easy hours a day and get all the lobster
you can eat and all the rum punch you can drink. And
the sunshine goes on and on and on. I hope you say yes.
What more could you ask?*

What more? There are a few things, actually, but nothing a job
will ever supply. I reread my friend Marilyn's express mail letter.
For several months she had been teaching aerobics and dance
classes at a resort in the Bahamas. Now she wanted to take a
vacation (a vacation from a vacation?) for two weeks. The
Flamingo Cove Hotel needed a reliable replacement. Immediately. Marilyn, no stranger to the ups and downs of my career,
had thought of me.

As I read, my neighbor across the hall launched body, soul and
straining vocal cords into another attack on Madame Butterfly.
This neighbor's an opera singer, when she works. Mostly she
practices.

As for my work, it consisted of whatever my temp agency could
come up with. The day before I'd been placed in the back office
of a glitzy midtown retailer. The back office was unsullied by glitz
or, for that matter, windows, laughter, coffee breaks or personal
phone calls. Before that there had been a couple law firms, a
grindingly dull stint at a brokerage, an . . .

But why continue this litany of tedium? The truth is, I'd recently been through something more upsetting than job problems and noisy neighbors. I'll make it short and . . . no, there is no way to make it sweet. My longtime boyfriend and I had broken up. I won't bore you with the details. Blame it on that catchall, incompatibility. I hear he's already seeing someone new. A struggling actress. May she struggle forever.

Outside my apartment a sleet storm raged. The long-range forecast for New York City was "wet and cold." I was being offered sunshine and turquoise water.

Marilyn's title was assistant fitness counselor. Should I try for another notch in my assistant's belt? I've been an assistant office manager, assistant database manager, assistant fundraiser.

A glass-shattering howl came from downstairs. Poor Butterfly. The sleet changed direction, smashing into the window behind me. My gray cat, Moses, scooted for cover under the sofa.

The phone rang. It was a counselor from my temp agency. Seems this insurance company in the East Forty's had these file cabinets they hadn't looked through in years. . . .

Assistant fitness counselor. And the sunshine goes on and on and on.

ONE

THE GETAWAY

My flight got in at a little after ten A.M. The temperature on New Providence Island was seventy-five degrees and the sky sunny. As I walked across the runway a soft breeze embraced me, a warm "hello" from the tropics. I passed through customs with no problem, and was on my way to the waiting area to check on my connecting flight when, from behind me, I heard a shout:

"BonBon! Yo! BonBon!"

The voice was straight out of a New York City gutter. It stopped me cold.

My name is Bonnie. It's a perfectly good name, but there are times when I wish my birth hadn't thrown my parents into such a giddy mood. I can't understand it. Ordinarily, they are not giddy people. If they had stayed true to form, I would have a name that means business at the top of a resume: Elizabeth, maybe, or Margaret. I'm not complaining—Bonnie isn't all that bad—but I have no intention of falling any further off the name-sobriety wagon. Nobody calls me BonBon.

His name was Sonny. Sonny! That's one to be reckoned with, isn't it? He had been one of my seatmates on the plane. By the time the pilot told us to look out the window at the Carolina Outer Banks, Sonny had antagonized half the people in coach class. I'd managed to ignore him through most of the flight, but at some point, I'd made the careless mistake of introducing myself.

Fists clenched, I turned. Sonny, an eyepopper in a white shirt with red dots, had just cleared customs.

"My name is . . ."

Sonny's bellow drowned me out.

"You get the heroin through customs okay?"

Friends who hear this story always howl when I get to that line. It *was* funny, I suppose, but at the time, my sense of humor was vacationing on another island. I dropped my two suitcases and stood, speechless. Around me people stopped to stare. At the edge of my vision I saw a uniformed policeman take a step my way.

"Just kidding," Sonny called to the man. "It's a joke. Get it, buddy? You're supposed to laugh."

The policeman did not laugh, but he did stop moving toward me.

Sonny sauntered up, grinning like an idiot.

"You should see your face, Bonnie! I never saw anyone turn so pale so fast. Look at her, Cindy."

Cindy was Sonny's new wife. She was small and delicate looking, with clear pale skin and black hair pulled into one long, old-fashioned braid. She was wearing a white dress with yellow trim, and looked absolutely angelic. She didn't look as if she belonged with Sonny.

Sonny was short and muscular. Beneath the bad dream of a shirt—please don't think I peeked; his buttons were open down the front—was a gold medallion, the beginnings of a beer belly, and enough matted black hair to . . . to . . . well, if I ever want to make a gorilla suit, I'll know where to find the fixings.

Cindy plucked timidly at one of her husband's sleeves. "That wasn't very nice, Sonny."

"Gimme a break! Look at her, Cindy! Now she's turning red." He made a grab for my arm. "Come on, Bonnie. Cindy and me have some time to kill before our flight. Let's all go have a drink.

4

I've been down here lots of times before. I know where there's a bar open. . . ."

My shock had worn off. "No thanks. It's a little early for me." I picked up my two suitcases. As I walked away, Sonny said, "Jeez. Can't take a joke, can she?"

I had time to kill, too, before my Inter-Bahamas flight to Flamingo Island, but I didn't want to kill it anywhere that Sonny might happen to wander. At the far side of the waiting room, I spotted my temporary safe house.

The sign over the door read ISLAND GIRL RESORT WEAR. In the window, on a mannequin, was this ravishing bathing suit. Black and red, with the legs cut high and the top cut low. I wanted that suit. And I could wear it, too! One good thing had happened when my love life fell apart—I'd lost ten pounds.

I spent about thirty seconds eyeing that mannequin. Then I walked in and asked the clerk if she had my size.

Of course she did. They usually do. She had a pretty tropical print shirt, too. And there was this darling coverup that matched the bathing suit, and . . .

Twenty minutes after I walked into the shop, I was standing in front of the smiling clerk—my, but she had a dazzling smile— with a hundred and fifteen dollars worth of resort wear piled on the counter between us.

I handed the woman my credit card. Still smiling, she plugged some numbers into a machine. Then, right before my eyes, the sunshine in her smile faded. She shoved the credit card back across the counter.

"The machine says your credit card is not good."

"Really? I guess my payment hasn't reached them yet."

Actually, guesswork had nothing to do with it. My payment hadn't reached them yet because I hadn't mailed it.

"Couldn't you just . . . " I began.

She shook her head, all business. There was an announcement over the airport loudspeaker:

"This is the first call for Inter-Bahamas flight to Flamingo Island. Passengers proceed to gate six."

I watched in dismay as the clerk began refolding the bright bathing suit. I was in a tropical paradise for ten days, and I was going to be forced to strut my newly slenderized stuff on the beach in a rump-sprung blue suit that didn't deserve me. I dug through my purse into my meager supply of traveler's checks and signed three of them. The woman's mile-wide smile returned.

Gate six was at the far end of the airport, and the single engine prop plane way out on the field. By the time I got there the engine was already making sputtering noises.

"You're going to Flamingo Cove by yourself, miss?" the copilot asked as he helped me into the plane. "I hear they're having a Couples Getaway Package this week. Two meals for the price of one and that sort of thing."

I glanced around the twelve-passenger compartment. Most of my fellow passengers were couples. Most of them were young, too. There were couples nuzzling, whispering, holding hands, doing the usual couple things.

"I'm not part of the package," I said to the man. "I'm part of the packaging."

And then I cringed. There they were at the back of the plane: Sonny and Cindy.

It hadn't occurred to me that they might be going to Flamingo Island. It was far off the beaten track, and from what I'd seen of Sonny, he belonged smack in the middle of the beaten track. They were almost surely going to the Flamingo Cove Hotel. Apart from a fishing camp on the other side of the island, Flamingo Cove was it.

Cindy looked up from her magazine and smiled in recognition. I was glad to see that whatever Sonny had done in the airport had knocked him out. He dozed, slack-jawed.

The copilot helped me slide my bags onto a tiny overhead rack. I wasn't the only uncoupled passenger on the plane. A native woman with a yellow bandanna around her head sat near the front. When I took the window seat behind her, she looked over the back of her seat.

"It's okay if you're not part of a couple. You're a pretty girl.

You'll find a sweetheart on the island." She tilted her head. "Maybe I've got a sweetheart for you. There's a fellow I know. . . ."

I smiled at the woman. "No, thanks. I'm not looking for any sweethearts right now."

"What will *we* find on Flamingo Island?" asked the female half of a young couple across from her. "What's there to do there? Any discos?"

"Flamingo Island is quiet," the copilot said. "If you want discos you should stay here in Nassau."

The native woman nodded in agreement. "You get drinkin', dancin', party boats in Nassau. On Flamingo Island you get quiet beaches, nature walks . . ."

"Nature walks," the young man groaned. "This could be a mistake."

A moment later, just before the copilot slid the door shut, a big black dog bounded on board. From the look and the smell of him, monthly trips to the groomer were not part of his routine. The man who followed him was big and black-haired, too. He sported cutoff jeans, at least a day's worth of beard, and the red-veined eyes of a man with a hangover. He was probably not much older than I am, but he had a hard-used look about him.

"Sit, Beast," he shouted at the dog.

The dog rampaged down the short isle, sniffing passengers and luggage and generally sticking his nose where it didn't belong.

The dog's owner slid into the seat next to me.

"Can't do a thing with that animal. Same thing every time he flies. I'm Charlie O'Dell."

"Bonnie Indermill."

He held out his hand and I took it. His skin against mine felt rough, almost raw.

The plane's sputtering engine coughed and died. It coughed again. There was laughter from the cockpit. The dog ambled up and plopped his head on the lap of the female half of a fortyish couple. The woman, who was directly across the aisle from us, was impeccably dressed in starched white slacks and a blue blazer. Drawing back her head, she said, "Friendly, isn't it?"

"It's a he," Charlie said, grabbing the offending dog by the red kerchief around its neck. "I told you to sit, Beast," he bellowed. "He'll be quiet once we get moving," he told the woman. "Takeoff always gets him going."

The woman sniffed and flicked her fingers across the black hairs the dog had left on her white slacks.

The engine sputtered and died again. Generally I'm not too bad a flyer, but the next sputter brought a bone-shaking lurch and a few leaps down the runway. By the time we jerked to a stop, I had a white-knuckled grip on the armrest.

A man called out from behind me, "Hey, is this thing safe?"

"Safe as the rocking chair on your granny's porch," Charlie answered.

There was another sputter and then a roar as the engines caught. Seconds later we were climbing.

"Going for the Couples Getaway?" Charlie asked me once we were in the air.

I forced my fingers off the armrest and flexed them, trying to relax. "No. I'm working at Flamingo Cove for ten days, if the plane makes it."

"This plane should be your biggest problem." Leaning closer, he said softly. "Money. That's what you should be worrying about."

I gaped at this virtual stranger. I'd never even been in this country! How did he know? Had he spoken to the clerk in the boutique? Half an hour in the airport and my reputation was shot.

"What do you mean?"

"Rumor around the island is that most of the staff at the Cove is ready to walk. Colin Ledbetter—he and his wife run the place—couldn't meet the payroll last week. They're trying to attract a crowd with special deals like this week's package, but they aren't doing too well."

The hotel was paying me so little that whether they met the

payroll or not didn't make much difference. I gave an inner sigh, relieved that I wasn't already known in the Bahamas as a bad financial risk.

"Do you live on Flamingo Island?"

"Yup. I operate a dive operation and help with the boats at the fishing camp."

We hadn't been in the air long when Charlie nodded toward the window. "Over there, that's Flamingo Island."

It lay just ahead, a gold and green vision floating on a shimmering turquoise sea. This had to be an optical illusion. Could any water really be that color? As we drew nearer I saw that the gold was beach, endless deserted stretches of it. We flew over a flock of vivid pink flamingos flying in V-formation, and over pastel-colored houses that clustered near the water. A few small boats dotted the sea.

For me, it was love at first sight. By the time we approached the airport I was making plans. I was going to give up my apartment, sell my furniture, give away my winter clothes and burn my interview suits. I would pack my cat and some cutoff jeans and move to Flamingo Island. I might not be able to earn much of a living, but I wasn't earning much of a living in New York, either. If you're going to be poor, why not be poor in a nice place?

The plane dipped, then rose abruptly.

"Look at that," the prim woman on the aisle said. "Down there! Surely he's not trying to land this plane on that!"

"That" was a paved flat place about as long as my living room. There was no runway, no tower. There was a white bungalow next to the flat place.

We dipped again, and this time came in about a foot over the bungalow. I'm not kidding. If the plane's window had been open I could have reached out and grabbed a loose tile from the roof.

I clutched the bottom of my seat with sweaty palms. A thump, a bounce and a squeal and we were all thrown forward, straining against our seatbelts. The dog slid to the front of the cabin, claws scrambling desperately for a hold. The plane rocked back, the

9

engines quit. The copilot stuck his head into the cabin and smiled.

"Flamingo Island." He slid open the cabin door. Sunshine flooded through.

I started breathing again.

The air outside was warm and fresh, the breeze soft. Charlie and his dog climbed into an ancient jeep and waved goodbye. The native woman got into a dilapidated green car and drove off. I stood in the shade of the bungalow with the couples. Cindy smiled again but Sonny was pretending I wasn't there.

We had been waiting only a minute or two when the hotel's jitney clattered into sight. It was painted pale pink with bright rose trim. A construction paper sign hung crookedly from its side: COUPLES GETAWAY WEEK, FLAMINGO COVE.

We all stepped into the roadway.

"Look at that silly thing," said the prim woman. "Couldn't you simply die of embarrassment?"

"It will be all right," her husband said. He was tall and pale. Already he was applying a smear of sunblocker across his face.

The jitney bore down on us.

"Like hell it'll be all right!" someone yelled. We leaped out of the way en masse. Embarrassment? We had almost died of a hit and run.

As the vehicle flew past, the driver stuck his head out the window and shouted, "Sorry! No brakes!"

"No brakes? They actually expect us to ride . . ."

Sonny yawned and stretched. He rolled his shoulders and grunted. When he'd finished this ape routine, he said to the woman, "Why don't you lighten up, babe. You're on vacation."

"Babe" blinked and straightened her shoulders.

Cindy, that tiny, cute little thing with her black braid screaming out *innocent little darling*, plucked at her husband's hand. "Sonny . . ."

"Ease up, Cindy." He looked back at the woman. "Way I look at it, when I'm on vacation . . ."

The woman opened her mouth, but whatever response she

had ready was lost in the sputter of aging engine parts as the prop plane prepared to return to Nassau. She turned away from Sonny, a look of cold disgust on her face.

The pink jitney circled the runway, gradually slowing. It finally came to a stop at the bungalow. A second later the driver told us to climb aboard. Brakes or not, the jitney was ready for us.

The driver followed a paved road through the pretty little village of Woodestown, where pastel cottages snuggled among the palms and narrow paths led toward the sea.

"There's a place that has a band," someone called as we passed a tin-roofed shack at the edge of town. "Barnacle Bill's."

"Okay in the day," the driver said. "But if you go there at night, be careful."

The driver's helper chimed in. "You go anywhere at night, be careful. Last week out at Rocky Point two men with machetes robbed . . ."

I was sitting directly behind the driver. I saw him look at his helper and give a quick shake of his head. The message was unmistakable: "Shut up!" For the rest of the ride we heard no more about robberies.

Beyond the village the road was rougher, broken by stretches of rutted dirt. It wound along cliffs that abutted the ocean. The driver worked the emergency brake diligently. We left the shore and crossed a shaky wooden bridge. Beyond that there was a forest where the midday sun hardly penetrated the canopy of dark green. We moved onto a stretch of bumpy, sunny road winding around and over hilltops. There were few houses, no hotels. I saw nothing geared to the tourist trade. It was an unspoiled paradise, exactly what my beaten spirits needed.

When we reached the far end of the island, the road emerged from the forest and followed the shoreline of Flamingo Beach. Bright sun glinting off gentle waves, turquoise water lapping at the pale gold sand. It hadn't been an optical illusion after all. I could barely keep from jumping off the jitney, running across the sand and flinging myself, fully dressed, into what was undoubtedly the most beautiful water on earth.

I think my fellow passengers felt the same. As we bounced along, even the impeccable prim woman was too taken with the scenery to complain. She had an expensive-looking little camera, and snapped picture after picture. I'd brought a pair of binoculars, but no camera. I was already regretting that.

The Flamingo Cove Resort was at the southernmost end of the island. Far beyond any pretense of paved road, we came to a place where a few sunbathers dotted the beach. On the other side of the road, up a long flight of steps, were some white stucco buildings. There was a paved parking area, and a small sign with pink lettering: FLAMINGO COVE.

The driver switched off the noisy engine. Everything was suddenly quiet.

"It seems a little secluded," a young woman said softly.

It did. It also seemed a little run-down. Some of the shrubbery around the parking area screamed out for tender loving care. The concrete steps were chipped. At the top of the steps, a pink and white awning over what looked like a restaurant drooped alarmingly to one side.

One of the men put what we were all feeling into words. "Seems a little dumpy to me."

A front tire on the jitney chose that moment to give up the ghost. As we carried our bags up the steps, the air was hissing slowly out of it.

TWO

ONE BIG HAPPY FAMILY

The pretty black woman behind the reception desk was the slowest moving human I have ever seen. With the possible exception of the elderly man sweeping the lobby, that is. What he did with that broom was beyond slow motion. Almost at stop-frame speed.

It took forever to get the various couples registered and off to their rooms. As I waited, I read one of the hotel's brochures:

> There is something for everyone at beautiful Flamingo Cove. Swim and sun on our mile-long beach, or follow a scenic nature trail. A multitude of organized activities, from exercise classes to bridge lessons, are always in the offing. Enjoy a moonlight cruise. Learn to scuba dive at a coral reef. Try your luck at our exciting casino. Wander the streets of Woodestown, where stately Government House presides over the picturesque square. Experience the romance of the islands with dining and dancing under the stars at our Terrace Restaurant. You will find that at Flamingo Cove, the

owners and staff are one big, happy family, working together to make your visit unforgettable.

"H-e-lll-p y-ouuu, M-a-mmmmm?"

"I'm Bonnie Indermill."

The woman's head turned slowly to the reservation book. Her fingers inched down the page, dragging a pen.

"I'm not a guest. I'm here to work . . ."

Before my eyes she turned into a fireball. Her head jerked up. She slammed her hand on the book. The pen shot to the floor. The word she hissed at me came so fast, with such force I didn't catch it.

"Pardon me?"

The woman leaned across the reception desk, eyes blazing.

"Scab! You know what that word means." She glanced quickly left and right, then called to the man sweeping the lobby. "Mr. Ledbetter's bringin' in scabs."

I was appalled. Though I've never been part of an organized labor group, anyone who knows me knows that I have no reason to side with management. I explained to the woman that I was taking my friend Marilyn's place for the week, and that I knew nothing about any labor problems.

"Marilyn didn't tell you about us getting no pay this week? She didn't tell you staff's on slowdown?"

I shook my head.

"You be sure you go on slowdown too," the woman warned. "Nobody around here is moving fast until the paychecks come." She tossed a key across the desk at me. "You're in 212. Second floor, far back as you can go. You share with the Australian. Leslie. You ask her about the slowdown. She'll tell you."

I carried my bags down a palm-shaded path. The hotel was larger than it had looked from the beach. In addition to a two-story building that housed the casino downstairs and the restaurant on the upper floor, there were three three-story stucco buildings with guestrooms. When I finally reached the last of them, I was almost at the edge of the forest.

I climbed the steps to the second floor. An open walkway stretched the length of the building. The door to 212 was propped open. I tapped on the frame and walked in.

Even before I took in the two dressers, the two beds at opposite sides of the room, the door to the bathroom, the tiny kitchenette, the many stacks of paperback novels, I noticed the hair. It was rather wavy, very blond, and very, very long. There was so much of it that, at first, I thought it must be a wig, but it was growing from the scalp of a woman who was sprawled on her stomach across the bed nearer the door. Her hair hung over the edge of the bed and curled onto the floor. A girl of about sixteen was sitting on a corner of the bed, braiding it.

"Hello," I said.

"Hello," said a voice from under the gold tresses.

"I'm Bonnie, Marilyn's friend. Are you Leslie?"

She lifted her head lazily. "That's me. And this is my mate Neticia. She helps out in the main house, and babysits the Ledbetters' kid."

Neticia was slender as a waif, with brown skin and shy dark eyes. Barely looking up, she nodded my way.

Leslie motioned to a chest of drawers at the far side of the room. "I think Marilyn cleared out a couple drawers for you. Anything you want to hang you can put in the closet."

Easier said than done. For two women living on next to nothing in a place where you didn't need much, Marilyn and Leslie between them had stuffed that closet. Finally it was done, though—summer clothes ready for action in the closet and drawers, winter things stuffed in my suitcase. My last bit of unpacking was symbolic of leaving the cold, cold city behind. I put my parka into my carry-on bag, and dropped my apartment keys in after it.

"Won't be needing these for a while."

By that time the languorous Leslie was up, examining herself in a mirror over her chest of drawers. There was a lot of her to examine. I don't mean that she was overly large, or, for that matter, beautiful. The mass of gold hair framed a face that was

15

long and thin, with eyes set too close together. Her mouth was small, and her lips formed a strangely lewd little circle. On first glance, though, I *thought* Leslie was beautiful: I would learn that she had that effect on a lot of people.

From the neck down Leslie was—all I can think of is that boys' locker room favorite—stacked. She wore her pink shorts and her plain white shirt with pink stitching on the pocket—FLAMINGO COVE—tight enough to make that obvious.

"What do you think?" she asked, giving her hair a toss.

Neticia had woven some brilliant red and blue beads into the braided strands of Leslie's hair.

"Very pretty."

"The beads shine in the dark," Neticia said.

"Em . . . five dollars, you said?" Without waiting for an answer, Leslie reached across the bed for a straw handbag. Then she tilted her head.

"I've got a better idea, Neticia. My mum sent me this beautiful scarf, all the way from back home in Australia. Pure linen."

Hooking a toe into a drawer pull, Leslie opened the dresser. "Look down there in the bottom drawer. There. That's it. Now, isn't that pretty?"

The scarf looked more like cotton than linen. On it was embroidered a big *L*. From the look of Neticia's faded cotton dress, it seemed that she might want five dollars more than a kerchief with someone else's initial on it, but it wasn't my business.

"Thank you," the girl said to Leslie. Folding the scarf carefully, she started toward the door.

"You're not going to forget now, are you?" Leslie said to her. "Remember what you promised."

I wasn't paying Neticia much attention, but she hesitated in the door so long that I glanced at her. "I'll go now," she said finally. She left, closing the screen quietly behind her.

As I put on light clothes, I asked Leslie about the employee slowdown. She dismissed it with a flick of her hand.

16

"Colin will come up with the payroll, don't you worry. He'll get it from his wife. Her parents have quite a bit."

I had started to slide my luggage under the second bed. My carry-on bag was new, a flowered tapestry print I'd paid too much for but loved.

"That's awfully good looking," Leslie said, nodding at the bag. "I'm going away later this afternoon. You wouldn't mind if I borrowed it, would you? I'll have it back by noon tomorrow."

"Actually, it's new and I'd like to keep it for myself for a while. If you want to borrow my bigger one, though . . ."

She gave my ancient tan bag a critical look—the stain on the side from when the bottle of ouzo broke on a Greek island, the torn strap from the top of that bus in Mexico . . . If that bag could talk, wouldn't it have some stories to tell.

"No, thanks."

The woman clearly had no feel for history.

I picked a book from the top of a stack near my bed. It was a romance, and so was the next one, and the one under that.

"You have a lot of books."

"Sometimes there's not much to do around here. TV reception's awful, so Marilyn and I read. Borrow any of them you want."

I thumbed through one of the books, feeling a little guilty about the suitcase.

"That nurse one's especially good," Leslie said. "The one on the table there. She ends up with the chief of surgery. He's an aristocrat to the bargain. Bit of good luck for a working girl, I'd say."

Colin Ledbetter had a way with words. It probably didn't hurt that he was tall and trim and tan, with brown wavy hair falling across his forehead. Or that his smile had a touch of sweet-little-boy innocence about it. I guessed his age as early thirties—no wrinkles, sags, bulges, bald spots. His accent was English, but nicely softened by the islands. As he spoke, the five angry

17

employees who were lined up in front of his desk were losing their resolve.

His office was at the side of the Ledbetters' house. I stood at the back of it, and marveled as he worked on the woman who had greeted me so angrily at the reception desk, the man from maintenance, the two maids and the chef. They had started out firm, with clenched-fisted demands and much shaking of their heads. Colin countered, with a performance that almost brought tears to my eyes.

"You people . . . I think of you as my family. All of us here at Flamingo Cove, we're in this together. One big family. We've been a happy family, and I'm hoping we can stay that way." He raised his hands at his sides, palms up. "You all know that a tour group from Chicago is due in tomorrow morning. And the special people from Texas are coming, too," he added, his voice softening to almost a whisper. "This is our chance, my friends."

A shaking head was stilled, a clenched fist loosened.

"If Flamingo Cove makes it, we all make it. You and you . . ." He looked from one to the next. He looked at me. He had truly devastating light blue eyes. ". . . and you," he said, his gaze softening my heart. "And your families, too. We all profit from this."

His dear, woebegone expression grew dearer, more woebegone. "I think about that little girl of ours, how much she loves all of you. If we had to leave the island . . ."

The rest of the clenched fists now hung slack. The uprising was stilled. A moment later the employees trooped from the office, rich on promises of raises, profit sharing, and a better life for all. I was not surprised to see the reception clerk dab a fingertip to her teary eye.

Colin Ledbetter sank into the tatty chair behind his desk, closed his eyes and groaned.

"Mr. Ledbetter?"

Those baby blues didn't look quite so dear when he opened them and stared at me. "You're still here? Who are you? What do you want?"

18

"My name's Bonnie Indermill. I'm replacing Marilyn. . . ."

He rolled his eyes and stood. "For a minute there I thought you were the new woman in accounts receivable at the utility company. So you're Bonnie, eh?"

There was a wicker sofa under his window, covered with a flowered print cotton. Pink and red roses. Sinking onto it, he looked me up and down and smiled and said, "Indeed, you are rather bonny."

Ordinarily I would have laughed at a line like that. And from a married man! I wouldn't have gotten a line like that from any man in New York. But I wasn't in New York. I was in a magic place where the water was turquoise and the air was sweet. In that office where a ceiling fan spun slowly overhead and the gentle turquoise sea lapped at the shore outside the window, Colin's line took on a funny charm. I felt my face growing warm under his gaze.

Oh, he was a smoothie. He'd done it to the angry employees and then, hardly missing a beat, he did it to me.

He reached to what looked like a small teak cabinet, and opened the door. It was a small refrigerator. From inside he took a bottle of champagne.

"You'll find some glasses in the cabinet. There, Bonnie. Behind you."

I took two champagne glasses from the cabinet. Was this customary? Did all new employees have a glass of champagne with the boss? Or was I about to experience something from one of Leslie's romance novels: Poor girl from seedy neighborhood meets landowner from paradise. . . .

"Take one of those flowers from the vase on my desk," he instructed.

"What a nice reception."

"And a tray from the cabinet. Make sure you get a clean one."

"A tray? Oh, that's not . . ."

"There are some newlyweds in the honeymoon suite on the ocean side. Sonny and Cindy . . . something. Be a pal and take this to them. Compliments of Flamingo Cove, tell them.

That's an expensive room they're in." He winked at me. "Make nice-nice for them, Bonnie. That's a good girl. When you've done, you can find my wife Eleanor around somewhere. She'll have plenty for you to do."

My face was warm all right. It burned as I carried the tray all the way from the Ledbetters' house to the front of the hotel where the rooms faced the water. Five minutes on the job, and I'd been only a word or two away from making a fool of myself.

And now, even worse, I had to make nice-nice for Sonny. What a disgusting predicament! I was worrying it over—could I get away with leaving the tray at the door, knocking and running? Or did I have to actually hand it to him? I suppose I was distracted. I made it to the third floor fine, but as I rounded a corner, my foot hit a chair leg. The tray tilted and—whoops! One of the glasses crashed on the cement floor.

I looked down at the shattered glass for a second, then kicked the pieces under the chair. I didn't dare go back for another champagne glass. Sonny and Cindy would have to make do with one.

Over the next week and a half, I would see more than enough of Sonny's and Cindy's honeymoon suite. All I had seen that afternoon was more than enough of Sonny. He answered the door in black undershorts. I pushed the tray at him.

"Compliments of Flamingo Cove."

He hulked there for a second. "Is this part of the two-for-one package? Two people on one glass?"

"No. It's an old island tradition," I said. "If newlyweds share a glass on their honeymoon, they'll share a long, happy life together."

He grunted. As he closed the door, Cindy was saying, "That's the most adorable thing I've ever heard."

The sun beat down on Eleanor Ledbetter's dark jaw-length hair, exposing greying roots. She squinted at the schedule in her hand. When she widened her eyes, the lines around them showed in sharp relief against her tan. I mention these things not because

20

Eleanor looked as if she was ready for the boneyard, but because she looked a dozen years older than her husband.

She was a bit taller than my 5′4″, and thin with small, sharp features. Looking at her and listening to her, I got the feeling that she was running on nervous energy.

"Early Bird Aerobics on the beach from nine-thirty to ten-fifteen A.M.," she said. "Dancercize from three to three-thirty on the big terrace below the restaurant. The spot's not really suitable, but it's all we've got until we expand. Water ballet at about twelve-thirty. . . ."

She looked up from the schedule. "You do swim well enough to handle that?"

I nodded an enthusiastic yes. To be honest, I hadn't the vaguest idea what was involved with water ballet.

"Good," Eleanor said, pushing a stray strand of hair off her face. "For the next couple days you can take that over for me. You're expected to help out wherever we're short of staff. Any objections?"

"No."

"With the Texans here I'm going to have more than enough work."

The Texans again. Colin had mentioned them, too. I might have asked about them, but my mind was taken up with visions of water ballet.

I swim well enough to do laps, but that's about it. For me, the notion is pretty silly. There is ballet, and there is water. The two have nothing to do with each other. Ever hear of water waltz? Or water tango? Of course not. So why water ballet?

"What," I asked, "is included in your water ballet routine?"

She flicked her fingers. "The usual."

I nodded sagely. "Ah!"

A girl of about seven came skipping around the corner.

"Mommy, have you seen Neticia? She said she was going to take me to the beach but I can't find her."

Eleanor shook her head. "She's probably off at the nesting area again. Bonnie, this is my daughter, Beth. Her school is on

21

vacation for the next week. Unfortunately, the girl who is supposed to be watching her spends half her time running around in the forest."

"Hi, Beth," I said.

"Hi."

Eleanor bent to tie the little girl's sneaker. The child had her mother's dark hair and small features. She was cute, but I couldn't see the least resemblance to the god-like Colin Ledbetter.

". . . and oh yes," Eleanor said as she straightened. "We have a rather young crowd to consider, don't we? It's this couples promotion." She looked at me. "What do you suggest we do about them?"

I didn't know what she was talking about. My expression must have shown it.

"Young marrieds," she explained. "A few honeymoon couples, even. Not the crowd we generally have. Afternoon bridge on the terrace isn't going to do." She wrinkled her forehead. "I wish we'd bought the jet skis. If things go well with the Texans, we will have more than enough money for that kind of thing, but for now . . ." She paused. "We do have motor scooters, and there is that parasailing device. Colin's boat is surely fast enough to get it in the air."

"Oh, Mommy," Beth squealed. "Please please set up the parasailing. Please. I want to do it."

"We'll see. You go along now and find Neticia."

She watched her daughter run off, then turned back to me. "Are you familiar with parasailing, Bonnie? Perhaps you could help out."

Parasailing! That took care of my problems with the water ballet classes! Marooned a hundred feet in the air, anchored to a boat by a slender rope? There are things I won't do, even for a job. I shook my head violently. "I've never parasailed."

She grimaced. "Maybe I can get Leslie to help them with it. That girl will do anything. If she can't get free, though, we'll deal with it. We've never set it up, but there must be instructions. It's stored in the beach shack."

22

She made a note to herself, then continued down her list. "Most nights you're free. There's a kitchenette in your room, but you can take your meals with the staff or simply grab something out of the kitchen. You also have off Sunday afternoon and Wednesday. Any other time you want off, ask. I'll try to work something out." She gave me a quick glance. "I wouldn't advise going into town on your own. There has been a bit of a . . . crime wave. Robberies, that sort of thing."

I nodded.

"Tomorrow we're doing Monte Carlo Night at the casino. Marilyn said you had been on stage." Backing away, she looked me over closely. "One of the housekeepers sews. I'll get her to put some costumes together. A few feathers and what-have-you. You and Leslie can do a can-can dance. Nothing too naughty," she cautioned. "Night after that we've planned a dive. Then there's an all-you-can-eat Island Buffet two nights later. I'll need your help there. Calypso on the Beach is next Saturday. You do the limbo? No? There's nothing to it. I'll show you."

My head was spinning. Hadn't Marilyn's letter mentioned a lot of free time? It sounded as if over the next ten days I'd have just enough time to pound my body into shape and make a spectacle of myself. And if Leslie couldn't do the parasailing, I'd get a once-in-a-lifetime opportunity to frighten myself to death and perhaps send a young couple parasailing into oblivion.

"But look at this," Eleanor said, glancing at her watch. "It's almost three. We better get to the patio for Dancercize. The record player is already set up. Your ladies will be waiting. By the way," she added, "the Dancercize class attracts some of the older ladies. We try to accommodate them by slowing things down. Some of them have been coming here for years."

Eleanor led me around the main building. When we reached the steps leading up to the big terrace, she stopped abruptly.

"Bonnie," she said, her voice low. "I mentioned that there have been robberies on the island. Most of them have occurred in town, but one night last week two of our guests wandered out beyond Rocky Point . . ."

23

"I heard something about that."

"From whom?" she snapped. "Not from one of our staff members, I hope. They've been told not to talk about it."

"No," I said, covering up for the jitney driver's lapse. "It was in a newspaper in the airport."

"A newspaper!" Eleanor shook her head. "I wonder how they got hold of that. In any event, I don't want you to say anything to the guests about crime on the island, but you might try to steer them away from moonlight walks on deserted beaches. And if you should hear any of them say they want to go into town at night, try to divert them. Offer them tango lessons or play bridge with them. You do play bridge?"

"Well, actually . . ."

"That's fine. Let's get to Dancercize, now. We don't want to keep our ladies waiting."

THREE

DANCERCIZE AND RUM DRINKS

My ladies were waiting. There were seven of them sitting around tables at the Terrace Restaurant. As Eleanor had told me, the group was made up almost entirely of older women.

"This is Bonnie," Eleanor said to the group. "She's going to be leading your classes for a while."

"But why, Eleanor?" a heavyset white-haired matron asked. "I was perfectly happy with the class you conducted yesterday."

"Thank you, Mrs. Hussy, but Bonnie is an experienced dancer, and since I'm going to be busy with the . . ."

Mrs. Hussy—the name could not have been further from the truth—waved a disparaging hand. "I know. I know. The Texans."

Grumbling under her breath, the older woman rose from her chair and, with the rest of the group, descended the flight of steps to the flagstone patio.

The setting—it looked out over the beach—was quite beautiful, but far from ideal for an exercise class. Half of my students were shaded by the overhanging restaurant awning, the other half stood in the sun. The flagstone surface was chipped and uneven. A portable record player had been set up on a bench. As the turntable spun, the warped record on it undulated.

25

I glanced at the label, then looked at Eleanor. "Mendelssohn?"

"Marilyn was using some disco music," Eleanor explained, "but the ladies found it too tiring. Yesterday I tried Mendelssohn and we did fine. I hope that's all right with you."

"It is a vast improvement over that frantic nonsense," said Mrs. Hussy. "Much better."

"I'll watch for a few minutes, just to be sure you're okay with this," Eleanor said.

If there was one thing I was going to be okay with at Flamingo Cove, it was Dancercize. I've taught scores of tap classes, sometimes even supported myself doing it. Not necessarily in the way I would like to be supported, but well enough.

"Let's begin, ladies." I nodded to Eleanor and she placed the needle on the record.

Before leaving New York City, I had modified a couple of my tap routines. I had not modified them to the point where I was happy doing them to waltz time, but what the heck—it beat typing and filing.

"Step left three-four. Point toe five-six. Watch-my-feet seven-and-eight. To the right, to the left. Arms up. Up, Mrs. Hussy."

My ladies and I attracted an audience. The people at the Terrace Restaurant moved to the railing so they could stare down at us. The woman from the registration desk wandered by and stood with an idle handyman. She had said slowdown, and I certainly had. We were a funny sight, I'm sure. I was grinning broadly when I glanced at Eleanor Ledbetter. She beamed back approvingly and gave me the thumbs-up sign. The next time I looked, Eleanor had gone.

Mrs. Hussy moved like the great glacier, grumbling all the while. Thirty minutes later when I ended the class I hadn't broken into a sweat. Mrs. Hussy was done in.

"I'm simply dead," she said as she dragged herself up the steps to the restaurant. A little alarmed, I followed.

"Are you all right?"

"Of course I'm all right." She collapsed into a chair under the awning and called to the bartender. "Bring me one of those rum things of yours."

"Bahama Mama?"

"The pink one."

"That was very invigorating, my dear," she said to me. "You'll do fine. I may even lose an ounce or two."

The bartender put a tall drink on the table in front of Mrs. Hussy. It was pink. A piece of bright red fruit floated on its top. It looked strange and wonderful. Mrs. Hussy noticed how I was staring.

"Won't you join me for one of these . . . rum things? They're quite refreshing."

"I don't think while I'm working . . ."

"Nonsense! I've often had drinks with staff. Bring Bonnie one of these," she told the bartender.

I asked Mrs. Hussy how long she had been coming to Flamingo Cove.

"This is my eighteenth year. Back then, Eleanor and her first husband ran the place. Eleanor's a native, you know."

Mrs. Hussy told me that Eleanor's parents now lived in Nassau, but that they had once been involved with Flamingo Cove, too. I learned that owners had come and gone over the years.

"I've seen four or five of them myself. I don't suppose it's ever been much of a money-maker. Last year Eleanor was back. With Colin. God only knows where they got the financing. I'm sure he doesn't have a dime. Eleanor's family has some, but I can't imagine them wanting to sink much more into this place."

I looked out over the beach. "It's a wonderful location. I hope they make it pay this time."

"They will if Colin has anything to say about it. He'll sell out to the Texans in an instant."

The bartender set my Bahama Mama in front of me. I took a few sips.

"Wow! Delicious! Who are these Texans everyone's talking about?"

"Some dreadful consortium of hotel and casino operators that want to turn this"—a grand sweep of her arm—"into another Las Vegas, or, God help us, Nassau. I stopped going to Nassau eighteen years ago because it became so tawdry. A mass of fleshpots, one end of the island to the other. I only hope Eleanor doesn't allow her gigolo to tart Flamingo Cove up too badly."

Gigolo? That darling Colin? I took another sip of my rum drink. "You can't be talking about her husband?"

Mrs. Hussy gave a mighty snort. "I'm sure your eyes are better than mine, Bonnie. You must have noticed that he's young enough to be her son. Eleanor can't seem to strike a balance there. Her first husband was old enough to be her father. Died of a heart attack."

"Well, Colin seems very nice to me," I said.

Two other women from my class slid into empty chairs at our table. Over the next few days I came to think of this pair as Mrs. Hussy's dinghies. They were both tiny, or at least they seemed that way in comparison to Mrs. Hussy, and they sort of bobbed in her wake. One had pink hair and the other blue.

"You're talking about Colin? Not a penny to his name, from what I hear," the pink-haired lady said. "Failed at running a hotel in Freeport, and another one in Jamaica."

"You could say that Flamingo Cove is his 'last resort,' " said Mrs. Hussy.

"Perhaps his time has come," the blue-haired lady offered kindly. "Third time's charmed, they say."

"*They* often don't know what they're talking about." Mrs. Hussy gestured toward the bulletin board near the bar. A waiter was pinning up a poster. "His time has come to turn this place into a shambles. Just look at that! Monte Carlo Night! And can-can dancers! With what the Ledbetters can pay, I doubt if they're direct from Paris."

I didn't say a word.

"It is a shame," agreed one of the others. "It's always been quiet here. You could count on it. No riffraff, no loud youngsters."

"You should have seen the group that arrived on the jitney

today. Most of them barely out of their teens! We'll be lucky to get any sleep at all this week."

"If that gigolo has his way, the place will be crawling with youngsters," said Mrs. Hussy.

"I met the couples on the jitney," I said. "I doubt that you'll have any problems with them."

"Harumph! Before you know it, there will be hordes of them. Eleanor told me they want to put in a disco and expand the casino. They'll be playing music on the beach and riding those noisy motorbikes and who knows what else."

Her friends nodded agreement. "I understand Bermuda has some lovely, quiet hotels."

"Bermuda's chilly! Might as well stay in Philadelphia if I'm going to freeze. Look! Look out at the driveway. It's already starting!"

I peered under the sagging pink and white awning just as two of the couples from the jitney roared past on motorbikes. The second couple missed the turn onto the road and ended up with their bike mired in sand. Boisterous shouts reached us on the terrace.

"I expect we'll see them in that flying apparatus next thing. The one Eleanor told us about."

"Perhaps they'll all fly away."

"Wait until they start attracting *singles*," Mrs. Hussy grumbled. "Students on spring break."

"I don't think you have to be concerned about hordes of rowdy singles," I said. "The airport could barely accommodate the little plane I came in on."

"You think those Texans couldn't build an airport? Mow down the forest, that's what they'll do. Drive off all the wild flamingos. What do they care? We'll have jumbo jets roaring overhead night and day."

Three heads nodded in unison.

"We saw some flamingos on our flight in," I said. "Are there many?"

"More than there were fifty years ago, from what I understand.

Between hungry natives and the airplanes, the flock here had disappeared."

"The airplanes?"

"During World War II, fighter pilots used to fly over the nesting birds to set them in flight. Out of boredom, I suppose. Eventually most of the birds left."

"They're coming back, though," the blue-haired lady said. "There's a scientist here now, studying them. He was here last year as well."

Mrs. Hussy thumped her glass on the table. "Scientist? He spends more time studying the blackjack table than he does the birds."

The dinghies nodded in agreement, then turned back to the "tarting up" of Flamingo Cove.

"Eleanor mentioned they were looking for another name for the hotel," one of them said. "The Texans aren't so taken with calling it Flamingo Cove."

"You know the kind of names they *are* taken with," said Mrs. Hussy. "Couples, and Eden. Years ago Paradise Island was called Hog Island. Perfectly good name, Hog Island."

"On Jamaica there's even one called Hedonism," the pink-haired woman tittered.

I said good-bye, to the ladies. As I walked away, I heard Mrs. Hussy say, "Hedonism? Why not name the place Fornication and be done with it!" .

"More to the point," one of her friends agreed.

Neticia, Leslie and Beth were in the room when I got there. Beth was sprawled on Leslie's bed. Neticia and Leslie were standing in the kitchenette. I had the impression those two were whispering about something, but their conversation stopped abruptly when I pushed through the screen door. I glanced from one to the other. Neticia averted her eyes, but Leslie seemed unfazed by my entrance.

She was dressed in skintight white slacks. An old black duffel bag had been thrown on the bed. Strolling to the closet, she took out a sundress. "I suppose I could bring this," she said absently.

"Do you know anything about parasailing?" I asked.

"Sure. Tried it a few times at Cable Beach. A bit boring, once you're up in the air."

I dug my new tapestry bag from under my bed and emptied the contents onto a chair. "You might as well use this. It does look better than your bag."

"You changed your mind. Thanks." She immediately began transferring her things to my overnighter. "Isn't this pretty, Neticia? I'll make a better impression."

"Are you going to be going somewhere nice?" I asked Leslie. To be honest, I didn't care where she was going. I just wanted to be sure she'd be back in time to deal with the parasailing equipment.

"Nice? You might say that. There's this man I've been seeing. Things could turn out quite nice. Eh, Neticia? Look at you," she said to the girl. "You worry like an old lady. I'll take care of everything. I promise you."

She glanced at the clock on the dresser. "Oh, no! I've been dawdling and I've missed the bus into town. I'm too pressed for time to wait an hour for the next one. I'll see if I can get one of the guys to take me in the jitney."

"You can't," Beth said. "Colin says no one can go in the jitney until they fix the brakes and the flat tire."

Leslie picked up the carry-on bag. "Oh, well. I'll just go out there and take my chances in the cold, cold world. Someone's bound to come along," she added with a toss of her hair.

Neticia glanced at Beth. "I'll be back in a few minutes." She followed Leslie from the apartment.

Beth watched them leave, a dejected look on her face.

"Neticia has been having a secret with Leslie," she said. "All yesterday and today. She won't tell me what it is. Anyway, I don't like Leslie anymore. She probably won't bring back your suitcase, you know."

"Really?"

The little girl nodded solemnly. "One time I loaned her five

31

dollars from my allowance and I had to tell my mommy to make her give it back. Mommy says she's an . . ." The girl wrinkled her brow in concentration. "Opportunity."

I smiled. "You mean opportunist?"

Beth nodded. "Anyway, she probably won't bring back your bag."

"Neticia seems to like her."

"That's 'cause Leslie has lots of clothes and she gave Neticia some of them. They weren't very nice, though."

I yawned and collapsed on my bed. The sun and the Bahama Mama had done me in.

Beth flopped back down with a sigh. "I have to stay here until Neticia gets back. Want me to tell you what's in the forest behind this building?"

"Instead of doing that, why don't you tell me about your mom's water ballet class."

"That's just dumb. They kick a lot, and swing their arms. In the forest there are spirits hanging upside down from the trees. They have red eyes. Neticia calls them devil eyes. If they don't like you they turn your head around backwards so you can't breathe."

These devil eyes sounded a lot like something I'd come across in a Bahamas guidebook.

"On Andros Island there's a myth about creatures who hang from trees. Is Neticia from Andros, by any chance?"

"Yes, she is. But on Andros the creatures aren't real. Here they are. I saw them. And there's this man who stays in the forest sometimes. He has a devil eye, too. He knows my mommy and Colin. He comes here sometimes. Sometimes he even visits my house, but Neticia said we better not look at him. Whenever he's here we hide."

"Why?"

"Neticia says if we look at him, we could die."

FOUR

A MULTITUDE
OF ACTIVITIES

Flamingo Cove Beach stretched endlessly, unbroken for more than a mile by anything but the occasional oasis of palm trees. What a great place to teach a class. My Early Bird Aerobics class—six of the younger women and one man—was a lively one. They followed the routine I'd filched from an exercise videotape with little trouble and lots of enthusiasm. We spent forty-five minutes kicking up the sand, our laughter breaking the sound of waves lapping against the shore. As we exercised, Colin Ledbetter jogged past and waved. While he was in sight, all my ladies tightened those abdominals and stood straighter. I did too. When you're in the presence of physical perfection, you don't want that tummy sticking out.

When we finished, my class thanked me and I left the beach feeling a glow of self-satisfaction. A great way to start my first full day at Flamingo Cove.

After that things went steadily downhill.

The problems began with my nature walk.

I'd showered and was sitting on the open walkway behind our room letting the sun dry my hair. I'd begun one of Leslie's romances—the nurse one. I had almost two hours to myself before Water Ballet. Not a bad way to spend a working morning: some exercise, then a few hours to catch my breath and lose myself in the dilemmas of the beautiful, dedicated nurse, suffering silently under aloof and patrician (not to mention darkly handsome and filthy rich) Doctor . . .

"Come on, Neticia. Hurry before mommy sees us."

The little girl's voice came from the path below. I peeked over the railing in time to see Beth and Neticia running up the trail that led into the woods. Beth was in the lead. Neticia trotted along behind, a big straw bag dangling from her shoulder.

"We're going to get in trouble," Neticia said as they disappeared into the trees.

I didn't think they would get into trouble. Mischief, maybe, but not trouble. Mild curiosity made me follow them. I was going to be living near those woods for a while. I might as well find out what I could about the devil eyes that inhabited them. Leaving the poor nurse mid-page—she was fighting back tears—I grabbed my binoculars from a drawer and hurried after the girls.

As I've said, the woods began only a few yards from the hotel's back rooms. The trail was wide at its start, the underbrush thin from the continuous trampling of feet. A small sign, almost hidden by vines, read NATURE TRAIL.

For the first quarter mile or so the trail ran parallel to the road. I could see the beach rental shack where Leslie worked and hear the voices of people on the beach. The jitney passed within yards of me, creating its usual uproar. Then, beyond the place called Rocky Point, the road veered right and hugged the shore. The path I was on turned left into the deep forest. At once, it became harder to follow. I could see that people used the trail to get to the beach, but seldom went further on it.

Eleanor had told me to keep the guests from wandering away by themselves. And what was I doing? Wandering away by myself, into the land where devil eyes hung upside down from trees and men put machetes to tourists' sunburned throats.

To the south I could hear the sea crashing into Rocky Point. I peered through the underbrush. It was thicker now, but twenty steps south and I'd be standing on the road. I had almost decided to give this up and go back when the girls' laughter called to me from the other direction. I took the trail north, leaving the sea and the road behind.

I walked easily for twenty or thirty feet before the path narrowed and abruptly turned into a track less than a foot wide. I was forced to place one foot carefully ahead of the other. A few more steps and snakelike tendrils grabbed at my ankles while taller bushes brushed my arms.

I was freeing my leg from a vine when Beth's high-pitched scream broke through the cries of birds and the shifting of tree limbs in the breeze. I raced ahead.

The tree cover was much denser now. Huge multi-rooted mangrove trees fought for light. Vines thick as my calves ran up and around tree trunks and wound over the moist earth. There were pale green ferns and darker green philodendron-like plants, grown to monstrous size. As I moved down the trail I was dwarfed by them.

The air was growing heavy with moisture. Small brown lizards scurried up tree trunks at my approach. At a low spot in the trail, my sneakers squished through a half-inch of mud. I had fought my way past a mass of damp leaves when I saw the two bright red eyes staring down at me. Red eyes in a hideous little monkey face.

I didn't scream, but the rate of my heartbeat must have doubled. For a moment I almost turned and ran. The forest was closing in around me, and this horrible red-eyed thing was hanging upside down from a tree limb, staring straight into my eyes. I forced myself to stare back. It didn't move. I walked toward it, closer until I was almost directly under the limb. . . .

"Damn!" I whispered.

The devil eye was a toy monkey, doctored up with some paint and tufts of hair. That was what frightened the girls. Letting out a relieved breath, I continued down the overgrown trail.

I hadn't gone far when the insects struck. They seemed to arrive with a rush of tropical heat. At once I was moist and sticky and slapping bugs from every part of my body. Hundreds of almost invisible flying creatures swarmed around my face until I felt as if I were peering through a buzzing, frenzied veil.

I lost track of time and direction. The only thing that kept me moving forward was the sound of the girls' voices and, once, a glimpse of them through a cover of leaves and vines. If I'd felt like laughing, I would have laughed at myself for bringing binoculars to a place where I couldn't see more than two feet in front of me.

At a bend in the trail I passed another red-eyed devil. This one had fangs. A stream of red paint trailed from its malicious mouth. It didn't frighten me; I was too involved with slapping away the horrible flying things that were trying to get to my neck.

Deep in the forest with no bug repellent. I gave myself one more turn in the trail, a few dozen steps. If I hadn't found anything more interesting than dimestore monkey dolls and bugs and overgrown houseplants, I was turning back.

That last dozen steps did it. A chorus of gabbling birds filled the air. Unexpectedly the green world that had wrapped itself around me opened and let through a cone of late morning sun. I had crossed the narrow section of the island.

Another step or two and I saw the dots of pink way in the distance. I raised my binoculars to my eyes. There were the flamingos, all sizes and every hue of pink. I couldn't even guess at how many there were. At least a few thousand. They were nested in a marshy area that lay between the forest and the shore. Even with the binoculars I couldn't see the chicks, but I did make out the foot-high mounds of mud the adults build for nests.

At that juncture the trail led away from the nesting area. When I had watched the birds for a few minutes, I moved on.

I walked into the research site before I realized it was there. One minute I was among the trees, and the next in a clearing with a neat shelter—a combination wood and canvas structure—in its center.

"Hello?" I called.

The girls came scurrying from behind the shelter, looking guilty as anything.

"What are you doing here?" Beth asked, indignant.

"Taking a walk. What about you?"

"We came to look at the chicks. You want to see?"

Neticia stayed behind while I followed Beth to a chicken-wire cage at the back of the shelter. "They're orphans," she said, pointing to the two pale grey bits of fluff in the cage.

"They're very cute, but you shouldn't be here, you know. Your mom . . ."

We both heard the car motor. Beth's belligerent look changed to one of pure panic as the motor quieted.

"It's him! Don't look at him, Bonnie!"

"You!" a man shouted. "Stealing again? Come here! I want to talk to you."

Neticia came racing around the shelter, her straw bag swinging wildly. A lanky young man was in hot pursuit. He stopped when he caught sight of Beth and me.

"Hello, Beth. Didn't your Mom and Colin tell you not to come out here any more?"

The suddenly shy child clutched at my legs and stared at the ground. Neticia scuttled around and hid behind me. I didn't half blame her. The man was crimson-faced with anger. Other than that I didn't see anything particularly devil-like about him. He had longish brown hair which lay in damp tufts on his head, and a neat beard. He was wearing a T-shirt with a silly cartoon bird on it. Over the bird were the letters WAO, and under it, in little print, the words ORNITHOLOGISTS DO IT WITH FANTASTIC BIRDS.

"We were taking a walk," I said. "I didn't realize where we were. . . ."

"He doesn't own this place," Beth mumbled into my leg. "It belongs to the government."

Ignoring her, I said. "I'm Bonnie Indermill. I'm working at Flamingo Cove."

I had extended my hand. He reached for it. "Paul Tyndall. I'm doing research out here. What is it you do at Flamingo Cove?"

For a moment I was thrown off balance. It looked as if he was speaking to someone standing behind me. I glanced over my right shoulder. There was no one there. I looked back at him and realized that his left eye didn't focus properly. This was Neticia's "devil eye."

"I'm the temporary fitness coordinator."

Tyndall had withdrawn his hand, clearly offended by my backward glance.

"Fitness coordinator? Then you have no business here, do you? I'd appreciate it if you and the girls would stay out of this area. The work I'm doing is sensitive, and mobs of resort people tramping around here . . ."

The three of us hardly constituted a mob, but why argue. I gave him a polite enough good-bye and herded Beth out of the clearing. Neticia was already waiting on the path. She walked ahead of us for a good while. Beth, still nervous about her close call with the devil eye, stayed at my side until we were well away from him.

When did I realize the girls were up to something? Maybe when I looked down at Beth and saw the huge smirking grin spreading across her face. Or maybe when I caught Neticia looking at Beth and winking. Quiet, serious Neticia? Winking?

We had pushed through the thickest part of the woods and were almost at the south end of the trail when Beth trotted ahead and caught up with her babysitter. Both of them ran on for a moment, then glanced back at me. I could tell they were gauging the time it would take me to catch up with them. When I dawdled, the two girls turned away and huddled together to examine something. Tyndall had accused Neticia of stealing. I hurried up the path.

"What do you have there?"

They were about to run ahead again when the thing they had stolen fluttered from Neticia's straw bag and landed on the ground between us.

It was a fuzzy grey flamingo chick, no more than six inches

tall. I stared at the little creature in dismay. It blinked back at me, more curious than frightened.

"You took a chick! Is that what he meant when he said you'd been stealing? Shame on you both. You have to take it back."

"It's an orphan," Beth said defiantly. "It's as much ours as it is his. Anyway, my mom said there used to be flamingos at the hotel and I don't see why . . ."

Neticia picked up the chick and gently tucked it into her bag. "We'll take good care of it. We already built a cage."

She wasn't pleading with me. Her mind was made up, and I had no control over her. I decided to leave things to a higher authority.

"All right, but you have to tell Beth's mom what you've done and let her decide about the chick."

The girls looked at each other, dubious.

"Will you do that? If you don't, I will."

Beth opened her mouth, ready to argue, but I suppose my determined glare stopped her. Finally both girls nodded reluctantly.

We were in sight of the hotel when Beth said, "Did you see his devil eye? I'll bet you believe me now."

"It's not a devil eye. One of his eyes doesn't focus."

Neticia was a few feet ahead of us. She turned in her tracks. "He is a devil. Once he said he was going to put a spell on me if I didn't stay away. And he puts devil eyes on the elves in the trees, too. Didn't you see them?"

"They're toy monkeys. He painted them to scare you."

She pursed her lips and shook her head stubbornly. She and Beth trotted ahead the rest of the way back to the hotel.

The walk had been unexpectedly trying. I'd been bug-bitten and scolded. Now I needed that rest that I'd passed up earlier. Too late. The sun was high overhead. I had just enough time to smear on the number fifteen sunblocker and change into my swimsuit for water ballet.

I'd put together a silly little routine. Beth's explanation—"They kick a lot"—didn't offer much guidance. My dance experience has been in two things—tap and chorus line work. I had discarded the possibility of anything based on tap dance immediately. There was simply no way I could translate shuffle-shuffle-heel-toe to water. Chorus work, though, might do. We could link arms and . . . kick a lot.

I had fallen asleep the night before envisioning a waterlogged business of leg-kicking and arm-waving. If I'd known Cindy was going to bring the class to a standstill with her attempted suicide, I wouldn't have bothered.

I found her waiting when I got to the pool at twelve-thirty. There were other women there, but Cindy was standing apart from them. Though she was in the shade of the awning that covered the poolside snack bar, she was wearing sunglasses and a big straw hat.

A couple of the women had been in my earlier classes. I introduced myself to the others. There were six in water ballet, enough to link arms across the pool. I thought everything would be okay.

"Okay, ladies. Let's get in the water."

There were the usual squeals, mine included, as the cool water hit our skin. I asked them to link arms in a little more than four feet of water.

"Join arms?" one was asking.

"This should be interesting," said an older woman who had been in my Dancercize class. She nodded toward the woman next to her. "You'll have to hold yourself up, dear. I can scarcely manage myself."

It was Cindy. By one of those nasty bits of fate, she had ended up dead center in the line. She hung between her two companions, her head drooping and her black hair falling over her face. Straightening a little, she pushed her hair away from her eyes.

Cindy had been crying, long and hard. I'd done it often enough, and recently enough, to know it when I see it. Her eyes were red, her lids swollen. It had nothing to do with chemicals in the pool, either.

Although I meant to address the entire group when I asked, "Are you all ready?" I looked at Cindy.

She gave a brief nod, taking a shuddering deep breath at the same time.

"All right then. We're going to start with some simple synchronized kicks. Left knees up and to the right."

"Like the Rockettes! What fun!"

Five left knees went up, and one right knee. Cindy's! She banged knees with the woman beside her.

"Left knee, Cindy," I said.

From the corner of my eye I caught a glimpse of someone passing on the second floor terrace. It was Colin Ledbetter. He waved and paused to watch us. For just a second I became flustered and forgot what I'd been saying to my class. When I recovered, maybe my voice was a little pitched, but honestly, I wasn't haranguing poor Cindy.

"Left, Cindy. Got it?"

Her left knee had barely cleared the water. I could see her chin quiver.

"Yes," she said, her voice choked. The women on either side turned to look at her.

"Cindy? Are you feeling . . . ?" I began.

She broke loose from her companions. "I can't do anything right, can I," she sobbed. "Nothing I do is good enough. I just want to die, that's all."

With that, she flung herself face first into the water directly in front of me. I took her by the shoulders and pulled her upright.

"I wish I'd never been born," she howled. "I'm a failure at everything. Let me go! I'm going to kill myself!"

Not in my very first water ballet class she wasn't. She tried to sink beneath the surface. I held tight and we struggled in front of my gaping class. This went on for a few seconds, until Cindy's body went limp and she collapsed on me, a soggy, sobbing rag doll.

"I'm sorry, ladies," I said as I dragged her from the pool. "Water ballet is canceled for the day."

41

FIVE

THE ROMANCE
OF THE ISLANDS

I got Cindy to her building and up the stairs without too much trouble. At the door to the honeymoon suite she balked.

"I don't want to go in there," she said, her voice quaking.

"Is Sonny in the room?"

That question unleashed a flood of tears. Sharing a room with Sonny would have had me sobbing, too, but she had married him. It took her forever to choke out that Sonny was "gone," and come up with the room key.

The honeymoon suite was lovely, all white wicker and tropical flowers on chintz. The honeymooners shared the wide walkway with the other guests, but they also had a private balcony off the side of the building. On it, a little table and two chairs faced west so the newlyweds could enjoy spectacular sunsets over the ocean.

When I was about Cindy's age, I had a honeymoon. I had it in a Motel 6 off an interstate truck route. The next time I have a honeymoon—assuming I have another one—I'd like to have it in a wicker and chintz suite.

But let's be honest: When you get down to the nitty-gritty, it isn't the decor that makes or breaks a wedding night.

To be blunt about it, the macho Sonny's manly equipment had failed to rise to the occasion. This non-happening had happened the afternoon before, some time after I brought the champagne. Cindy's pathetic story came out in gulps and sobs.

"I disappointed Sonny. That's what he said. Because I wasn't enough of a woman. That's why he couldn't . . ." She looked at me through her tears. Her chin quivered. "You know."

"I know, but I don't think that's the way things actually happen. I'll bet he was nervous. . . ."

"No," she blubbered. "He wasn't nervous. Sonny's had lots of experience. I was the one who was nervous. Sonny always said he wouldn't marry a woman who wasn't a virgin. And I saved myself."

"For *Sonny?*" Talk about pearls before swine.

She wiped a tear from her eye. "My family is old-fashioned. I would have saved myself for my husband no matter who I married. My parents . . . they gave us such a beautiful wedding." She blinked watery eyes at me. "You'll see. My mom's sending polaroids down by express mail. We had more than three hundred guests. Can you imagine what everyone is going to say?"

I put an arm around her shoulder. "I doubt if everybody will find out, Cindy. Sonny had a case of wedding-night jitters. Next time things will be fine."

"I hope you're right. My daddy gave Sonny a job in his company because we were getting married. Daddy still doesn't think Sonny's good enough for me."

As she cried she stared down at the floor where a filmy white nightgown lay crumpled.

"My godmother bought me that for a shower gift. I went in the bathroom and put it on. I was nervous but I thought . . . well, you know. I thought everything was supposed to be so romantic. When I came out Sonny had finished the champagne. He grabbed at me and one of my straps tore and I got more nervous and then . . . and then he got mad and then . . . " A fresh wave of sobs shook her body. " . . . and then everything went wrong. Everything."

"Sonny drank *all* the champagne?" I asked, offering her a tissue. "That was a big bottle."

"I had a few sips. He drank the rest of it. I thought it was so sweet, that custom about drinking from one glass. Sonny said it was cornball. He drank out of a bathroom glass."

"That bottle of champagne could be the problem. Liquor is a depressant. It can depress *everything*."

My gut feeling was that the champagne was only one of Sonny's problems, but my words seemed to make Cindy feel better. She blew her nose.

"Do you think so? Sonny always says he can handle his liquor."

I shrugged.

"You think he'll come back? I've been worried sick all night."

For the first time, I was alarmed. I had assumed Sonny had collapsed into a drunken stupor in the room. "You mean he's been gone all night?"

My question got her sobbing again, so hard she could barely speak.

"Right after we couldn't . . . you know. He said he was going to find a real woman. He never came back. After it was dark I went out looking for him. I looked at the casino and in the bar and out on the beach. Sonny doesn't like anybody to know but he's not a very good swimmer. I'm worried he might have gone for a swim and drowned. I'd rather he was with another woman."

"Cindy, I'll bet he fell asleep in a beach chair and now he's embarrassed to show his face. I'm going to go find Colin or Eleanor and tell them about this. . . ."

She clutched my arm. "No, please don't do that."

I shook my head. "I've got to tell someone that a guest is missing." And though I didn't tell Cindy about the rash of robberies, I was concerned. Sonny wasn't exactly a silver-tongued orator. What if he said the wrong thing to a guy with a machete?

"Sonny has a lot of pride. Please don't tell anyone that he couldn't . . ."

The door to the suite opened with a crash.

45

"He couldn't what? Huh? I heard you through the window. What kind of lies are you telling her about me?"

Sonny looked a wreck. His oily hair hung matted over his forehead. All the buttons on his Hawaiian print shirt had been ripped off. The shirt hung open. Red welts ran down his chest.

He strode into the room and stood glowering, first at Cindy and then at me.

"Lemme tell you something. . . . It's a lot of lies, what she's been saying. A man can't get what he needs from his wife, he goes and gets it somewhere else. And I got plenty of it last night from a great big beautiful blonde."

Cindy's sobs rose in pitch, threatening to turn into shrieks.

"You want to come with me?" I asked.

She shook her head.

I slipped past Sonny and through the open door as fast as I could. When I'd closed the door behind me, I stood by the open window for a moment. If he got violent with her, I was going to scream for help.

"I'm beat," I heard him say. "Got to get some sleep. Gimme a break, Cindy. Stop crying. You want to talk, we'll talk later."

There are worse things in life than being single, and Cindy was discovering that the hard way. I felt sorry for her, but there was nothing I could do. I walked away from the open window thinking that my part in the marriage of Sonny and Cindy was over.

Eleanor Ledbetter got to me before I got to her. Unfortunately, the brief saga of the water ballet had also gotten to her.

I had descended the steps from the honeymoon suite, intending to find Eleanor and give her a rundown of that morning's activities, when she rounded the corner. She wore a toothy smile—the one all the guests got. Spotting me, she glanced right and left. No guests were in sight. The teeth disappeared behind drawn lips.

"I'd like a word with you, Bonnie." She nodded to the side. "Over here."

"Over here," was behind the row of bushes that hid a bank of

46

trash cans. I followed Eleanor past the cans, through the buzzing insects that surrounded them. She made sure we were well hidden before saying a word.

"I heard about the incident at water ballet," she began. "Colin mentioned he saw you and one of the guests—scuffling. I asked someone who was in the class. She said there was a problem with the woman in the honeymoon suite. Something about her left knee."

"I planned to tell you. Cindy had a problem with Sonny. She was upset when she got to class. . . ."

Eleanor held the flat of her hand to my face, stopping me mid-sentence.

"And you thought a sharp word from you would take care of that?"

"No. That's not . . ."

"You are not a sergeant major drilling a troop of recruits, Bonnie. These are paying guests you're dealing with. And what they're paying for isn't merely the beach and the sun. They come here looking for rejuvenation of body and *mind*, not some grueling New York City gymnasium workout. To send a guest sobbing from water ballet class in inexcusable."

My heart started pounding so fast I didn't trust myself to speak. I was convinced that her next words were going to be "You're fired!" Twenty-four hours earlier I'd fantacized about starving happily in this tropical paradise. Faced with the chance of doing just that, my mind went into a grueling New York City workout. My nonrefundable return flight ticket wouldn't be valid for nine more days and my credit card was no good. All that stood between me and the street, or the beach, were two fifty-dollar traveler's checks.

Hot tears of anger burned my eyes. The evil God of the workplace had followed me to paradise. I started to say something. I got as far as, "But . . ."

Again Eleanor's hand stopped me.

"I like you and I'm sorry to speak to you this way." She had lowered her voice. Her expression softened a little. She placed her hand on my shoulder. I was not comforted.

"I realize you come from a different environment. But you have to understand that your job isn't to get the guests into shape. Perhaps later, if we should decide to take the direction of a full-blown spa, that might be the case. And if that happens, you and I might talk about your taking a permanent position. For now, however, you are here to make the guests feel good about themselves. I don't care if they weigh three hundred pounds and haven't moved off their bottoms in ten years. Believe me, the muscle that writes the checks is still in tip-top condition. If you say 'Left knee up' and they lift their elbow to the sky, your job is to say, 'Very good!' Is that clear?"

I could only nod.

". . . like an animal, I tell you, Bonnie. He all but ripped my nightgown off of my body. I had packed my red one, with the open panel down the sides. . . ."

And another nightgown bites the dust in the tropics. From what Leslie said, hers had bitten it with a lot more success than Cindy's. I adjusted the wet towel on my forehead so that the cooler side rested against my throbbing temples, and wished that my talkative roommate would go away.

". . . smothering me in kisses, all the way from my toes to . . ."

She sounded like a jacket blurb from one of the romance novels. I could almost smell the aftershave of the man she called her "special mate." Their night had been a feast of orgasms, a sweating, moaning triumph for the proverbial "other woman."

"Oh, we have our problems to work out," she said. "He's got this sort of entanglement he's got to get free of before we can tell anybody about us. The woman—well, it involves his job and you know how that is. But once he's rid of her . . ." She lowered her voice. "He's unbelievably romantic. He kept repeating, 'You're the woman for me, Leslie. The only one.' Got so swept away making love he crushed me right against the headboard, he did. It was padded, mind you," she assured me. "Purple and black print. Wallpaper, too. What do you think, Bonnie? Marvelous, huh?"

"Purple and black wallpaper? Did you find that around here?"

"I'm talking about *him*. But the hotel! Well, it was simply the most gorgeous hotel imaginable. Dazzling beyond belief!"

Leslie knew her way around the shadowy nooks of an illicit affair—lots of superlatives, but no names, no places.

"I've had my problems with men," she said. "Always had more than enough, mind you, but never found quite the right one until now."

"Uh huh."

"I've played it smart for once. Didn't go chasing him around. Bided my time until—"

There was a pause in her chatter. I prayed that was the end of it, that she would shut up and get out of the room and let me get a nap before Dancercize class.

"—until I knew I had him. There's a lot of ways to skin a cat, and I've learned most of them. Sometimes you have to let a man sweat a bit, don't you? He's not the type I've usually gone for. He's more sensitive, and intelligent, too. Oh! Thanks for the loan of the overnighter. I'll put your things back in it and slide it under your bed. All right with you?"

"Uh huh."

There followed the rattle of keys and the shuffling of clothing, the snap of a latch, a bit of shoving under the foot of my bed.

"Bit of a headache, have you?"

"A bit."

"You try taking a bath? Always relaxes me. I brought a couple new books back. If you want . . ."

"I'll be okay once I get some sleep."

My hint went right by Leslie. "My special mate and I took a bubblebath after midnight." She gave a lewd giggle. "He's a real sensualist. Purple and black, it was."

I tossed the towel aside and sat up. "What was?"

"The bathroom. You should have seen it. Bubble bath must

have had coloring in it. Pink bubbles everywhere. I'd tell you who he is, but I'm not sure whether I should just yet."

"What do you think I'll do? Leak it to the press?"

She giggled again, but she still wouldn't tell me.

So far as I was interested in thinking about it, I thought that the noxious Sonny was the other half of this bubble-brained duo. She was his great big beautiful blonde, he was her sensitive, intelligent male. He had the better end of the deal. I couldn't imagine many things more disgusting than a pink midnight bubblebath with Sonny. I'd sooner plop myself down in a hog wallow.

"By the way, Bonnie. I ran into Eleanor on my way in."

The very mention of my boss's name made me fall back on my pillow and groan. Leslie never noticed.

"She wants us to try on our costumes for tonight. Monte Carlo Night at the casino, you know. She said we should see her at the house after Dancercize. About four-thirty. Right? I'll meet you there."

"What is it we're supposed to do tonight?"

Leslie shrugged. "Make 'nice-nice' to the guests," she said sarcastically. "It's something Eleanor and Colin cooked up to impress the Texans. They came in, you know. About a half-hour ago. And there's a tour group from Chicago in, too."

She was in front of the mirror. "We're both to wear our hair up tonight. French-looking. That's what Eleanor wants. Said we should try to look as much alike as we can. Suppose that means I'll have to hide these beads Neticia braided in. Oh, and Eleanor said you're to teach me a short dance routine. Let's keep it simple, okay?"

I watched her play with her hair. "Have you ever done any professional dancing?"

"No, but it can't be so hard, can it? Tell you the truth, Bonnie, right now I feel like I can handle anything. Ever feel like that? Like you're on a roll and it's only a matter of time before you have everything you ever dreamed of?"

"Not lately."

"Don't you worry. Your time will come. Mine has. Of course, I helped it along. I can be awfully persuasive." She flashed me a big smile, then turned back to the mirror.

She was wearing one of the plain staff blouses, but as I've said, Leslie wore hers a size too small. "Wish they didn't make us wear these ugly shirts. It's Eleanor's idea, I'm sure." She unfastened an extra button, then straightened her shoulders and examined her ample cleavage.

"Yes indeed." She gave her reflection a self-satisfied nod. "Things are going to work out dandy. How can I miss? You might say I've got hold of the key to paradise."

The key to paradise. That had to have come right out of one of her books. As I got into my Dancercize clothes those silly words ran through my mind. Leslie was fooling herself if she thought that opening an extra button on her shirt was going to open up the door to paradise.

SIX

MONTE CARLO NIGHT

Leslie stared down, first at my feet in their beige low-heeled sandals, and then at hers in white sling-backs.

"There's our only problem, Bonnie. Shoes. Otherwise we could be twins. Do you think we look French?"

A flamingo feather tucked behind my ear slipped, tickling my neck. I didn't know how French we looked, but Leslie and I sure looked like birds of a pink feather.

Eleanor had come up with a couple of old black bathing suits. They must have been her castoffs; they were tight beyond belief. Onto these suits rows of hot-pink ruffles—worn curtains, I think—had been sewn. Strategically placed flamingo feathers completed our outfits.

I cracked the kitchen door a few inches. As the reggae band wound down at the end of their set, Eleanor Ledbetter joined the musicians on the small stage.

"Ladies and gentlemen, if I could have your attention for a moment, please."

The two dozen or so customers at the Flamingo Terrace Grill looked up from their dinners.

"Tonight is Monte Carlo Night at the casino. Complimentary rum punch. We hope to see all of you there. To get you in the mood, I'd like to present our very own Flamingo Cove can-can girls in 'Can-Can Reggae.' ''

I nodded to Leslie. She gave a final push to the push-up bra built into her bathing suit.

"One more push," I whispered, "and you'll be dancing topless."

"Nothing too naughty, girls," she said in a mocking imitation of Eleanor. We were giggling when we heard our cue, the roll of the steel drum.

Once a hoofer, always a hoofer. A familiar surge of adrenalin rushed through me. I pushed through the swinging door. Leslie was behind, hands on my waist. We pranced knees high across the floor, pink curtains bouncing and flamingo feathers swaying.

Eleanor had set a spotlight in front of the stage, so bright it made my eyes water. I couldn't see our audience well, but I could see well enough to make out the startled looks on the faces of Mrs. Hussy and her friends at the table nearest the stage. One of them said something. I couldn't make it out.

"Harumph!"

Leslie and I linked arms. Guitars joined the steel drum in "Can-Can Reggae." We began our routine.

Can-Can Reggae was far from the low point of my dance career. Highlights of past performances include a shuffle-shuffle-kick-slide across a stage dressed as a begonia (San Francisco Flower Show) and an appearance as a tube of tapping toothpaste in a short-lived television commercial. I have a secret dread that one may someday surface on late-night television. A consoling thought lingered at the back of my mind as Leslie and I did our act: I don't have to live with this one. After next week, none of these people will ever see me again.

It wasn't that any one thing was especially awful. The problem was, everything was a little awful. The costumes I've described. Then there was the well known can-can theme, done with a relaxed island beat and punctuated by the echoing booms of the drum. And the routine itself—step for step the same as I'd planned for my disastrous water ballet class—"left knee, right knee, kick, kick."

Leslie had picked up the simple routine without too much trouble. She wasn't terribly graceful, but she had the advantage of fearlessness. No butterflies for her.

High kick left, high kick right. It was almost over. The guitarist was plunking those final chords. Leslie and I turned our backs to the audience, bent at the waist and flipped up the back of our ruffles.

From between my knees I saw the burst of a camera flash.

"Gotcha, BonBon! Right in the buns."

The audience—even Mrs. Hussy's table—was clapping and cheering. We took our bows, elated. They had liked us. I've done that sort of thing often enough to know.

Eleanor stepped onto the stage. "Aren't they terrific? And they'll be helping out at the casino. I hope you'll all join us there. Remember, drinks on the house."

The casino was a shoddy place, even more neglected than the rest of the hotel. The carpets were worn, the pink print wallpaper— flamingos, what else?—faded to the point that the birds looked anemic. The odor of stale cigarette smoke hung in the air. A chandelier in the middle of the ceiling lit the place. The crystals were dirty, though, and the light barely reached the far corners of the casino. To the shabby atmosphere, add Sonny's presence. It's no wonder I didn't like it in there.

"Waddya mean, Goombay Smash's not included in the free drinks?"

"I'm sorry," I said, though I wasn't in the least, "but you can have a rum punch."

"Yeah, sure," he grumbled. "Drinks are free, as long as we drink the cheap stuff."

I shoved the tray of glasses at Sonny. "Take it or leave it, stupid," was on the tip of my tongue. I controlled myself only because Colin and one of the Texans were in earshot near the roulette table.

Sonny glared down at my tray, then jutted his chin over my shoulder. "She'll give me what I want."

He pushed past me and made his way over to Leslie. She was all smiles, tickled no end to be passing out cheap drinks in a down-at-the-heels casino. She giggled flirtatiously when Sonny grabbed at one of her flamingo feathers. The next thing I knew he had backed her into a slot machine. She didn't seem to mind.

I was watching surreptitiously when there was a whisper in my ear.

"She's the one!"

"Hi, Cindy! She's the one what?"

Cindy was wearing a bright pink sundress with thin straps. Her black braid was wrapped around her head. She looked darling, except for her red-rimmed eyes.

"Leslie's the one Sonny spent the night with. I'm sure of it."

"Did he tell you that?"

"No, but you heard what he said. A great big beautiful blonde. She's your roommate, isn't she, Bonnie?"

I nodded.

"Someone told me that yesterday they saw her walking down the drive with a suitcase. She didn't spend the night here, did she?"

"I don't remember."

"It was just last night!"

"I don't keep track of Leslie."

"Look at them now, Bonnie. Look what they're doing."

I took another quick look. Sonny had pulled a feather from Leslie's costume and was trying to shove it under her ruffles. Leslie had her hand on his chest, pushing him away. She wasn't pushing hard, though, and she was laughing the whole time.

"She's such a tramp. I could kill her."

If Leslie deserved killing, Sonny deserved worse, but I didn't point that out. "Things aren't any better?"

"No. What do you think I should do, Bonnie?"

"Get a good lawyer."

Cindy blinked, and I realized I shouldn't have said that. She wasn't old enough to be cynical about these things.

"I'm sorry. That was a bad joke."

"But maybe you're right. Should I call my dad?"

The sudden appearance of Mrs. Hussy rescued me from the unsuitable role of marriage counselor. The older woman had dressed for Monte Carlo night, in blue silk and pearls.

"Quite enjoyable, your can-can." She took one of the rum punches from my tray. "I didn't think I'd enjoy it, but it was surprisingly entertaining."

I thanked her. We were chatting about the performance when Cindy interrupted.

"Oh . . . Look at them now. He's pushing the feather down the top of her suit. I can't stand this." She rushed away, her eyes shiny with tears.

"Ay, yes. The situation in the honeymoon suite." Mrs. Hussy shot a killing look at Sonny and Leslie. "So many men, so little time." She *was* old enough to be a cynic.

"You heard about it?"

"A word or two. This is a small, quiet place, my dear. There's usually not much to talk about. Now, though, between the honeymooners and the Texans—there they are now. Just look at Eleanor and Colin, acting as if they're escorting royalty."

The Texans consisted of two men—one thin, one fat—and one woman, a size-two wife who went with the size-fifty Texan. *How* she went with him is something I shudder to think about.

"Look at the face on that woman," Mrs. Hussy said. "It's been lifted so many times her ears almost meet at the top of her head."

I laughed out loud. "That's the meanest thing I've ever heard anyone say."

"Oh, I'm capable of saying much meaner things."

We both watched as Colin and Eleanor escorted the Texans around the Casino. It didn't take long; there wasn't much to see.

"Too bad there isn't more business here tonight to impress them with. That young man—the one studying the flamingos—he should be here."

"I met him. Sort of," I added, remembering the way he ignored my outstretched hand. "So he likes to gamble."

"Addicted, if you ask me. Ran up such a debt that Colin has barred him from the place until he pays up."

Mrs. Hussy set her empty glass on my tray and took a full one. "Nightcap. See you tomorrow, my dear." She ambled away.

I spent the next few minutes passing out drinks. Eleanor, Colin and the Texans were on their way out of the Casino when Eleanor stepped aside and motioned to me and Leslie.

"Bonnie, I'd like you to stay here until closing time. Take care of the customers. Leslie, someone mentioned that they left a snorkel and fins outside the beach rental shop because you'd already locked up. Would you go down and put them away? And make sure you've locked the shutter. I noticed the latch doesn't hold. Double-check it, please."

Leslie and I nodded. Eleanor hurried away to catch up to the Texans. As soon as she was out of hearing we both started to complain.

"It will be hours before everyone's gone," I grumbled, looking around the smokey, noisy casino. "And I've got to stay here."

"You're lucky," Leslie whined. "I'm having such a good time. Sonny's such a scream! And here's Eleanor sending me off to the beach shack! She must have seen that I'm having fun." Leslie looked down at her breasts bulging from the black suit. "She's jealous, you know. Colin likes a pretty girl. Can't imagine why he married her."

A cigar-chomping man in a tight yellow shirt nudged himself between us and stared at our empty trays. "Any more of that rum punch around?"

"Leslie," I said, "Why don't I put away the beach equipment? You can stay here and get this gentleman a rum punch."

"What a great idea, Bonnie. The girl at the front desk will give you a key. You can drop it off on your way back to the room."

When I left the casino, Leslie was smiling broadly through a swirling cloud of cigar smoke.

I'd gotten the better part of the trade with Leslie, I was sure. The night was incredibly beautiful, with a sliver of moon in the star-filled sky. The fresh clean air felt good after the casino, and the sound of waves lapping against the shore eased the strains of the evening.

When I reached the beach, I took off my shoes and strolled through the sand. I hadn't yet been to the shack, though I had seen it from a distance. It stood among a cluster of palm trees at the far end of the hotel property. Beyond it the forest began, the same forest that circled the back of the hotel. As I neared the shack, I could hear nocturnal birds and insects calling through the trees.

The shack was closed up tight, the long shutter on the front which served as a counter when lowered, was raised. I gave it a tug. Sure enough, the latch inside gave an inch or two. I'd have to relatch it. The snorkel and flippers Eleanor had mentioned were in the sand next to the shack's wood door. Picking them up, I fitted the key into the rusty lock.

As I pushed the door open, a noise from nearby gave me a start. I spun. There was nothing in sight but the stretch of sand and the forest. Only the crack of a tree limb. Or else one of Neticia's red-eyed devils kicking up a fuss. Despite these consoling thoughts, I was spooked. If I hadn't had to latch the shutter, I probably would have tossed the flippers and snorkel through the door and left.

I stepped into the shack and felt along the wall for a light switch. There was none, so I propped the door open with the flippers. A dim light filtered through the opening.

After setting the snorkel on a shelf, I made my way to the front of the shack. A thin grey light showed around the wood shutter. I pushed at its top plank. It was held in place by simple slide bolts, but on one side the bolt wasn't connecting with the catch. I was stretching, struggling with it, when suddenly there was a sound somewhere behind me. Another tree limb? Or the tap of a shoe against concrete?

Could it be the men with machetes? A shiver of fear ran up my spine. I quickly turned. As I did, there was a scraping noise. And then the sound of the forest birds was gone and I couldn't hear the waves. There was nothing but darkness. The shack's door had been closed. The only light inside came through the top of the shutter.

There was the noise again. There was no mistaking it now. A footfall on the concrete floor. Someone was in there with me. Mute with terror, I tried to put something between myself and this person. I backed away and stumbled into a stack of beach towels. A shadow broke the light from the shutter.

He was on me, his hands around my neck choking off my breath. I was paralyzed with fear for a moment. Then I began to fight, my arms flailing frantically.

He was strong. He took both my hands in one of his. My legs shot out from under me as he pushed me to the floor. I fell among the towels. He followed me down, crushing me with his weight. His knee pressed into my chest, forcing the air from my lungs. With his free hand he grabbed my throat again. He let my hands go for just an instant. I reached to push him off me but then he pulled something over my head and the darkness was complete.

Gasping, I tore at the thing covering my face. It was heavy plastic, hot and terrible against my skin. He held it tight around my neck. I struggled futilely, collapsing deeper into the towels. I briefly wedged a hand under the plastic and air flowed into my lungs. He rolled hard onto my hand and once more pressed the plastic tight.

My strength was leaving me. "Oh, please don't kill me," I managed to whisper. That effort sucked away the last of my breath. For a moment everything was still and it seemed as if those words muffled by the hot plastic would be the last sound I would hear. Suddenly most of his weight lifted off me. I managed to push the plastic up and gasp.

This time he didn't stop me. Yanking the bag off, he grabbed my hair roughly, so that it fell from its pins. As he did this I took in air in huge gulps. When my breaths were finally regular, I lay still with my eyes pinched closed.

He had let go of my hair. His weight was off my chest now, but

I didn't know he had backed away from me until I heard him moving around the shack. Some time passed—I'm not sure how much—before I realized that the forest sounds had returned. I could hear the waves again. Carefully lifting my head, I opened my eyes and peered around the shack. The door was open again. The man had gone.

When I felt strong enough, I got to my feet and crept to the door. The beach outside looked deserted, but I didn't take any chances. I ran like hell for the Ledbetters' house.

"Kill you?" Eleanor shook her head as she topped off my glass of sherry. "I'm sure you're wrong about that. I grew up on Flamingo Island. There has never been random violence here. House breaking, that kind of thing, but we simply don't have the type of crime you find in the States."

"You're sure it was a man?" the police chief asked.

"I'm not sure of anything, but I think so. He—the person—was a lot stronger than I am. And taller, too."

"Well," Colin said. "The man was undoubtedly a thief. Probably one of the pair who robbed our guests out at Rocky Point last week. He could have been inside the shack. You opened the door and surprised him."

Sure, in the midst of stealing beach towels and flippers in a locked, pitch-dark shack. And for that he tried to smother me with a sheet of plastic. I shrugged, worn down. It was strange, but I felt as if the details of my attack had been taken away from me. A man trying to smother me had become a burglar surprised in the act.

Eleanor had still been with the Texans when I pounded on the Ledbetters' door. One look at my tearstained face and my torn can-can ruffles and Colin had sent Neticia looking for his wife. She'd come in a hurry. I don't have to tell you that she came without the Texans. This was one bit of the Flamingo Cove tour they missed out on.

Now Colin was standing in the middle of the living room with

61

the police chief, Roscoe Richards. He put his hand on Chief Richards' arm.

"Roscoe, my friend, you've got to do something about these crimes. You know as well as I do that the economy of this island depends on tourism."

Richards, a tall, ebony-skinned man who seemed to have a permanent mist of sweat on his forehead, nodded. "What we hear is they're coming in a motorboat from off island. Wave their machetes, rob the tourists and disappear back in their boat."

"I didn't hear a motorboat," I said.

The distressed lines in the chief's gaunt face deepened. "You were in the house when Miss Indermill got here," he said to Colin. "Do you remember hearing a boat?"

Colin shook his head. "They probably would have left the boat some distance from the resort. Maybe over by Rocky Point. It's easy to cut through the woods."

Eleanor nodded in agreement. Naturally. Maybe Leslie couldn't understand what Colin saw in Eleanor, but I could. And I could see what she saw in him. They were attached like Siamese twins when it came to preserving Flamingo Island's unsullied reputation.

"You can get out around Rocky Point if you take the right path through the forest," she said.

"Of course," agreed Colin. "Out there the forest reaches almost to the water." ·

"That may be where they left the boat." That was Eleanor.

Colin turned to the police chief. "After we go through the beach shack, you should have your men check that area."

"Yeah," I said. "Could be he dropped his machete there."

They either missed the sarcasm in my voice, or decided to ignore it.

When Colin had followed the police chief through the door, Eleanor asked if I was feeling better.

"You can stay here in the house tonight if you'd like," she added. "Otherwise I'll walk you to your room."

She was being kind, but it was self-involved kindness. I told her I was fine, and that I'd just as soon spend the night in my own room.

"All right," she said. "I'll walk you there."

We were leaving the living room when a shadowy figure scooted up the stairs to the second floor of the house.

"Neticia? Is that you? Are you snooping again?"

The girl poked her head around the banister.

"You've been warned about listening behind doors. Come down here now."

"Eleanor, please," I said. "I'd like to go to my room."

"This will only take a minute. Neticia," she said, backing the girl into a wall, "under no circumstances are you to discuss this with anyone. Do you understand?"

"Yes, Ma'am."

"And from now on you keep Beth out of the woods. And stay out of them yourself. Is that clear?"

We left the poor girl shaking by the stairs.

"I noticed your expression there," Eleanor said as she walked me down the path from the house to the hotel. "I'm not such an ogre, Bonnie. You cannot imagine how hard it is to run a place like this. I'm concerned this will get out and alarm the guests."

We passed a couple taking a late night swim in the pool. Eleanor greeted them casually. Near the casino, breezy "hellos" were exchanged with other guests. You would have thought nothing out of the ordinary had happened.

When we reached the door to my room, Eleanor laid her hand on my arm.

"You've had an awful experience. Perhaps you'd like to leave tomorrow. If you would, we'll pay you for the entire week."

Her offer wasn't a complete surprise. Between the rumpus at water ballet and the attack, the Ledbetters were probably thinking that I was more trouble than I was worth.

"My plane ticket's not good for another nine days. It can't be cashed in and I don't have the fare home."

Eleanor pondered that and I half thought she would offer me

a return ticket. I wonder if I would have taken it? It's irrelevant. She didn't offer.

"In that case, I suppose you'll have to stay." She said that with a faint smile, but I sensed an underlying irritation.

"We would appreciate it if you would use discretion in talking about what happened tonight," she continued. "It's not as if attacks are an everyday occurrence. We're going to hire some extra security men to patrol the resort. Just the same I wouldn't want the guests to be unnecessarily alarmed."

I was tired of her, tired of the guests, tired of everything. I wondered, briefly, what she would do if I balked. Would I get the same treatment Neticia got?

"I won't say anything to the guests, Eleanor."

With that, I went into my room, checked for devil eyes and men with machetes under the bed, peeled off what was left of my can-can outfit and collapsed.

For a while I drifted in and out of sleep. I have no idea what time it was when Leslie came in.

"You awake, Bonnie? It's okay, luv. I'll be quiet. Nice time at the casino tonight, wasn't it?"

I was aware of noises in the bathroom, of the light by her bed going on. Then she started to talk, and talk and talk.

"You still awake? Wouldn't mind having a chat, would you? I've got this problem. Kind of been bothering me. Remember what I told you? About my special mate, I mean. Fact is, the sex and all that . . . you remember the way I described it? It wasn't . . ." She paused. "It didn't actually work out that way. I mean, the room and what have you—well, I'm not totally bonkers. I wouldn't make up a hotel room. The room was every bit as lavish as I said. Thing is, though, my boyfriend . . . he's not as affectionate as I made out. We're having these difficulties. I'm pretty sure he's going to come around after a bit, but . . ."

I couldn't stand it any more. I sat up and flicked on my bedside lamp. Leslie was in bed, one of her novels in her hand. A redhead in a business suit being either embraced or strangled—

64

for obvious reasons it looked like the latter to me—by a severe-looking man in a trench coat.

"Leslie! Listen to me. Less than two hours ago a man came into the beach shack and tried to smother me with a sheet of plastic. We had a terrible struggle and I'm still not sure why he didn't go ahead and . . . kill me."

Once I had the words out, I started crying. "I couldn't care less about your problems with that moronic boyfriend of yours."

The book fell from her hands. Jumping out of bed, Leslie hurried over and put her arms around me. "At the beach shack? Imagine that. Are you all right? Here." She shoved a tissue at me. I wiped my eyes and blew my nose.

"Yes, I'm all right," I said, falling back down on the pillow.

"Did he have a machete? Did he try to rape you? There's this pair of native men going around. Blacks. You know what they're supposed to be like, with white women. Not all of them, of course, but there was one in this book I read. Slave on a plantation . . ."

"Please, Leslie! For all I know he was as white as I am. I couldn't see a thing. But he didn't try to rape me and if he had a machete he didn't use it on me."

Standing, she started pacing the space between our two beds. "All he tried to do was kill you?"

"That's all."

"Whatever for?"

"Who knows?" I turned my lamp off.

"How odd," she said. "I've never heard of that here. You don't suppose we've got a lunatic on the island, a Jack the Ripper? Garroted a lot of women, that one did. Sliced them bottom to top. Imagine what he could have done with a machete."

65

SEVEN

RESORT COURSE

Leslie was gone when I woke. I sat up and opened the curtain over my bed. It was after dawn. Rays of gold shone through the forest. Lying back on my pillow, I let the sunlight warm my face.

When I felt more awake, I stretched cautiously, waiting for pain to shoot through my limbs. I was relieved that nothing ached other than the sore spot over my ribs where the man's knee had rested. Sliding the sheet off my legs, I looked at them. Not even a bruise. Getting up, I examined my neck in the mirror. There wasn't a mark on it.

I'd let the pink ruffles and feathers fall where they might the night before. I was straightening the mess on my side of the room when Leslie walked in.

"I'll do your aerobics class if you're not up to it," she said. "After last night you might want some extra sleep."

"Thanks for the offer, but I'm probably better off keeping busy. You're out bright and early."

"I went down to the beach shack to make sure everything was there. Doesn't seem as if anything's been taken. On the way back I ran into Colin. He and the police went over the shack pretty carefully last night."

"Did they find anything? Like the plastic bag?"

Leslie shook her head. "Colin said they didn't find one lying about."

"The man must have taken it with him."

"That's what Colin thinks. He said the bloke's fingerprints may be on file, and he didn't want the police finding them on anything. I took the precaution of hiding my extra cash, in case they start breaking into rooms. You should do the same."

I nodded, but I probably wouldn't bother. Even if I had surprised a robber, which I doubted, my extra cash didn't amount to enough to worry about.

"I had quite a nice chat with Colin, about this and that," Leslie said. "He wants me to help out on the dive tonight. You too, if you're up to it."

"I'll decide later. Do you know what he wants us to do? I don't dive."

"You don't have to. Colin needs someone to watch out for the guests and keep count of them. That sort of thing. If you don't go along, I'll do it. Otherwise, I'm going to dive. Colin said I could take the resort course for free."

"Resort course?"

"In the pool at two. They teach you the basics. Only takes two hours."

"Two hours, and you're ready for night diving?"

"Technically no, but they take the boat out before the sun sets. If things run smoothly everybody's in the water while there's still some light. Tell you the truth, the idea of diving, day or night, scares me. Most things don't, but diving . . ." For a moment her expression darkened. She quickly perked up again. "I'm going to do the course this time, though. I've been kicking around these islands for three years. Might as well learn to dive while I've got the chance to do it for free."

"I'll go along tonight," I decided. "A boat ride would be nice."

There was a tap on the door. When Leslie opened it, Beth Ledbetter walked in. She was wearing a pink striped bathing suit with ruffles. She glared at Leslie and gave an exasperated sigh.

"Neticia's taking me to the beach, but first she has to talk to you. I'm supposed to wait here."

Leslie answered with an exasperated sigh of her own. "She's simply going to drive me crazy. That's all there is to it. Where is she?" Leslie demanded.

"At the bottom of the stairs."

Leslie left, slamming the screen door behind her. Beth flopped herself down on the edge of my bed.

"My mommy will fire Neticia if I say so."

I was going through my drawer looking for clean clothes. I stopped and stared at the little girl. "You like Neticia, don't you? You wouldn't want her to lose her job."

Beth wiggled her toes. Someone had painted the nails a flaming orange. "I like her when she takes me with her in the woods. Once she took me to the swamp to see the nests where the flamingos lay their eggs, but the devil eye caught us and made us go away."

"What did your mom say about the flamingo chick?"

"She said it was okay, as along as we take care of it."

"It sounds to me like you and Neticia have a lot of fun together."

"Sometimes we do. You want to know the most fun we had? Once Neticia and Leslie came to Nassau and we all stayed at my grandparent's house. We went to the Paradise Water Club 'cause my Grandmamma Simmonds is a member. There's a water slide there. I wish we had a water slide. Colin says we will if the Texans give us money."

"You have a nice pool here."

"I'd rather have a water slide. Neticia's more fun than the babysitter I had before. She was an old lady. All she wanted to do was sit in air conditioning and watch television."

"Sounds boring for you."

"It was, but now all Neticia ever wants to do is tell secrets with Leslie. If she doesn't start playing with me more I'm going to tell my mom I want another babysitter. My mommy probably won't fire her, though. She's teaching Neticia about working in the office. Neticia quit going to school, but she's still smart. She can do arithmetic. Sometimes she helps me with my homework."

I asked Beth where she went to school. She told me she went to a private school in Nassau, and generally returned to Flamingo Island for weekends. "Sometimes Mommy and Colin pick me up in Colin's speedboat, and sometimes I take the mail boat."

"Mail boat?"

"Uh hum. One afternoon it goes to Nassau, and the next afternoon it comes here. Fridays it comes here. The pilot lets me ride up front with him. Can I turn on the television?"

She flipped it on without waiting for an answer. I couldn't object. I felt sorry for Beth. From what I had seen, there were no children of her age around. When Beth wasn't in school, her only playmate was Neticia, twice Beth's age and paid to keep the child company. I stepped into the bathroom, thinking that in the total scheme of things, my problems didn't amount to much. The attack was a one-time thing, over and done with. I examined my ribs. The skin over them was red but nothing felt broken. Unless of course there was a hairline fracture, or maybe internal bleeding. . . .

Leslie's voice from outside the window interrupted this dismal line of thought. Our bathroom overlooked the passage between our building and the next. At first I couldn't distinguish what she was saying, but then there was an outburst. Her words echoed up the wall.

"What a ridiculous idea, Neticia. You're mad to even suggest such a thing. Why don't you try to relax? You want to go on the dive boat tonight? I'll ask Eleanor if you and Beth . . . No? Okay, suit yourself. Sit around here worrying worse than me mum."

There was a moment's lull. Leslie's voice again broke the quiet. "Once and for all, I'm taking care of it. It's like I told my roommate," she said. "I have hold of the key to paradise."

I never heard a word from Neticia.

Frenchie—that's what everybody called him—was the male half of Flamingo Cove's two-person dive crew. Someone told me he was originally from Haiti. He was brown as a walnut from the top of his bald head to the tip of his gnarled toes. He was no kid—I guessed his age at around sixty—but he lifted the scuba tanks as if they were weightless. He ended the lecture portion of the class by putting a good scare into everyone.

"Diving is fun if it is done in a safe way. At any depth, the air is regulated so you feel just like you are breathing on the surface. You are breathing compressed air. Always remember to exhale on the way up."

To get the point across, Frenchie took a red balloon out of his equipment bag. He blew it up, held it inflated, and let the air out. Then he put on a scuba tank and swam to the bottom of the deep end of the pool. We watched him fill the balloon from his mouthpiece, tie off its end and anchor it to the bottom of the pool by attaching it to a weightbelt.

He came to the surface slowly.

"Now look at the red balloon down there. It's filled with compressed air in twelve feet of water. All pressures are equal: twelve feet of water pushing in, air compressed to an equal pressure pushing out. When the balloon rises to the surface and the pressure of the water decreases, the air is going to expand. But it's trapped by the balloon. The balloon can't let out its breath.

"Pretend the balloon is one of your lungs. Let's see what happens."

Diving back into the water, he released the balloon from the weightbelt. It rose straight to the top. As it broke surface, it exploded like a firecracker. The ruined balloon settled back on the water like a lifeless bird as the class watched, stunned.

"Now, what is it we all do as we come up?"

"Exhale!"

"Frenchie?" Leslie called out. "I've got to open the beach shack. Can I go first and make it quick?"

"All right."

She slipped into the shallow end and tugged a mask over her head. Frenchie held the mouthpiece in front of her, demonstrating to the crowd of people around the pool.

I was at the side of the shallow end, my feet dangling. A tremor of anxiety hit me when the mask was in place over Leslie's eyes and nose. She gave a pull to the rubber strap to tighten it, and I suddenly felt as if I couldn't breathe, as if something was sucking away the last whisper of my air. I could hear every word Frenchie was saying, but I wasn't able to focus on them until I had forced myself to take a few calm breaths. There would be no night dive for me.

When the diving equipment was adjusted, Frenchie told Leslie to take the regulator in her mouth and breathe naturally. When she'd done that, he told her to swim half the length of the pool and back. She had no problem with that, so for about fifteen minutes he had her do a number of exercises. Sitting underwater, Leslie removed her mask and tank and surfaced slowly without them. Then she went back down and put the tank on again, cleared her mask and came back to the surface. Again, no problem.

Next came Frenchie's discussion of the various meters and tubes attached to the scuba tank. Scuba diving is a complex and exacting sport, requiring not only a lot of heavy, cumbersome equipment but a lot of technical knowledge. Even if I hadn't been weak-kneed over the idea of not being able to breathe, it wouldn't be something I'd take up. I like my relaxations less demanding.

A few in the crowd around the pool shared my feelings, but most did not.

"Fantastic feeling, breathing under water," Leslie said when she had completed a circuit of the pool and removed the equipment.

When Frenchie asked "Who else?" at least a dozen hands shot up. Frenchie and his assistant, a young local woman, had their hands full. Several of the Chicago tour group wanted to take the course, and so did all three Texans and the prim woman who had been on my flight. Her husband, after a second's hesitation, decided he'd dive too. Sonny and Cindy jumped in at opposite sides of the pool.

Leslie climbed from the water and sat next to me. "Great fun, once you get used to the idea. You should try it, Bonnie."

I shook my head. "It's not for me."

She had bent over and was squeezing water out of her long hair. Long, long hair. Hair to where her bikini bottom started. I stared for a moment. The night before, after I'd spoken to my attacker, had he purposefully felt for my hair? He'd grabbed it as if intending to anchor me, but when my shoulder-length hair had come unpinned from the top of my head, he'd stopped. He'd let me go.

"Oh, please don't kill me," I said under my breath.

"What?"

"Leslie, do me a favor. Say, 'Oh, please don't kill me.'"

"Whatever for?"

"Just say it."

"Oh, please don't kill me."

"You sound like an Australian."

She laughed and turned back to the pool. "Frenchie told me he tries to see who might panic. Claustrophobia."

We spent a few minutes watching the lesson. There was every conceivable level of swimmer and diver in the water. The Texas woman and her tubby husband had both dived before, and so had two of the Chicago group. Cindy moved well in the water. She had dived once before. Sonny, who had never dived, announced there was "nothing to it." He thrashed through the water like a buffalo.

"What's next for you?" I asked Leslie.

"Got to open the beach shack."

I nodded at the water. "I mean in the class."

"Oh. That's it for the class. I told Frenchie I had to hurry."

Altogether with lecture, demonstration and swimming around the pool, her lesson had lasted less than an hour. Leslie must have picked up some concern in my expression.

73

"That's all it takes," she said defensively. "I've got my temporary certification now."

I looked back over the pool. Frenchie was next to Sonny, pointing at the meter attached to Sonny's tank and looking stern. His assistant was trying to cope with Cindy, the prim woman, and her husband.

"I thought this was supposed to take two hours."

Leslie shrugged. "Sometimes it runs a bit less."

"An hour less? Look at this mob, Leslie. There are going to be a dozen people in the water tonight, with only two instructors."

As I spoke, Sonny was taking off his tank.

"This thing's heavy. Good thing I work out." Holding the tank at both ends, he hoisted it over his head. "Next?" he yelled.

Frenchie took one look at Sonny and shouted, "Lower that tank slowly and put it down gently!"

Everyone was suddenly quiet. Sonny stood still for a moment, the tank over his head. Finally he lowered the thing to the concrete at the side of the pool.

"Jeez. I was only joking."

Frenchie didn't appreciate the joke. "That tank is full of compressed air," he said angrily. "If it is dropped, it could explode."

I shook my head and said softly, "This is going to be awful tonight."

Leslie laughed. "God, Bonnie. Sonny was only kidding. You should take up with Neticia. Two of a kind you are. Worriers. Frenchie's super cautious, you know. He makes the divers surface while they've got at least ten minutes of air left. Everything will be fine tonight."

"Of course it will."

Colin had walked up next to us.

"What's the matter, Bonnie? Nervous? I'll be along and I've dived every inch of the reef, day and night. So has Eleanor."

The man had such a calm demeanor that I felt a little foolish. "I'm sure you're right."

"I want to talk to you," he said. "Let's get away from this crowd for a second. I have good news."

I followed Colin to an umbrella-shaded table and sat across from him.

"I just had a call from the police. Early this morning there was another robbery."

"Did they catch the men?"

He shook his head. "A guest at the fishing camp thought he'd get in some early flycasting on the other side of the island. He noticed a boat anchored just offshore. Then two natives came out of the woods with machetes and robbed him. They got away in the boat."

"I hope that wasn't the good news, Colin."

He smiled. "Until now all the victims have left within a day or two. The fisherman's going to be here for another week. He'll be able to identify the men. He got a good look at the boat, too."

I know good news when I hear it. Colin's didn't even qualify as borderline. I don't necessarily think of myself as a pessimist, but I shook my head in disbelief.

"What is it?"

"Colin, they have to catch the men first. And the men who robbed that fisherman might not be the same men"—I caught myself; he even had me talking about my attacker as a team— "man who attacked me."

"But who else would it be, Bonnie? I've been on this island almost two years, and the only violent crime in that time was a stabbing in a bar fight. Eleanor has lived here most of her life. When she was a teenager a local woman took an iron skillet to her husband. He'd been abusing her for years. Crime doesn't happen here. Not the way you're used to it in New York. Don't you see what I mean?"

I didn't. What I saw was a hotel owner so bent on turning a profit that he was grasping at every straw. I gave up and smiled back. Colin reached across the table and patted my shoulder.

"You're a trooper, Bonnie. Now I had better go circulate. Wouldn't want anyone to feel neglected."

I watched Colin for a few minutes from under the shade of the umbrella. Everybody from the guy collecting wet towels to the Texans got that friendly smile, or a pat on the back or a thumbs-up signal. He laughed heartily at Sonny's wet towel-snapping, and said something to the prim woman that released a carefree giggle. I saw him motion Leslie aside. They talked for a few minutes, partly shielded from the crowded pool by a flowering hibiscus bush. Whatever he said put a nice smile on her face. Before they parted she touched his hand with hers, and moved closer to whisper in his ear. Minutes later he was huddled around a table on the far side of the pool, a smiling Texan on either side of him.

I caught Leslie as she was walking away from the pool area.

"Mind if I walk to the shack with you? I'd like to look at it in daylight."

"All right with me," she said. "Colin mentioned just now that those two men attacked someone else. Bet you're relieved there's someone who can identify them."

Good God! He had her doing it, too. "Yes. That's a big relief to me."

On the way to the beach shack, I stopped at the reception desk and dropped off the key I'd borrowed the night before. If the clerk had heard about the attack, she didn't show it.

Leslie and I crossed the dirt road to the beach. It was crowded for Flamingo Cove: a couple dozen people sunbathing, six or eight people in the water. Several guests were playing volleyball with a few natives, while someone's toddler made castles in the sand. The sun gleamed off the water and a soft breeze blew.

The day was particularly warm, and as we crossed the sand I could feel the sun draining my energy, not to mention my anxieties. By the time Leslie unlocked the door to the beach shack, I was yawning. I'd had a hard night, and I was going to be working that night as well. A nice nap before Dancercize. . . .

". . . that where it happened? That's where the towels were tipped over."

Cracks of light showed around the edges of the shutter. When

Leslie unlatched and lowered it, the shack was flooded with warm yellow sunshine. I looked around at the neatly stacked towels, at the snorkels and fins hanging on their hooks, at the soda machine. A lightbulb hung on a cord at one side of the room.

"Where's the light switch?"

"On the wall next to the drink cooler."

"I wish I'd known that last night."

She shrugged. "Wanted a look at the bloke who was trying to ravish you, huh? Ever hear about white slave rings? Kidnap white women and sell them into prostitution. Next thing you know you're in a harem in Turkey."

"Leslie, the man was not a white slaver."

"I expect you're right. He was most likely a robber. One of those black guys with machetes. Last night I started telling you about a book I read. There's this woman running a plantation while her husband's off at war. She takes up with a slave. . . . "

Leslie's babbling was so crazy I tried shutting it out. She had read too many bodice rippers. A customer—"snorkel, mask and a pair of fins, please"—occupied her for a few minutes. While she was busy I looked around.

Even in broad daylight, with all the nooks and crannies exposed, there wasn't much to the shack. It was about twenty feet square, with the one shuttered window across the front, and one door. The shutter, which bolted at both ends, was made of heavy wood. I pushed my palm against the wood. It scarcely gave. Even with one bolt gone, no one could have squeezed through.

I tried the door and found it solid. No glass, no screen, no give. Kicking the rubber stopper from under it, I pushed it shut and examined the rim. There was enough space to let light show through, so I could assume the light in the shack had not been on when I got there the night before. I would have noticed if it had been. Which meant that if I'd surprised a thief at work, it was a thief who knew his way around because he was working in pitch dark.

"Who has a key to the shack?"

"Just me," she said carelessly, "and the reception desk. And of course the Ledbetters. The head maintenance man has one. And I think Frenchie does, too."

In other words, everybody. I reopened the door. Bending to push the rubber stopper under it, I spotted some black plastic trash bags in a cardboard container that had been placed neatly on a shelf behind the door. When the door was open you wouldn't notice them unless you looked. Yanking one of the bags from the container, I fingered it. It was big enough to fit over my head and shoulders. It was strong, too. I pulled at it hard but it didn't tear. Taking it into both hands, I held it tight against my face. The sun-bright shack disappeared and I was in smothering darkness. I lowered the sack quickly.

The young man Leslie had been helping walked away.

"You don't keep cash here, do you?"

She shook her head. "Towels are free for guests. Anything else they want is added to their room bill."

"Are the trash bags always kept here behind the door?"

"Yes. It's convenient when we want to load them up with towels or trash and carry them outside." She started rubbing the facemask of a snorkel with some liquid cleaner.

I walked to the other side of the shack and searched though the stack of towels.

"What are you looking for?"

I held out the bag in my hand. "I think the man held one of these over my head. It might still be here."

"Colin said they looked the place over carefully. Oh! That lady I was telling you about a minute ago—she got to like that bloke, she did. Helped him escape."

"What are you talking about?"

"On the underground railroad. You know—the plantation mistress and the slave. In the end she made it up with her husband."

I threw the plastic bag aside. "Are you nuts? Where is your mind? Someone tried to kill me in here last night. Do you understand? He put a plastic bag over my head and held it tight

78

around my neck and wouldn't let me breathe. Does that sound like something I'd get to like, Leslie?"

She shook her head. "Of course not. I didn't mean that. I was just telling you how it was in that book." She bent to pick up the sack.

"Leslie," I said hesitantly, "Do you think maybe someone was trying to kill *you* last night?"

I expected her to laugh at the idea, but she didn't. Not right away. She straightened and stared at me, and I thought there was doubt in her eyes. Then she hooted with laughter.

"Why would anyone want to kill me?"

"I don't know, but this shack is *your* territory, and last night we were dressed alike. In the dark someone could mistake us. The man only stopped when he heard me speak, and when he realized my hair is shorter than yours."

"You're bonkers. No one would want to kill me." She paused as if something had occurred to her. "Though there's a book I finished a few days back. Set in France, it is. This orphan girl takes a position in the home of a Baron. Next thing you know . . ."

"Life's not like a romance novel."

"A pity, isn't it? Things always work out so nicely in those stories. Of course," she said with a shrug, "they work out nicely for the *good* girl. If one of those writers put me in a story, I suspect I'd be the bad girl. You know—the girl who plots and schemes and ends up losing the man in spite of it all."

I gave her a long look. "I hope you're not doing something that could get you hurt, Leslie. Sometimes the bad girl who plots and schemes ends up dead, doesn't she?"

"What an idea! Positively bonkers! Besides, if I was doing something risky, I'd do what the spies do in thrillers. You ever read any thrillers? They always say, 'Watch my back.' I'm no fool, Bonnie. You can bet I would do just that."

EIGHT

NIGHT DIVE

We gathered on the pier at Flamingo Cove before the sun began to set. From there, a motorized dinghy took us, in groups of five and six, out to the big dive boat that had been chartered for the evening.

I was in the last group. The water was surprisingly rough once we got away from the placid shore, and the dinghy pitched as I reached for the ladder hanging from the dive boat's side. It swung out of my grasp as a wave buffeted us. Holding onto Cindy for support, I grabbed for it again. When the rung was secure in my hand, I pulled myself up the five swaying steps. Frenchie was at the top of the ladder to give me a hand.

"Be careful, Bonnie." He leaned back over the edge, and a second later was helping Cindy. When she was on board, Frenchie jumped lightly over the side, pushed the dinghy away and leaped back onto the ladder.

The engines of the big boat roared as it headed away from Flamingo Cove. As we sped over the waves, a party atmosphere was building among the guests. Bursts of laughter traveled from one end of the boat to the other. Music rang from a speaker in the sheltered cabin—a happy song about sailing and foreign ports.

Colin, Frenchie and his assistant were busy securing the dive gear under benches and along a wall.

"What should I do?" I asked Colin.

"Nothing right now," he said without lifting his head. "Make sure all the guests are comfortable."

Eleanor had told me I would be keeping count of the divers. I had a paper and pencil in my tote. I leaned down and put the tote under a seat where it would stay reasonably dry. When I stood, I bumped heads with Cindy.

Cindy had chosen me as her confidante, periodically treating me to the news from the honeymoon suite. The situation in that wicker and chintz love nest hadn't improved a bit.

"Can I hang out with you for a while?" she asked.

"Sure. Want to go on a tour of the boat?"

She glanced left and right. "Okay. I don't see Sonny around. Did you notice that he rode out with that tramp in the first dinghy?"

"No, I didn't. Try to forget about them for a few minutes. You're supposed to be having fun."

"I'm supposed to be having a honeymoon," Cindy grumbled. "If I see them together I'm going to kick them both overboard."

"So you've decided to kill both of them, instead of just Leslie." I was kidding, but I still found myself giving her a searching look. She was shorter than I am, and smaller-boned, with almost stick-like wrists. There was no way Cindy could have been my attacker.

"Why are you staring at me? You don't think I'm serious, do you?"

I shook my head. "No. Let's go look around."

The boat was impressive, by far the best maintained piece of property I'd seen on Flamingo Island. It was sparkling white, at least fifty feet long, and had two decks, one just above the water where we boarded, and an upper deck accessible by a wood ladder. On the main deck was a roomy cabin with a bar, and for those who wanted to feel the spray of water on their faces, a catwalk led around to a deck at the front of the boat. For the adventurous, a four-foot ramp extended straight out from there. It was wide enough for only one person at a time. Cindy and I took turns going out to the tip and letting the spray hit our faces.

We found Leslie on the second-level deck—the flying bridge, someone told me it was called. From what I saw up there, Cindy didn't have to worry about competition from my roommate, at least for the moment. Leslie, in her skintight white jeans and bikini top, was in the pilot's seat. Her golden hair flew back in the stiff breeze. The strap to her bikini had slipped off her shoulder. She didn't bother straightening it.

The captain, a man of about my age, was giving her an impromptu lesson in steering a big boat. When she spotted us she waved.

"Come and see how fast I'm catching on to piloting a boat." She turned back to the captain. "Aren't I fast, Mike?"

He wasn't fast enough with his answer to suit Leslie, so she grabbed playfully at the rumpled sailor hat he wore.

"You are that," he said, straightening the cap.

"Bonnie, this is Mike. We're old friends."

Cindy stood there for a few seconds before she clattered back down the ladder. Her place was immediately taken by the prim woman.

"What a beautiful sunset. Hold still, you two," she called to Leslie and the captain. She brought her little camera to her eye and focused on the couple. Mike started to turn away, at the same time lifting his arm to his face. The shutter clicked before he had shielded himself.

"Got it," the woman said.

"Hope I didn't break the camera," he said. "I have a way of doing that."

When the prim woman left the bridge, I joined Leslie and Mike. By that time the sun was a giant red ball on the horizon. After a few minutes I realized we were circling the island, never getting too far from shore.

"I thought we were going out to the reef."

"After I pick up this other bunch we will be."

"There they are now," Leslie shouted, pointing excitedly.

I squinted into the sunset. A small boat, crowded with people, was bouncing toward us through the choppy water. As it drew nearer I counted eight passengers.

"Who are they?"

Leslie jumped out of the pilot's seat. "It's Charlie and his gang from the fishing camp. I'm going below to say hi."

"They're coming with us?"

Mike nodded, matter of fact. "More profit for the boat owner this way, and less expensive for the resort operators. Cheaper by the dozen, somebody once told me."

I had started down the ladder. The people from Charlie's boat were coming on board. With each one up the ladder, the turmoil on deck seemed to double. When the dog, Beast, was shoved and tugged over the railing, he hit the deck barking and the turmoil turned into frenzy.

"We already had a dozen. Now we've got . . ."

"Trouble." Mike was staring down from the bridge to the lower deck, shaking his head. "Hey, Charlie. What's with the dog?"

"What dog? This is my son."

Charlie greeted me with outstretched arms. "Hey! Here's my girl."

A huge hug followed. As he pressed me to his massive chest, I got a lungful of rum. I looked beyond him. Leslie was standing near a stack of life preservers, patting Beast and eyeing me curiously. When Charlie finally let me go to busy himself with other things, she said, "Didn't realize you two were acquainted."

"We met on the plane from Nassau."

"Oh. Well, if you fancy each other, don't let me stop you. Charlie and I went together for a while, but it's over. He still comes around, visiting at the beach shack, but I've told him it's pointless." She scratched Beast's nose. The dog nuzzled her for more. "Bit old for me, if you want to know."

"I don't 'fancy' Charlie at all."

Leslie, with her attention span of about thirty seconds, was already peering past me.

"Oh, luv, what goodies did you bring?"

Charlie and one of his group lugged an ice chest over the railing onto the dive boat.

"Yohoho and a bottle of rum," he growled.

They had brought more than a bottle of rum. They'd brought gallons of it, and bottles of mixer as well. The last thing over the rail was a huge aluminum bowl and a cellophane pack of paper cups.

"Rum punch for everybody," Charlie called. He opened a bottle of rum and splashed it into the bowl. A bottle of mixer was next, and then some ice cubes. Beast tried sticking his nose into the bowl. Charlie dragged him away, but not before the dog managed one big slurp.

"Nasty animal," Leslie giggled, but the nasty animal didn't stop her from dipping a cup into the mixture.

Frenchie had joined the group around the punchbowl. He stared, grimfaced, as Charlie dipped a paper cup into the mixture.

"Why don't we leave the drinking for later, after the dive?"

"You heard him," Charlie shouted. "Nobody from Flamingo Cove's allowed to drink any of this." Taking a big swallow, he smacked his lips. "You've got to pour yours back, Leslie."

She nudged Frenchie with her hip. "Don't be such a poop. We're here to have a good time, aren't we?"

"Drinking and diving don't mix. It can be dangerous."

Charlie responded with a laugh. "Hell! I just ran the mixer past the open bottle. No more than a whiff of liquor in this bowl. Just enough to get everyone a little relaxed." He filled another cup and downed it.

It didn't take Sonny long to get to the punchbowl. He slugged one cupful down and ladled himself another. The group from the fishermen's lodge—four men and three women—all took drinks, and then several more Flamingo Cove people dipped into the punch. The tubby Texan helped himself twice. Then Leslie ladled another cup.

She was in her glory, laughing, flirting, flitting from one

admirer to the next. The beads Neticia had woven into her hair were growing luminous, glittering in the darkening evening like the lights on a Christmas tree. It was like Monte Carlo Night all over again. Leslie loved the sparkle of an "occasion," she loved dressing up and performing for an audience, and the more men in the audience, the better. When she breezed into the forward cabin looking for something to crush ice with, Sonny and Charlie trailed close behind.

I was watching this parade, in a way awed by Leslie, when I felt Cindy's hand on my arm. "I'm probably the only bride in history whose husband has an affair on their honeymoon."

"Cindy, I don't want to hear . . ."

The girl looked down over the edge of the boat. The water was dark blue now, flecked with gold from the fading sun. "I wish she'd drown tonight. If I wasn't so embarrassed, I'd call my daddy. He has connections. I have an uncle who could get someone to take care of her."

"Enough!" I groaned. "I'm not going to listen to any more of this. Either get on a plane and leave tomorrow, or make the best of things while you're here."

She opened her mouth to protest, but a piercing giggle from Leslie stopped her. The fat Texan had joined the party in the cabin.

"Name's Ted. Ted from Texas."

I peeked through the door. Ted the Texan was pretending to examine the metal buckle on Leslie's belt. The buckle, brass with a big silver L on it, was impressive, but I doubt if that was what had impressed the Texan. He had managed to work one of his slug-like fingers under the waistband of Leslie's jeans. She squirmed and wiggled away from him, giggling all the while.

The Texan's size-two wife gave the couple a chilly look, then wandered away.

Frenchie finally cooled things off in the cabin. "We cannot have this," he said angrily. He walked to the other side of the boat where Colin and Eleanor were working with equipment. As he talked briefly with them, Colin's perpetual smile showed strain—unusual for him. Eleanor's faded completely.

"Leslie?" she called between clenched teeth. When there was no answer, Eleanor went to the cabin door. A smile crossed her face when she saw the Texan, but there was ice in her voice.

"Leslie, dear. I need your help with some of the wetsuits. You too, Bonnie."

This unpleasant reminder that she wasn't on the boat as a guest scarcely fazed Leslie. As she pushed past the men surrounding her, she grinned disarmingly at each in his turn. She managed to bump Sonny with her hip before we followed Eleanor across the deck.

"Forty lashes for me, I suppose," she giggled.

"Keelhaul her, Eleanor," Charlie called out. There was a shout from the upper deck, "Make her walk the plank." And then a voice from the cabin took up the cry: "Feed her to the fish."

Each suggestion was greeted with raucous laughter from around the boat. Leslie laughed hardest of all. By the time someone screamed out, "Throw the wench to the sharks," even Eleanor was grinning.

"Not the sharks," Leslie said as she grappled with an air tank. "Anything but that. Promise me we won't see any sharks, Colin."

"I promise. If I see one, I'll give a signal." He placed his thumb against his forehead and extended his hand, fin-like, from it. "This is the standard signal for a shark sighting."

"But you won't be seeing it," Eleanor said. "Sharks seldom attack divers. They are attracted more by swimmers."

Sonny came lurching across the deck. Eleanor put out a hand to steady him.

"Should I just take any of these rubber pants things I want?" Without waiting for an answer, he grabbed for a bright blue wetsuit.

"That's Eleanor's," Colin said. Fishing a large black wetsuit from the pile, he tossed it to Sonny. "As Eleanor was saying, sharks are more attracted to swimmers than divers."

"It's all that thrashing around," Eleanor offered. "Even so, I can't recall swimmers ever being attacked in these waters, and I've lived here all my life."

I noticed that she said that with her voice raised, so that it would carry over the deck. *We are all secure on Flamingo Island and in its waters. No sharks, no criminals, no worry.*

Leslie had lost interest in the conversation. She was staring at the wetsuits, in particular at the bright blue one Colin had tossed back on the pile.

"Are you diving tonight, Eleanor?"

Eleanor hugged her arms to her chest. "Too cool for me. Why?"

"Blue is my favorite, you know. And that shade's smashing on me. You wouldn't mind . . . "

"Who's going to see you underwater?"

"You never can tell about that, can you?"

Eleanor gave a careless shrug. "If you damage it you pay for it."

"When I get out of the water, I'll examine every inch of it. I promise."

"Don't bother," Eleanor said. "Just throw it on the pile. Frenchie will check the suits over tomorrow."

With a happy squeal, Leslie unbuckled her belt and peeled off the white jeans. When she had rolled them into a tight ball, she threw them under the seat where I'd stashed my things.

"Should stay dry enough there." She began pulling on Eleanor's wetsuit. "Oh, Bonnie. My wallet's in my jeans pocket. Keep an eye on my stuff, will you?"

"Sure."

"I'll zip you up," Eleanor said. She turned Leslie so that she could reach the zipper up the back of the suit. In doing this, she steered Leslie a little away from the crowd so that no guests would overhear.

"When you come back on board, I want you to be low-key. No flirting, no drinking. Is that clear?"

Leslie was testing the batteries in an underwater flashlight.

"I'll bloody hide myself in the loo," she said. As soon as Eleanor had gone, Leslie whispered to me, "Jealous bitch."

For a while I was busy handing out wetsuits and helping some of the guests get into them. When I finally had an idle second, Eleanor appeared at my side.

"Listen, everyone. Bonnie here is going to take the names of all divers. When you come back on she'll call off your names."

"Counting noses, like kindergarten?"

That came from over by the punch bowl where Charlie O'Dell's group had stationed themselves.

"That way," Eleanor continued, "we'll be sure to return with as many divers as we left with, won't we, Charlie."

I didn't give much thought to the barbed undertone in her voice. Eleanor's sharp tongue was as much a part of her as Colin's reassuring smile was of him. I dug my pencil and paper from under the seat and began getting the divers' names down.

There were divers everywhere, on both decks, in the cabin, up at the front of the boat. Most of the wetsuits were black, and as more and more divers got into them I became frazzled. Getting all their names on the list wasn't easy. Charlie and his group were particularly raucous. They teased me as I went from one to the next. "You'll never make much of an island girl like this." "You're too compulsive to ever be a real island girl."

Sonny naturally took up the cry. "Yeah," he called. "She's too serious to be an island girl. Should of seen what I done to her in the Nassau. . . ."

I was learning to ignore Sonny. As for the rest of them, for all their bravado I got the feeling they were relieved that somebody was actually "counting noses."

By the time I finished with my list, the breeze had a definite nip to it. The deck rolled and pitched as the boat cut through the waves. Tropics or not, it's cool and rough out there in the evening. The mood on the boat had changed in some slight way, too. Oh, it was still noisy. The shouts and laughter still carried from one deck to the other, from the front to the back of the boat, and out of the cabin. But there was something new in the air. Apprehension. It became noticeable when Eleanor handed releases to all the divers.

"What's this for?" someone asked.

"It releases the boat owner and operator, the hotel and the fishing camp, and the instructors of responsibility in the event of an accident. It's always done, and it is mandatory for anyone who wishes to dive."

As the divers signed these forms, I noticed how short, uneasy silences descended over them, as if each in turn was withdrawing into a private place. It was in the midst of one of those silences that the engines on the big boat stopped and we were suddenly aware of how dim and quiet the night was.

We had circled back around the point and anchored just off Pirate's Cay. The moon had not yet risen, and the cay was a jagged and desolate outline against the setting sun. Where we were anchored, the water was about thirty feet deep, but I knew that just beyond Pirate's Cay was the great Tongue of the Ocean, an undersea cliff where the depth dropped to over six thousand feet.

"All right," said Colin, breaking the hush. "All divers with permanent certification come over here to put on your equipment. Eleanor will check you out before you get in the water. Everybody who took the resort course move to the rear. Frenchie and Charlie will help you get your tanks on."

At this point Frenchie's assistant, already in her tank, jumped from the diving platform at the back of the boat. A strand of orange neon cord had been attached to her tank. Colin followed her into the water. They stayed on the surface by keeping the buoyancy compensators they wore fully inflated.

"Once you're in the water, stay near the boat until everybody is in," Eleanor said. "All three instructors will be carrying orange neon cords. Make sure you are always in sight of one of them. Once you are under, please do not touch the coral. It is alive. If you touch it, you kill it. You'll see some wonderful plants and animals that glow in the dark, but many of them can sting so don't touch them. We also ask that you be selective about bringing up souvenirs."

Someone held up a black mesh bag. "Is that what these are for?"

"Yes," Frenchie said, "but please don't bring anything up without first pointing it out to an instructor or Colin." He paused and took a long look at the divers. "If any of you have changed your minds about diving, now is the time to say something."

The certified divers were already putting on their tanks and weight belts, but I could tell that some of the others were having second thoughts. There was nervous conversation and glancing back and forth. Finally Charlie spoke up.

"What are you trying to do, Frenchie? Scare everybody? The water's only thirty feet deep here. We have a strobe light under the boat and a thirty-foot rope hanging off the ladder."

"Yeah," Sonny growled. "I'm not chickening out." He stepped over to Frenchie. "Load me up, Pierre."

That seemed to make up everyone's minds. In seconds the resort course group was lining up for the cumbersome forty pounds of equipment. Two at a time, they put on tanks, regulators, weight belts and buoyancy compensators. Once they had the fins on their feet, movement was all but impossible. At that point the divers stepped off the rear diving platform into the water.

One minute the boat was clambering with activity; the next it was almost deserted. Eleanor and I looked over the edge. The strobe under the boat flashed, sending a bright intermittent cone of light to the ocean floor and putting the divers in sharp relief as they bobbed in the waves. The water was deep blue now, streaked by the last gold rays of the fading sunset. When the strobe blinked off, the almost two dozen divers were no clearer than shadows. Only the strands of orange neon were bright against the water.

"Yo. This rubber suit's too damned tight. I should of took a large. It's squeezing my . . ."

Sonny gagged on his words. I saw him in a burst of the strobe. Awful as I found him, my heart thudded.

"Keep your regulator in your mouth," I heard Colin say

sharply. "Don't worry about your wetsuit. It has to be tight to keep you warm."

Eleanor was a few feet from me, shaking her head. "Glad I'm not in there."

"Everyone says it's safe."

"Of course it's safe. It's just that Charlie scares me."

"He does seem sort of easygoing."

"Easygoing? That's putting it kindly. Six years ago Charlie O'Dell was head of the diving operation at one of the biggest resorts in the U.S. Virgin Islands. One night they did a group dive—something like this," she added, with a nod that took in the water.

"They were supposed to be diving in forty feet of water, but Charlie let some hotshots talk him into going deeper. Some poor woman went into the water with her equipment messed up. Either there was too much weight on her belt or her buoyancy compensator wasn't working. She went straight to the bottom in over a hundred feet. Her husband followed, trying to get hold of her. They both drowned. Or so the story goes. I'm told Charlie isn't allowed to lead dives in the U.S. territories."

"How awful."

"But we've got two other certified instructors down there, and Colin, too. He's logged over a hundred dives. Nothing can possibly go wrong."

She was looking at me as if I might argue about that. "I'm sure you're right," I said quickly.

"I'm going below. See you in a while."

Eleanor disappeared into the cabin.

I stood at the railing and watched as the divers let the air out of their buoyancy compensators and slid beneath the surface. When the strobe brightened the ocean I could see their distorted spidery outlines moving slowly deeper. Finally the last figure vanished from my view. I strained to see the little I could—the dot of light from an underwater flashlight, a camera's flash, a streak of orange neon. And then there was nothing but the strobe pulsing against the ocean floor.

Beast paced the deck anxiously. I scratched his head, but he didn't seem comforted. I felt lonely out there, but for some reason I didn't want to leave the railing until the divers had returned. The damp night air began chilling me and I pulled my sweater tighter.

I'd been there for quite a while when Mike came down the wood steps from the bridge and joined me.

"Where did Eleanor go?"

I nodded toward the cabin door. "I don't see her now."

"There's a bunk room below the cabin. She's probably trying to catch a nap before the craziness starts up again. It will be worse when they come back. That's when they start with their war stories."

"I can't wait."

"How come you're not down there with them?"

"Would you believe the one about a perforated eardrum, or should I save myself the trouble and admit to no guts?"

"Good for you. You couldn't get me down there with that mob."

"I heard about Charlie and the lost divers."

Mike lifted up the white sailor hat and ran his fingers through his hair. That didn't take much effort. There wasn't much hair up there. When he realized I was watching him, he quickly put the cap back. He wasn't particularly handsome, but he had a nice face. A little hard around the eyes, maybe, but nice.

He shrugged. "Charlie's a friend of mine, but he doesn't talk about that. I've dived with him during the day, though. He seemed careful enough to me. Anyway, everything will be fine tonight. Frenchie and his assistant are the best, and Colin . . ."

"I know, I know. He's swum every inch of this reef."

"Same old pitch. I hear it on every dive boat I take out." He glanced at his watch. "Speaking of charters, this one could run overtime."

It was almost as if telepathy was working, for at that instant a door slammed inside the cabin. A moment later Eleanor joined us on the deck.

"They should start coming up in five or six minutes. Once everybody's on board get moving right away, Mike. They can deal with their equipment on the way back. I don't want to pay one minute extra on this boat. You're dropping us off first, before Charlie's group. Right?"

"Right." He saluted her retreating back before returning to the bridge.

It wasn't long before a shout came from over the side. "Eleanor?"

"Colin's back, Eleanor," I called.

She hurried to my side. "I'm always so relieved when these things are over. Back to business for us, Bonnie. Once everybody's on board, get them to count off so we can get out of here immediately."

Excited returning divers soon crowded the deck. Cindy was one of the first to board. I could feel her trembling as I helped her out of her wetsuit.

"I'm frozen," she said, shuddering as she put her flashlight on the growing mound of equipment. She had carried one of the mesh sacks with her but I didn't get to see if she'd brought anything up from the bottom. Charlie came on board, sending his dog into a leaping, yapping ecstasy that distracted me and everyone else. Having managed that, Beast then collapsed into an exhausted heap of matted fur in the middle of all the action.

The big boat's engines started with a roar. That had to mean everyone was out of the water. My paper had been pushed into a damp corner next to Leslie's pile of clothes. I dried it as well as I could, then shouted above the engines: "Everyone please listen. I'm going to call out names now. Colin?"

No answer.

"Colin?"

"That's me," Colin shouted from up in front. "One."

The next two responses came from the cabin. I wandered in that direction. "Here" was called from on the bridge, "yes" from right behind me. That's how it went, voices from every part of the boat shouting above the engine's roar. By the time I checked off

94

the last diver, we were moving toward the welcoming lights of Flamingo Cove.

I gave the reef one last look. The quarter moon had slipped behind a cloud and the water was raven black. Satisfied that everyone was on board, I put my list back in my tote under the seat. Leslie's clothes were no longer there.

"That's the lot of us, then?" Colin called.

"Wait for me!" I was the last one in our party off the dive boat. Just as I started over the railing, Mike stopped me.

"The reef's a lot more interesting in the daylight. Would you like to come back tomorrow and go snorkeling?"

A date? Was Captain Mike asking me out? He couldn't possibly be asking if I was interested in chartering a fifty-foot boat. Or could he? I decided to play it safe. I asked casually, "What would that cost?"

He raised an eyebrow. "Cost?"

"This isn't exactly an innertube we're on."

"You think this is my boat? I should be so lucky. I have an eighteen-foot motorboat."

"Oh." Oh. It *was* a date he wanted. Did I want a date? Colin didn't give me time to worry about it.

"Come on, Bonnie," he yelled from the dinghy.

"Sure," I said to Mike. "I have off tomorrow afternoon."

"I'm taking some fishermen out in the morning. What do you say to one o'clock? We can come out here first, then go into town for a late lunch."

We made hurried plans: He would pick me up at the Flamingo Cove dock the next afternoon.

As soon as I was set in the dinghy, Colin gave a shove against the side of the dive boat and we were off. When we pulled away, Charlie and his group broke into the strains of "Waltzing Matilda." Their voices, raised above the sound of the engines, floated across the waves. A bank of mist had risen over the surface of the water, and the dive boat was soon a ghostly shape against the dark night.

95

I settled into the dinghy, leaning against the side. The put-put of the little motor, the gentle buffeting of the waves close to shore—I'd sleep well that night.

"You really see a shark out there, Colin?"

One of the guests—I didn't know him—asked that.

Frenchie's assistant was next to me. "A shark?"

The man nodded. "Yeah. Your boss here gave the hand signal. Almost gave me heart failure."

Colin rolled his eyes back. "How embarrassing. I actually thought I saw a big one. It must have been all that talk about sharks before we dived. Turned out to be a big old grouper who hangs around the reef. I sure hope nobody else noticed."

The man laughed. "I didn't wait around to see."

Ted the tubby Texan was at the front of the dinghy, sitting near Sonny.

"Speaking of seeing," he said, "where's that blond gal gone to? You know who I mean?"

"I know," said Sonny. He cupped his hands in front of his chest.

The Texan nodded. "That's the gal, all right. I wouldn't mind waltzing her Matilda around the floor once or twice. No offense intended, ladies," he added, acknowledging our presence at the back of the boat.

Colin shrugged. "Leslie must have been in one of the first groups off. Or else she stayed behind."

"With Captain Mike?" the Texan asked. "I thought those two looked pretty friendly when we boarded."

Maybe it was the mention of Captain Mike that woke me up. For whatever reason, though, I was suddenly uneasy.

"I don't remember seeing Leslie after . . ."

Frenchie's assistant interrupted with a laugh in her voice. "More likely she's with the fishing camp group. Remember how she and Charlie were at the New Year's Eve party?"

Colin turned off the motor. The fading strains of "Waltzing Matilda" again reached us. The dive boat had disappeared into the night, and the voices from across the water sounded thin and eerie. We bumped gently into the pier. Within seconds we'd all be separating for the evening. I didn't want that to happen until I was sure about Leslie.

"Did anyone actually see Leslie after the dive?"

Colin was tying the boat to the dock. He paused, the rope in his hand. Frenchie's assistant rubbed her forehead.

"I think . . ." she began.

"I saw Leslie," Sonny announced. "I helped her out of her wetsuit. The two of us had a nice long talk up on the flying bilge."

When he'd said this, he gave me a quick, sneaky look and I realized that he wanted me to tell his wife about his latest transgression.

"It's bridge," I said. "Flying *bridge*. Your talk was on the flying bilge."

"Lucky guy, however you look at it," said the Texan.

The last thing I heard as I walked from the pier was the obscene grunting that passed for Sonny's laugh: "Uh uh uh."

NINE

SNORKELING
AT THE CORAL REEF

I woke slowly, into a sticky morning. Everything stuck to my skin: the sheets, my cotton nightgown. My hair clung to my neck. It was going to be an unusually hot day.

Stirring, I looked across the room at Leslie's bed. It hadn't been slept in. Three nights I'd been there, and Leslie's bed had been slept in once. I didn't envy her, but she probably didn't envy me, either.

As always, Early Bird Aerobics went well. When the class was over I had a late breakfast in the kitchen. The clattering of pots, the easy chatter of the cook and his assistant helped me keep my mind off my impending date. I'd had time to worry about it by then. It was starting to seem like impending doom.

After breakfast I went back to the room to change clothes. A ride on a boat to look at some fish. What's the big deal? Shorts and a T-shirt over a bathing suit. I put on the new red and black one first. I had yet to wear it. Pulling back my shoulders, I posed in front of the mirror, chest out, the way Leslie had when she announced she had the key to paradise. The woman who looked back at me was not the one Captain Mike would take to the reef that afternoon. I peeled off the suit.

When I left the room I was in the baggy blue suit, topped with droopy shorts and a big old T-shirt.

I wanted to pick up a snorkel and fins from the beach shack, but found the building locked when I got there. I went to the reception desk for an extra key.

"Seen Leslie around this morning?" I asked the clerk.

"No," she said. "Colin's looking for her too. And Eleanor, and half a dozen people wanting to get floats. Are you going to fill in for her?" She motioned me closer with a crooked finger. "Don't be taking on any extra work. We're not getting paid this week, I hear."

"No problem there. I've got the afternoon off. I'm just borrowing a snorkel. I'll bring back the key."

It was bright daylight, perhaps the clearest day yet, but when I slipped the key into the beach shack door, my fingers started to tremble. I propped the door open wide and then rummaged through the snorkels and masks. Light poured in through the open door, and I could hear people on the beach. Even so, I jumped at the sound of Neticia's voice.

"Have you seen Leslie?"

She spoke so softly that I had to ask her to repeat her question.

"Leslie? Have you seen her?"

I shook my head. "Not today. She may be with Charlie O'Dell."

Neticia gave me a puzzled look. She was about to say something when Beth ran up behind her and slipped through the door. Within seconds a stack of deflated rubber rafts tumbled from a shelf.

"Beth! What are you doing?"

"Mommy says I can take whatever I want," the child answered. She dragged a bright yellow raft toward the door. "I want to take this one. You can blow it up for me, Neticia. Come on. Let's go!"

Whatever Neticia had been about to say about Leslie was forgotten. Snatching a foot pump from the floor, she hurried after Beth.

I had started replacing rubber rafts on the shelf when I spotted a box up there that made me pause. It had PARASAILING HARNESS lettered on it. Eleanor hadn't mentioned parasailing in a while. Just in case she did, though, and Leslie wasn't around to help, it was nice to know where the equipment was. Not that I intended to use it. If things ever reached that point, I would take the damned thing out to the forest and hide it under a bush. For now I piled rubber rafts high around the box.

I found a snorkel that seemed to be in good shape, and a pair of fins and left the shack, locking the door behind me.

There were lots of people on the beach. Neticia was pumping mightily as Beth looked on. The prim woman and her buttoned-down husband were under an umbrella. In her white bikini the woman didn't look so prim any more, and the buttoned-down husband was looking downright carefree in his funny flowered trunks. That's what the islands do to people, I mused as I walked slowly across the sand. And maybe I was starting to feel more like an island girl myself.

Cindy was on the beach in a sun-drenched spot by the water. I wasn't eager to talk to her, but her lounge chair was almost in my path and she was facing my way. I couldn't ignore her "hello."

"Beautiful day, isn't it?" I said.

"Em," she answered absently. "What time did *she* get back to your room last night?"

So much for small talk.

"Cindy, I've told you I don't keep track of Leslie."

Cindy lifted her sunglasses off her nose and nodded up toward the balcony of the honeymoon suite. She had set her chair at an angle so that she could keep an eye on the room.

"Sonny came back to our room before midnight. I think he'd been at the casino. He had some chips in his pocket." She looked at me. "You know what, Bonnie? I got the feeling he wanted to make up. He was . . . you know . . . sort of affectionate. I've been thinking maybe you were right about that first night. Remember how you said he might be nervous, too? Maybe he's been trying to make me jealous with Leslie. Maybe there's nothing going on between them."

"Maybe not." There was nothing to be gained by mentioning what Sonny had said in the dinghy the night before. Frankly, I was having second thoughts about Leslie's "special mate." The special mate was sensitive and intelligent. That didn't sound like Sonny to me.

Cindy's hands were very still on her lap. "He was taking his shower when I came down here. He's still in the room. Should I go up there and try to make up with him?"

I shrugged. "That might be a good idea." I left her sitting in the lounge chair, chewing a knuckle and staring at the door to the honeymoon suite.

About one o'clock, Mike had said. I had a few minutes to spare. I wanted to drop off the beach shack key, but the reception desk was closed so I pocketed it. I then filched a couple of corn muffins from the kitchen, and strolled casually down to the dock. If he was waiting, how nice. If I had to wait, there was a shady spot and a place where I could get a soda, and that was nice too.

And then I'd go on my nice, casual date. That's all it was. Casual. I looked down at my old grey shorts, flopping just over my knees. Baggy Bonnie.

The sun beat down on the daypack I was carrying, and the muffins bloomed in there, filling the air around me with the scent of cornmeal. If Captain Mike was expecting a hot tamale in a skimpy suit, too bad for him. It was less stress for me this way, and that's what I wanted from the rest of my stay on the island: less stress for me.

He was already at the dock. I saw him from the distance, leaning against one of the pilings. He was barefoot, and wearing a T-shirt over bathing trunks. The rumpled white sailor hat covered his head. My outfit was perfect.

As I approached, he glanced at the watch on his wrist. I started to move faster, but stopped myself. I was an Island Girl now, on island time.

"Am I late?"

"Not much. I'm always early. A bad habit I can't shake."

In the water behind him was a small sleek boat with burnished leather cushions on its seats.

"I'm impressed," I said.

"So am I. Unfortunately, it belongs to that fancy man you work for. That's mine."

He pointed to a boat with an outboard motor mounted on its back and MIKE'S MISTAKE painted on its side. The boat had been white at some point in its not too distant past, but the white was greying and dented. The awning mounted on aluminum poles had once been as bright green as the one on Colin's boat, but now it was cracked and faded. A rip had been patched with a torn piece of yellow rubber.

"Mike's Mistake?"

"One of many. Don't worry," he added. "I've got life jackets." He stared at my pack. "Is that food I smell, or are you wearing cornmeal perfume?"

"I have some muffins. You hungry?"

"Starved. We can go into town and get something later, but for now. . . ."

A hungry man, with a crummy old boat. Poor thing. I opened my pack. He wolfed down one muffin, and then eyed the other.

"Go ahead," I said. "I had mine already."

When he'd finished off the muffins, we hopped onto *Mike's Mistake*.

We sat in the tattered seats behind the pockmarked windscreen. When Mike turned the key, the motor coughed a few times, and then we were off, noisy and fast with the wind whipping around us. I didn't have time to worry about the snorkel, or anything else. There was too much noise for talk at anything less than a shout, and it didn't seem that either of us had anything to say that justified shouting.

Less than ten minutes and we were at the reef. Mike steered the boat up close to Pirate's Cay where the water was calm, switched off the motor and dropped anchor.

"It doesn't seem as eerie in the daylight," I said. "Where exactly were we last night?"

He pointed about twenty feet from the boat. Just below the surface I could see some rocks. "On the other side of those rocks. The water's about thirty feet there. We'll stay in here where it's shallower."

"Fine with me." I stepped out of my shorts and was pulling my shirt over my head when Mike stopped me.

"You'd be wise to leave your shirt on. Your back will be raw otherwise."

So much for the lecher lusting after my willowy charms.

He lowered a short wooden ladder off the side of the boat while I smeared sun blocker over my legs, arms and face. I put the pair of flippers on my feet. Then came the moment of reckoning.

"Where's your snorkel? In your pack? I'll show you how to use it."

Nodding, I opened the pack and took out the snorkel and mask. There was the slightest tightening in my throat, but I managed to get the mask over my head. I took a deep breath before I pulled it down over my eyes and then my nose. The snorkel hung by its rubber strap alongside my face.

"Okay," Mike was saying. "You want to put the snorkel in your mouth. Try to breathe normally."

He was sitting next to me. He took the snorkel in his hand and held it by my mouth. "Here. Try it."

I reached for the snorkel, but the chain reaction had already begun: a thudding heartbeat, and the mask tight over my face so that I couldn't get my breath.

I yanked the thing off my head. "I don't want to wear this. I can see fine in the water without it."

He look at me curiously. "Maybe, but it's hard on your eyes. You'll get tired faster, too, trying to breathe without it. What's the matter?"

I shook my head. "Nothing. I don't like the mask."

"You a little phobic?"

He might have accused me of being a little depraved, the way I snapped, "I am not a little phobic!"

He sat back away from me, and his glance fell onto the snorkel. I had a hard grip on it. My hands were shaking noticeably.

"Maybe this wasn't such a good idea," he finally said. Getting off the bench, he fished around behind him and found a life jacket. "You can swim wearing this."

Tears welled in my eyes. I swallowed hard, trying not to cry. I've never been good at that—not crying. Sure enough, a tear streamed down my check. And another. I looked at my date through a watery veil.

"Why don't we skip this," he said after a second. "I'd be more comfortable if you put this life jacket on for the ride back."

He thought he was out in the ocean with a crazy lady. I wiped my tears away with my hand and tried to smile. "I'm not nuts."

His response came all too fast. "Of course not. I didn't think you were."

I took a deep breath. "It's just that something crummy happened to me the night before last." I told Mike about Monte Carlo night, and the man in the beach shack.

"He was trying to smother me. Since then I've had this fear of putting something over my nose and mouth."

He sank back onto the seat beside me. "Smother you? Who would do a thing like that?"

I shook my head.

"How awful! The guy didn't steal anything, or do anything else?"

"No. I keep telling everyone, he just tried to kill me."

"It's hard to think that could happen here."

"Hard for you and everyone else, maybe, but it's not hard for me to think it."

"I guess you're right about that. And the police say it might have been one of those off-islanders who have been robbing tourists? Seems like an odd thing for a robber to do, doesn't it?" Then he rubbed his forehead. "What would a robber be doing in the beach shack? I was there with Charlie one day when he visited Leslie. There's nothing in there that isn't falling apart. They don't even use cash at the shack, do they?"

"No. The guests sign for whatever they take. It's charged against their rooms."

"The whole thing sounds strange."

He couldn't have known how glad I was to hear him say that.

"That's what I think, but Eleanor and Colin want to believe I walked into a robbery. I couldn't tell about Chief Richards, but he seemed to go along with them."

"Don't underestimate old Roscoe. He's no fool."

I leaned back and let the sun fall on my face. "Thanks for listening. You're not having much of an afternoon off, are you?"

"I've had worse. You feel like getting lunch? We could go into town."

I looked out at the horizon. High white clouds dotted the blue sky, and the afternoon sun streamed over the water at us. Sailboats tilted in the stiff breeze and gulls dived for fish. Way out on the horizon a big fishing boat was anchored. Mike nodded in that direction.

"That's Charlie, out with a group from the fishing camp."

"I wonder if Leslie is with them. She didn't come back last night."

He squinted into the sun, then looked back at me. "She didn't? Well, she didn't stay with me. I don't even remember seeing her after your group left. Of course, I was on the bridge when Charlie's bunch got off."

"I know she got out of the water. Someone in our group talked to her after the dive. Up on the bridge, in fact. You didn't see her?"

Mike shrugged. "I don't think so, but there were people everywhere. I can tell you she's not out there with Charlie on that fishing boat, though. Leslie hates fishing."

"How do you know?"

"On Flamingo Island everybody knows everything about everybody. Whisper something at the airport at noon. By evening the staff at the hotel knows it. Right now the entire island's wondering what you and I are up to."

"I hope they didn't see my anxiety attack." I nodded back at the cay. "It's awfully desolate-looking. Nothing like the island."

"The cay's greener on the other side, but not by much. There's supposed to be buried pirate treasure there, but I sure didn't find it."

"You looked?"

"Not very hard. Charlie and I came out here fishing one time. Paul was with us. When Paul and I got tired of fishing, we kicked a few rocks over. No luck."

"Paul Tyndall? I'm surprised. He doesn't seem as if he'd have a lot in common with you and Charlie. Or most other people. You should see these monkeys . . ."

"The devil eyes," Mike said with laughter in his voice. "I've seen them. Paul's just trying to keep the kids away from the research site. He's not a bad guy. I haven't seen much of him lately, but I'll tell you, Bonnie: You take your friends where you find them down here. Stay long enough and you and Leslie will be sharing romance novels."

"We already are."

He nodded. "See. Now, do you want to get lunch?"

I lifted my feet. The big rubber flippers still weighted them down. The mask was still in my hand. I stared at the rubber nose piece.

"Actually, if you can stand it, I'd like to try the mask and snorkel one more time."

Five minutes, and not too many thudding heartbeats later, I was in the water, mask and snorkel in place. Mike was a patient teacher, and once, when anxiety threatened to send me back onto the boat, he talked me through it.

"I know CPR," he said. "The worst thing that can happen to you out here is me giving you mouth-to-mouth resuscitation."

A nice guy, I remember thinking as my anxiety lifted. Too bad he lives down here.

When I was able to float on the surface and breathe through

the snorkel, he showed me how to dive under and surface and clear the snorkel. Soon we were moving through the water close to the cay. It was shallow there, and I could see the ocean floor easily. What a wonderful sight! Mike showed me forests of staghorn coral, and the purple seafans that swayed with the surging water. A school of curious blue damselfish came close to look us over. A red grouper ducked shyly behind a clump of brain coral.

The flippers gave me a lot of leverage against the water, and made movement easy. We swam around like this for about half an hour. It wasn't exhaustion that made me swim back to the boat. It was the sensation of the hot sun burning my neck and arms. Taking the snorkel out of my mouth, I called to Mike.

"I'm going to the boat for some sunblocker."

He was drifting near some rocks, sure he'd spotted some spiny lobster waiting to be turned into dinner.

"I'll join you in a minute," he shouted.

I put the snorkel back in my mouth and headed out. The boat had been tugged by the tide until it stretched far on the anchor line where the water was deeper. It was still calm, though, and I reached the ladder easily. Grabbing it with one hand, I bent to remove my flippers with the other. The first came off with no problem. I threw it onto the boat and started on the second one. There was something wrong with the buckle. I fumbled with it for a second before the rubber strap snapped off in my fingers. So much for Flamingo Cove's rotting equipment. Ducking my head under water, I watched the flipper spiraling to the bottom.

Eleanor would be sure to take that out of my paycheck, if I got a paycheck at all. The flipper finally settled near a bed of coral on the ocean floor. Maybe I could ditch the mate, too. Would anyone check? I was staring down at the thing when a few tiny red and blue fish caught my eye. They were so bright, like dots of neon nestled among the strands of a filmy pale plant that floated out of an old fishing net. What could they be?

Mike had swum up next to me and removed his flippers.

Raising my head, I cleared my mask with saliva the way he had showed me.

"See something interesting?" he asked as he started up the ladder.

"I don't know."

In the distance a big cruise boat was passing by.

"We're going to get that wake. You better hurry." He offered me a hand up.

"Just one second."

"I've created a monster," he said as I slipped the mask back on.

I thought my flipper had moved when I ducked back under the water. But it hadn't. It was still directly beneath me. Then I saw that there were two other flippers down there, protruding from under the old net. I focused again, on the pin-points of neon light. The wake from the cruise boat hit. I gripped the ladder harder and watched the net undulate with the current.

Suddenly I started. A face was peeking up at me, pushing through an opening in the folds of net. It couldn't be, though. It was a big fish with a pale, puffy human face. The current settled. The big fish disappeared. And then I saw the bright blue wetsuit floating beneath the net. In a horrible flash of recognition, I knew what it was.

I jerked my head from the water and sputtered, "Leslie's down there."

Mike looked over the side. "What?"

"Leslie's down there. She's caught in a net."

"Get in." He half pulled me up the ladder and I was afraid he hadn't believed me. As soon as I was on board, though, he dived into the deep water. It seemed forever, but it really was only seconds before he was climbing up the ladder. He looked at me, his eyes wide.

"We left Leslie behind last night. Just left her to die."

The motor started easily and we sped toward Woodestown.

TEN

WOODESTOWN

Leslie had become tangled in a discarded fishing net that was snagged by massive growths of coral on the ocean's floor, and had been left behind by the dive boat. The police divers who went back to the reef with us suggested that the net had first caught on her regulator, where she couldn't reach it.

She'd had at least ten minutes worth of air remaining in her tank when she became trapped. That was ten minutes worth of life, and during that short time she had fought desperately to free herself from the heavy net. These struggles had only made her situation more impossible. Both feet had been completely ensnared and her right arm immobilized by the net. She had managed to get out of her weight belt, but it had merely fallen into the net, further weighing her down. She had had the presence of mind to get some air into her buoyancy compensator, too, but it had lifted her only as far as the net could stretch away from the coral. According to the divers, the net had been on the reef for months. It was not a light casting net. It had fallen from a good-sized fishing boat.

Toward the end Leslie may have been irrational, not only with fear but with delirium. The police told us that if a diver panics and gulps air, the tank regulator isn't able to handle the exaggerated breathing and can't provide sufficient air. With Leslie's air hunger feeding her panic, and her panic adding to her air hunger, she didn't have much chance. Maybe she ripped the mask from her face at that point. Or maybe she did that earlier. Maybe as the bright light from the dive boat disappeared and the sound of those big engines faded away, she panicked and tried to scream after us. In that case, she died with precious air remaining in her tank.

No one will ever know what happened to Leslie during her last few minutes. She had a cool head, though. I know that. I suspect she didn't rip the mask off right away. She knew the Pirate's Cay was close by. She could have made it easily, if only she hadn't been so hopelessly trapped by that net. I imagine her fighting it as long as she could. What a terrible, lonely way to die.

It was hours before Leslie's body was recovered by the divers and taken away for autopsy. Then there was another long wait while the divers searched the reef. By the time Mike and I got back to Chief Richards' office to make our statement, it was almost evening.

The police station in the little village of Woodestown is located in the impressive-sounding Government House. Government House is, in fact, the only stone building in town, and boasts an arched double door, which sets it apart from its neighbors, and a worn placard, carved from stone, that tells the visitor it was built in 1857. That afternoon its one jail cell stood empty of everything but a cot and a pail. Light trickled through a small barred window. Graffiti, some of it obscene, some of it sad, had been left by over a century of prisoners. As we passed the cell I saw a primitive drawing of a marijuana plant, and got a whiff of dank air, stale sweat and urine. I turned my head away.

A blast of icy cold air hit us when Mike opened the door to the chief's office. I stepped in gratefully. A big air conditioner rumbled in one of the windows.

"Have a seat," Chief Richards said, indicating a couple of hard ladderback chairs in front of his desk. The chief himself was in a rather grand carved chair behind an old mahogany desk. There was a woman stenographer at the side of the room. Through the window behind her I could see the pretty, almost New England-type houses along the main street. The ebbing yellow sun was low over the horizon, and shoppers passing back and forth left long shadows in the street.

We began by giving our names and addresses to the stenographer. I went first, then Mike. Michael Schrader. I hadn't known his last name until then. He had lived in Woodestown for ten months.

"And you are from the States. You carry a U.S. passport?"

"You know that," Mike said irritably.

The chief sat passively. "Tell the stenographer, please."

"Originally from Long Island, New York. I have a work permit."

That was about as outgoing as Mike had been since we discovered Leslie's body. The whole time we'd waited for the divers to surface at the reef, he had stared quietly into the distance, lost in his own thoughts.

We all react differently to something like Leslie's death. My initial horror had given way to a dull ache in the pit of my stomach. I hadn't cried, though I eventually would. What I wanted to do by the time I got to Chief Richards' office was talk about it.

Mike's statement was short and simple. Mine was long, rambling, complicated by the many questions that had been taking shape in my mind.

"What about her clothes?" I asked. "How did they disappear from under that bench? And where's her flashlight? She had one when she went in the water. I saw her testing it. The divers didn't find one."

The chief shrugged. "She must have dropped it. The waves can be rough out there. The flashlight could have drifted. My men are going back in the morning to search the area again."

"I looked, you know. I looked at the reef before we pulled away. I didn't see any light under water."

113

There was a desperate edge in my voice, and I knew why. I was on the defensive. I had kept the list of divers. I was the one who had drawn a line through Leslie's name.

The chief said sympathetically, "Accidents happen, Miss Indermill."

Accidents, sure, but was this an accident? I had told Chief Richards about Leslie's "special mate," and about her talk of plots and schemes. I had suggested that Leslie might be trying to manipulate this man, and that maybe Neticia knew about this. I also told the chief my theory about my attacker—that possibly the man had been after Leslie.

The chief listened quietly to everything I said. I couldn't tell what he was thinking.

Now I leaned across his desk. "But somebody answered when I called Leslie's name. I'm sure of that. I wouldn't have scratched it out otherwise."

Mike put his hand on my arm. "It's okay, Bonnie. Nobody's blaming you."

I was blaming me. I went on, trying to explain what it had been like on the dive boat. "Voices were coming at me from all over, until I could hardly keep track of them. But I'm sure someone answered 'here' or 'yes' or something when I called out Leslie's name."

The chief just nodded. He'd heard it already. I forced myself to stop talking and settled back into the chair. I kept saying I was sure of things, but how sure was I of anything? There had been such confusion on the dive boat. "Here" and "yes" had been shouted from the bridge and called out from below. Could I swear there was a shout for every name on my list? Could I even swear that when I called Leslie's name it was a woman's voice that answered?

The stenographer in the corner took down everything Mike and I said. My statement was going to be the longer one. That was certain.

"This couple you referred to, Miss Indermill." Chief Richards looked down at his notes. "Sonny and Cindy. You heard the woman say . . ."

He glanced at the stenographer. She flipped back through her notes and read out loud: "Before she left the bridge, Cindy said, 'I hope she drowns tonight.' "

"I'm not sure about her exact words, but I think that's right."

He then asked the stenographer to read another few lines from her notes.

" 'I helped her out of her wetsuit. The two of us had a long talk on the flying bridge.' "

The chief gave me a thoughtful look. "You are sure he was referring to the time *after* the divers surfaced?"

I nodded. "I may not be quoting him exactly, but there were other people in the dinghy. They can confirm that Sonny said he had been with Leslie after the dive."

The chief rose slowly. "I'll be at the hotel tomorrow morning. If you still have that list, I'd like to have it. You will both be available for further questions?"

I nodded. "Seven more days."

For a moment Mike said nothing. When the chief continued staring at him, he muttered, "You know I'm not planning on going anywhere."

A blast of dank hot air hit us when we walked from the chief's office. As we hurried past the empty jail cell, we almost collided with Colin and Frenchie. The two men were on their way in to see the chief. They told us they had been called about Leslie's death. They were there to give statements about the night dive.

I'd never seen Colin without his perfect resort-owner look, but this time he must have put himself together hastily. His dark blue pants were rumpled and his sneakers dirty. He hadn't shaved. He was pale, and the stubble on his cheeks stood out against the pallor of his skin.

"Eleanor is devastated. I had to get the doctor to give her tranquilizers," he said, explaining his wife's absence. "Poor Leslie. What a tragic accident."

"I would not call it an accident," Frenchie snapped. In

contrast to his ashen boss, Frenchie's dark skin was flushed crimson. "Charlie O'Dell brought liquor on board. He coaxed an inexperienced diver to drink. That is criminal. The man should never have been permitted to lead dives."

The two men disappeared into the chief's office.

Mike and I walked through the building and out into the street. It was late evening by then. The sun was a red half-circle peeking from behind the pastel buildings.

"I have to go to work," Mike said. "I'm taking a party boat out to Nassau. Moonlight cruise. You want to go along?"

"No. I've had enough of boats for the day."

"So have I, but I don't have a choice. I'll get you a cab."

I would have loved the comfort of a cab, but I didn't have the money to spare and I didn't want to take money from Mike if he offered.

"I'd rather take the bus, if you'll point me to the stop."

"It's at the next corner. I'll walk you there."

We set out up the street together, but not companionably. He was preoccupied again, lost in his own world. I wasn't certain what was wrong, but I knew something was and an ugly idea had been worming it's way into my thoughts.

"Had you ever been out with Leslie?"

He hesitated before answering, long enough so that I knew his answer was going to be yes.

"Leslie went out with many men. Before I knew about her and Charlie, I took her out a few times."

We stopped under a big tree at the corner. A bus stop sign had been nailed to the trunk. A couple of native women stood waiting.

I kept my voice low so that the women wouldn't overhear. "You weren't still involved with Leslie, were you?" It was a crazy question but I couldn't help myself.

"What? Me?" He blinked, then stared hard. "You're asking if I was the guy Leslie was so crazy about?"

"Not really." I hesitated. "Well, yes. I guess I am."

"If that was the case, why would I be seeing her on the sly? If

116

I want to date a woman, I do it in public. Look at us." He made an expansive gesture with his hands. "By morning everybody on this godforsaken island will know we went out."

"Sorry. It's just that you two were friendly last night, but you didn't want your picture taken with her. That was obvious to me. And you've been so preoccupied all afternoon, ever since we found Leslie's"—I couldn't brink myself to say body—"since we found Leslie, that it struck me maybe you were this man."

"You're very observant. If you thought that, didn't it also strike you as funny that I asked you out?"

I could feel the blood rising to my face. In the process of grasping for answers, I had managed to come up with something that made no sense at all.

"I apologize. My mind is in a jumble right now."

"It sure is," he said. "I am guilty of taking part in some things that might bother you, Bonnie, but dating two roommates at the same time isn't one of them. A minute ago I told you that Leslie and I went out a few times when I first got here. I wasn't special to her; she wasn't special to me. We had nothing in common. Even if I hadn't found out that Charlie was crazy about her, our fling would have died a natural quiet death. I hadn't been near her in months." He nodded over my shoulder. "Here comes your bus."

Even before the white van pulled up under the tree, Mike had stalked away. When the driver opened the door, I followed the native women aboard and took one of the single seats by a window. The bus followed Main Street toward the bridge at the bottom of the hill. I caught sight of Mike on one of the side streets. His fists were clenched and his shoulders hunched. He walked with his head down, seemingly unaware of the children playing in the road around him.

He'd been so nice to me. What a crummy way I'd found to pay him back for his kindness.

Someone was in my room. I was outside the door, about to put my key in the lock, when I heard a drawer sliding shut. Leaning closer, until my ear rested against the wood, I listened. Another drawer opened, then closed.

I had moved quietly along the walkway. I didn't want anyone to notice me, talk to me, wave to me, ask me about Leslie. I'd had enough conversation for the day. I wanted to disappear into my room and settle into a quiet funk. Instead, I'd managed to sneak up on someone searching my room.

The person was in the kitchenette now. The refrigerator door clicked open.

I tiptoed to the window and peeked through an opening in the curtain.

Neticia! She had just shut the refrigerator. I watched her walk back into the bedroom. Like me, she was on tiptoes.

I crept back to the door, put my key in the lock, turned it as quietly as I could, and burst into the room.

"What are you looking for?"

I had frightened her badly. She was always shy; now her voice quavered as she tried to explain herself.

"I heard about what happened to Leslie. I was just looking for . . ." Her glance fell on the pile of paperback books next to Leslie's bed. She grabbed one hastily. "I was looking for this book. Leslie borrowed it from me."

Holding the flimsy paperback in front of her chest as if it was a shield, she edged along the wall toward the door. I glanced at the cover: a blonde beauty in a blue ball gown, a full moon shining through a window, a sinister man wearing a black cape.

"Oh. I'm surprised you didn't find it in the fridge. Do you have a key to this room?"

Neticia dug one from her pocket. "Leslie gave it to me."

I held out my hand. After a second's hesitation, the girl dropped the key into it. She scurried past me, not saying anything. Once she was within an easy leap of the door, she mumbled, "I wasn't going to steal anything. Leslie was my friend. We shared things with each other."

She slipped through the door and let the screen close quietly behind her. I listened to the sound of her footsteps retreating down the steps. Through the screen, I saw her shadow against the next building as she crossed the path. She was probably going around back to see the flamingo chick, but she disappeared into the evening before I could really know.

I closed the door and locked it. The list of names from the night dive was still crumpled in the bottom of my tote. As I sipped a cup of tea, I looked it over. There was Leslie's name, almost at the end of the list. What did that mean? Only one thing that I could think of.

By the time I had started calling out names, Cindy was out of her wetsuit. Cindy's name was near the beginning of the list. She could have answered to her own name, quickly moved to a part of the boat where she couldn't be seen, and then answered when I called Leslie's name. She might even have faked an accent. I was certain of one thing: Someone had answered. If they hadn't, I wouldn't have drawn that line through Leslie's name.

Night comes quickly in the tropics. I opened the curtains wide and sat at the edge of my bed with the list in my hand. I'd hardly known Leslie, but suddenly I missed her—her silly chatter, her absurd ideas and her petty vanities. The key to paradise had eluded her. I watched the blue twilight shroud the forest through my tears.

ELEVEN

THE ISLAND BUFFET

A noise jarred me from my sleep. Dead quiet followed, and as I lay in my bed there was an instant when I didn't know where I was and my heartbeat quickened. I had slept badly, disturbed by dreams that I couldn't remember.

There was the noise again—a rapid tapping on my door.

I forced myself awake and sat up. The sun peeking through my curtains was still low over the forest.

"Miss Indermill?"

"Who is it?"

"Chief Richards."

The clock on Leslie's dresser told me it was just after eight A.M. The police weren't paying much attention to island time.

"Just a minute, please."

I threw on my robe and opened the door to the police chief. Even in the relative cool of early morning, he was mopping his brow with a white handkerchief. With him was a young woman officer in uniform.

I gave Chief Richards the list of names I'd kept on the night dive.

"We'd like to take a quick look through your roommate's things while we're here," he said. "If we take anything, we'll give you a voucher."

Even in my half-awake condition, I could see the problems with that. "I'll be leaving here in a week. You better give it to Eleanor or Colin."

"I thought that would be best, too, but the Ledbetters told me to deal with you for the time being. We haven't been able to locate any of the young lady's relatives yet."

I had become Leslie's next of kin by default. It wasn't hard to understand why the Ledbetters wanted the police to deal with me. How would it look to the Texans if their hosts were being hounded by cops? An investor might get the idea that this wasn't such a great place after all.

I sat on the edge of my bed while Chief Richards and the officer moved carefully around the room, methodically searching Leslie's belongings. What a sad little accumulation it was: Her jewelry was costume, her clothes inexpensive. And there were the books, of course.

I saw the uniformed officer eyeing the stacks of paperbacks covetously. Books are expensive in the islands, when you can get them at all.

"Such a lot of books," she said. "Are they yours?"

"No. Some of them were Leslie's. Some belong to the woman I'm filling in for. Borrow any of them you want."

She picked up the nurse romance I'd started, and glanced at the chief. He shrugged. "Make sure you sign for anything you take."

He crouched on the floor and peered beneath Leslie's bed. There was nothing under it but shoes. His eye wandered to the foot of my bed.

"Is that your suitcase, or hers?"

"It's mine."

He got back to his feet as the young officer said, "Oh, look at this."

She'd been searching Leslie's dresser. Beneath a few folded T-shirts, she had found some wadded Bahamian currency hidden away in a rolled-up sock. She handed it to Chief Richards and his eyebrow lifted. He smoothed the bills and counted them, then glanced at me.

"Forty dollars?"

"It was her emergency money. She hid it after I was attacked in the beach shack."

His lips tightened at the mention of the beach shack. He put the money on the dresser, along with Leslie's passport.

"Strange there's no wallet," the officer said.

"Leslie had it with her on the dive boat. She told me it was in the back pocket of her jeans. That's in my statement," I added.

It didn't take them long to finish with Leslie's things. Before he left, Chief Richards told me that he'd already spoken to Neticia.

"She says she knows nothing about any of Leslie's boyfriends. She says that she and Leslie talked mostly about clothes and books. I'm afraid I frightened the girl."

What could I say to that? I had no proof of any secrets between Leslie and Neticia. All I had were Beth's complaints about neglect. I didn't tell the chief that I'd found Neticia searching the room the night before. She would deny that, too. I decided I would talk to her myself when I got the chance.

When the two of them had left the room, I picked up the receipt Chief Richards had signed. The police had taken Leslie's passport, forty dollars, an address book, a few loose photographs, and three paperback novels. It was a sad little showing, and yet Leslie had something that Neticia wanted so badly that she had sneaked into my room to search for it.

The room had been searched twice now. Whatever it was that Neticia wanted, it either wasn't in the room, or it was so small that Neticia, who presumably knew what she was looking for, had missed it. The beach shack was the obvious place, and I still had the key. If I hurried, I could search the shack before Early Bird Aerobics.

I started at the bottom—among the towels and cartons of soft drinks on the floor. I searched behind the soda cooler and among the stacked beach chairs. Nothing. I worked my way up through the snorkels hanging on their hooks, and up further to the rubber rafts on the shelf. My mind had become fixed on a piece of jewelry. A diamond ring, to be specific. This man had given one to Leslie. When he wanted it back, she said "no" and hid it. But what was Neticia's part in this? Go-between? Maybe. . . .

"Is there something I can help you find?"

I was so startled I almost fell off the chair I was standing on. Colin was staring at me from the doorway, head tilted. He was in his jogging shorts, and shirtless. A sheen of sweat covered his chest. Of course, he smiled.

He's not for real, I thought. He's too calm. Too composed. He smiles too damned much!

And, as quickly as I had fallen under Colin's spell that first afternoon when I arrived on Flamingo Island, I fell out from under it. My by-then-automatic reflex—suck in that tummy, Bonnie!—failed me. Slumping against the shelf, I shook my head.

"You're searching so diligently. What is it you're looking for?"

"I found it." I pulled out the box I'd hidden the day before. "The parasailing equipment. One of the guests was asking about it."

"Well, you had better forget it for now. Your aerobics class is waiting for you."

Leslie's death hadn't been broadcast to Flamingo Cove's guests. If any of my Early Birds knew about it, which I doubted, none mentioned it. We were doing some thigh-trimmers when suddenly I was the only one moving. Everyone was still. Every eye in the group was focused on the same spot somewhere behind me.

I turned and glanced at the building that fronted on the beach. The door to the Honeymoon Suite was standing open. The young woman officer was outside the room. When Chief Richards led Sonny and Cindy through the door, one of the women in my group asked,

"What do you suppose is going on?"

The two weren't handcuffed, and the chief and his officer didn't have guns. Still, Sonny's scowl as he hastily buttoned an orange and aqua print shirt, Cindy's dark glasses and ever-present soggy tissue, made it clear that the couple wasn't being taken off to a champagne brunch.

The chief had a clear plastic bag in one hand.

"What's in the bag?"

"Can't tell."

"Cocaine smuggling's a problem down here," someone offered. "Maybe it's drugs."

"Whatever it is," the prim woman said, "I'm sure he's guilty of something."

"It hasn't been much of a honeymoon for his poor little bride. I feel sorry for her."

How sorry would they feel if they knew Leslie was dead?

The couple was escorted past the restaurant, over the patio, down the drive and into a waiting police car, while the group of us stood, mesmerized.

"He looks the criminal type, doesn't he?"

"That shirt's certainly criminal," said the sole male member of our group.

We saw what happened when Chief Richards took hold of Sonny's elbow to steer him into the waiting car. Sonny yanked his arm away angrily. We couldn't hear what he said to the chief, but we all saw him bare his teeth and snarl something.

The scene had transfixed us. For me, it was as if all the vibrant colors at the resort had faded. The pink awning, the swaying green palms, the stretch of golden sand disappeared into a haze, and all I saw was Sonny's orange and aqua shirt and the white flash of his exposed teeth.

"Bonnie, may I please speak to you for a second?"

Whoops! Caught again! Eleanor had come up behind us. "Please," she said, and her smile was plastered into place, but there was a little barb in that voice. I followed my boss to the water, out of the group's hearing.

"I realize that something unusual is going on," she said softly, "but remember, Bonnie, that you are an employee. It is your job to entertain and *divert* the guests. You're being paid to lead them in an exercise session."

As she spoke, that toothy public relations smile was there for the benefit of my group and anyone else who wandered past. Eleanor's smile didn't come as easily as her husband's, though. That morning it showed more strain than usual. Her face was puffy around the eyes and drawn around the mouth. She was as upset about Leslie as I was. Maybe more. Eleanor had known Leslie longer. If she hadn't kept up her scolding, I wouldn't have snapped back.

"You are *not* being paid to gawk at other guests who are experiencing a bit of unpleasantness," she said.

I twisted my face into a smile so broad that it hurt my jaw. "You can't have it both ways, Eleanor. You can't make me the police contact, and at the same time ask me to pretend nothing's going on. You think I'm forcing my class to gawk? They're as curious as I am."

She started to say something but I kept going. "And while we're on the subject of what I'm being paid for, rumor is I'm not being paid at all! For exercising or gawking or anything else! Now, I've got to get back to my job."

That wiped her smile off. It was back a second later, of course. Even bigger. A Texas-sized smile for the Texans, because here they came with Colin, strolling down the beach. Eleanor waved an exuberant good-bye to me and my class, and an even more exuberant hello to her husband and the Texans.

"What a lovely woman," one of my group said.

"And her husband's so charming."

"He's gorgeous!" was another opinion. "I want to eat him up."

"You must love working for them."

"Adore it! Okay, ladies," I barked. "We're not getting rid of that ugly fat by standing around here. Form two lines. We're going to do some tummy tamers. . . ."

Bonnie the drill sergeant.

126

Seven P.M. at the All-You-Can-Eat Island Buffet on the terrace.

"That little bride killed out of jealousy. Her husband's covering for her," the pink-haired lady said as she took a scoop of conch salad.

"I wouldn't be too sure," the blue-haired lady responded. "Maybe he was sick of Leslie. She could be a bit much, you know. He could have done it to get rid of her." She poked at a plate of limp pineapple and added, "Tsk tsk. It's canned. You would think they could get fresh fruit down here. The only thing that is fresh is this conch. One does get tired of it."

"Maybe they were in it together," someone else in the buffet line suggested.

Mrs. Hussy gave a single nod of her head, scooped half-a-dozen jumbo shrimp and a mountain of cocktail sauce onto her plate, and moved on to the conch fritters. "If that's the case, it's the only thing they've done together since they got here."

Mrs. Hussy and her friends made their way down the buffet table.

A lot had happened between Early Bird Aerobics and the buffet dinner. The police had returned to the hotel that afternoon and interviewed everyone who had been on the dive boat. Leslie's death was now common knowledge. The staff whispered together behind closed doors and in quiet corners. Guests didn't bother whispering. They exchanged gossip under the umbrellas at the pool and around tables at the restaurant.

"They took the film out of my camera to develop," the prim woman announced, wide-eyed. "The shots I took of the night dive."

Early in the afternoon I heard a man who had not been on the diveboat say, "I hear they allowed drinking on that boat." By late afternoon, the same man was saying, "Drunk as lords out there, the bunch of them. It's no wonder there was an accident."

Stories about Charlie O'Dell and the lost divers in the Virgin Islands were rampant. People who had never before heard of

Charlie now cringed at the mention of his name. Opinions about Sonny and Cindy shot off in all directions.

I was hostess that night, freeing Eleanor to sit with the Texans. My job, seating guests as they arrived and taking their drink orders, gave virtually everybody in the place an opportunity to question me. As Leslie's roommate, and the one who found her body, I was an instant authority, a grandmaster in the death of poor Leslie.

It was an honor I didn't want. I said as little as possible. I wasn't trying to protect Sonny and Cindy, or Charlie O'Dell. The thing was, though, nobody really knew what had happened, and I didn't want even Sonny drawn and quartered unless he deserved it. And, when I thought about it, I couldn't imagine Sonny or Cindy being involved in Leslie's death. Even if Sonny was Leslie's "special mate," which I doubted, I'd seen the way he moved in the water: slow and clumsy. How could he have lured a strong swimmer away from the group, found that net, and gotten her tangled in it?

As for Cindy, perhaps her motive was much stronger—she had believed Sonny's bragging. But I knew from experience that she had the muscular strength of an infant. She swam well, but so did Leslie. In an underwater struggle, I would have bet on my roommate.

I answered the barrage of questions that came my way with, "I don't know what happened." I must have said, "I never heard any rumors about Charlie O'Dell" and "No, nobody was drunk" a dozen times. And as for Sonny and Cindy, I shrugged it off with: "The police simply took their statements. They've been back for hours."

This last bit was true. The same car that brought the police back to the hotel had dropped the couple off that afternoon. I'd been at the pool at the time, and had seen them make a quick and quiet retreat to the honeymoon suite.

When the young couple walked onto the terrace that evening, there was an immediate buzz of excited whispers from the other people on the patio. Then, as if on signal, everything grew completely quiet. Not a voice, not a clank of a fork against a plate. Even the table where Eleanor and Colin sat with the Texans fell quiet. A waiter who had been placing drinks on a table stood and stared, a Goombay Punch in his hand.

I never thought I'd have much sympathy for Sonny, but I kind of admired the way he toughed it out. Cindy's lips were compressed and she looked as if she were on the verge of tears. Sonny, though, had his chin high and his chest puffed. He was holding Cindy's hand, something I'd never seen. Maybe it wasn't affection. Maybe her hand was the only thing keeping him from falling down, but I can't say. I hadn't spent the afternoon with them in the honeymoon suite.

I smiled at them. "Good evening. Where would you like to sit?"

Sonny nodded toward a table at the side of the terrace. As I led them past the other diners, conversation resumed full blast, as if a gong had been rung signaling everyone to resume. Voices sounded forced—too loud, too much shrill laughter—but the sudden chatter made things seem more normal.

Whatever had happened that afternoon, either at the police station or in the honeymoon suite, Sonny sure was being nice to his wife. He held her chair for her and asked her so nicely what she wanted to drink that I could only suppose that he was suspected of murder and she was providing his alibi.

As I waited at the bar to fill their drink order, I watched the pair go to the buffet line. She took a plate, and he straightened her sweater on her shoulders. At first, everyone on the terrace pretended not to look. Then Eleanor stood, crossed the floor and fell into the line behind them.

"A little bird told me you got something by express mail today from the States. That wouldn't be those Polaroids of your wedding, would it?"

A slight smile crossed Cindy's face as she nodded. "I have them with me if you'd like to see . . ."

"I would love to."

She followed the couple back to their table. Colin pushed back his chair and joined his wife and the newlyweds. The Texans followed, and then Mrs. Hussy and her friends. By the time I got there with the drinks, Sonny and Cindy were surrounded by the other guests.

Eleanor held one of the Polaroids at arm's length.

"And who is this handsome couple?"

"My Aunt Rose and Uncle Vincent," Cindy said. "He's in construction. They gave us a microwave. And this is my Uncle Joe." She glanced up at me. "He's the one I told you about, Bonnie. The one who . . ."

She stopped abruptly. I think she'd been about to tell me that this was the uncle with "connections," who could have people killed.

I put their drinks on the table, then smiled dutifully at the picture of a skinny, pointy-chinned man with an off-center nose.

"He and his girlfriend gave us a complete place setting of our china. I picked out a pattern called—"

She rattled off a name that meant nothing to me, but it meant something to the Texas wife, who said, "Very nice."

Someone else had given sheets, and someone else a coffee maker, and . . .

The three dozen Polaroids showed a flock of smiling bridesmaids in blue, a troop of husky men in white jackets, enough aunts and uncles and cousins to populate a small country, a curbside full of limos, tables groaning with food.

"Isn't your gown gorgeous," someone said.

Cindy was beaming by then. "It has lace insets here and here"—she ran a finger across the picture—"and my headpiece had the same. . . ."

The picture had been taken in front of the church. Sonny looked out of character—stiff, nervous and cold. And Cindy looked like a bride, in miles of white lace.

Ted the Tubby Texan patted Sonny on the back. "You're a lucky man. I always say marriage is a great institution, if you've got to be institutionalized."

Colin laughed on cue. Everyone else followed his lead. What

a happy group it was that had gathered around the young couple. "Oooh's" and "ah's" rolled off the same tongues that minutes before had speculated about the newlyweds' part in Leslie's death. Hands were pumped and cheeks were kissed.

No doubt about it: Sonny and Cindy had had a wingding of a wedding. A year in the making. Mind-boggling costs for Cindy's family. And for what? I asked myself as I pushed my way out of the group that had gathered around the table. So that Cindy could marry Sonny!

We all make mistakes. Some of us marry Sonnys. That's forgivable, but for God's sake if you're going to do that, do it right. Go to a Las Vegas wedding chapel and have a justice of the peace read the vows and a little old lady in pincurls witness. Want to go all-out romantic? Want a special little something to mark the moment that you hooked up with your prize, this thing you found rutting around at the bottom of the evolutionary scale? Hire an Elvis impersonator to croon "Love Me Tender."

It was after ten by the time I escaped the buffet. As I walked up the path toward my building, the woman from the reception desk stopped me.

"You had a call from that nice man who pilots the big boat. Lucky you. I stuck his number on your door."

"Thanks."

I climbed the steps to my apartment and pulled the piece of paper from my door.

Call me. Let the phone ring. Mike. And a number.

With Leslie's death on my mind, I hadn't given Mike much thought since I'd seen him trudge angrily up that dirt road the afternoon before. What did he want? Surely not a replay of the rollicking good time we'd had on our first date.

As I put my key in the lock, I was thinking about how I'd started our date with a mini-hysteria and finished it by wondering, out loud, if he was involved with Leslie. If he wanted to see more of me, he was either desperate or crazy.

I pushed my door wide open and flicked on the light switch. A sense of unease hit me.

The room seemed different, in a way that was almost imperceptible. It wasn't as if Neticia was clanging around in the kitchen, or the police were moving stacks of books, but the room didn't look right.

I kept my hand on the door knob. "Hello?"

There was no answer. Shutting the door behind me, I looked from one side of the room to the other. There was nothing obvious, but Leslie's mattress was an inch or so askew on the bed frame. It hadn't been that way earlier. And the stack of books on her night table. Hadn't the policewoman left them on the dresser? I'd been back to my room a couple times that day, the last time at about six-thirty, but I hadn't touched the books.

On the other hand, I hadn't studied the room carefully. Maybe paranoia was getting the best of me.

I opened my top drawer. When I found my wallet, my passport, my binoculars and my traveler's checks safe, I decided it was my imagination working overtime, as usual.

Fatigue was catching up to me. After a long hot bath, I made myself a cup of tea, changed into my nightgown and tossed a couple of Leslie's books on my bed. Too bad I'd lost the nurse romance to the policewoman, but nurses weren't the only ones with hot blood rushing through their veins. The policewoman had passed up Leslie's new books, the ones she'd brought back from her night of purple lust. Leslie had finally admitted that the night hadn't been so wonderful, but maybe these books were hot stuff.

I sat down on my bed with a yawn. They'd *better* be hot stuff to keep me awake. Maybe there was one about a moody charter-boat captain and a down-on-her-luck dance instructor. Picking up the first book, I examined the cover. It was another of those corporate romances. I let it fall to the floor. On the cover of the second book, a young beauty stood in a shaft of bright light, a flimsy wrap falling off her shoulders. A light-haired man with a—was that an artist's pallet?

132

Oh, no! My recent ex had been an artist. I threw the book at the wall. It bounced back, landing next to my bed.

Get a grip, Bonnie! You can't let a book cover get to you. Reaching over the side of my bed, I dragged my hand across the floor. Instead of finding the book, though, I suddenly had hold of the strap of my tapestry bag.

My heartbeat quickened. That morning the bag had been at the foot of my bed. Chief Richards had seen it there. So what was it doing up here at the top?

Jumping up, I dragged out the suitcase. It wasn't latched. I flipped open the lid and dumped the contents on my bed. There were my city clothes, my city keys. A scene came back to me:

Eleanor has scolded me. I've put a wet towel over my forehead to stop its throbbing. Leslie is chatting, making my headache worse. "Thanks for the loan of the overnighter," she says. "I'll put your things back in." There is the rattle of keys, and then the sound of a clamp falling into place.

Leslie had latched my case before she slipped it under the bed. The room had been searched again! My bag had been searched! Damn Neticia! Whatever she wanted in my room, whatever the secret she shared with Leslie was, I was going to confront her and get it out of her.

Throwing on my clothes, I stormed from my room.

It was late Monday night, and the hotel was quiet. As I passed the casino, a bored blackjack dealer waved to me. No customers that night.

"Come on over," he called. "I'll teach you the game."

I shook my head. "Can't now."

The pool area was deserted. The last of the diners had left the restaurant. I saw the bartender leaning over the railing looking at the water.

The Ledbetters' house was dark but for a light shining from an upstairs window, and one from the back where the household help stayed. With the resort so quiet, I figured that Eleanor and Colin would be home. I didn't want to get Neticia in trouble, so I circled the side of the house, quietly making my way toward the back. I was almost directly under the lighted second floor window when the voices from the window reached me.

I thought for an embarrassing moment that I had overheard the Ledbetters making love. There were groans and snuffling noises, bedsprings squeaking. Then I realized that I wasn't listening to the sounds of sex. Eleanor was crying and trying to speak through her sobs. Colin was comforting. All her words were lost to me. His murmuring floated softly through the open window, only a few sentences drifting down.

"I never once touched her," he was saying. "Not once. Never even went near her. Please, Eleanor. You've got to pull yourself together."

Never once touched her. There are millions of *hers* in the world, but the *her* on everybody's mind was Leslie. Could Colin be believed? Had he never touched her once? I thought back to the resort course, the way he smiled at Leslie as he led her away from the pool. While they talked, her fingers had briefly touched his. Sure, Colin always smiled—warmly, seductively. He had a smile for every occasion. And Leslie was always provocative. But maybe the brief touch of those hands had been a caress. Maybe his smile had been more than public relations.

The list of Leslie's past boyfriends was growing: definitely Charlie O'Dell and Captain Mike. Possibly Sonny. And now, perhaps, Colin. So many men, so little time.

I imagined Eleanor's muffled sobs following me as I continued quietly to the back of the house, but when I paused I heard only the nocturnal birds calling from the forest. Rounding the corner, I tapped on the screen door.

"Neticia?"

As I called her name softly, something that had slipped my mind came back to me. The evening before, I had taken my room key from Neticia. That meant nothing, though. There were probably a dozen keys around Flamingo Cove that would open my door. Neticia could have taken one from the reception desk, or from the Ledbetters' office.

I rapped harder. There was no answer, but from inside I heard another sound, the voice of a radio disk jockey. A second later a middle-aged woman in a flowered robe appeared on the other side of the screen. I recognized her as the Ledbetters' housekeeper.

"Yes?"

"I'm looking for Neticia."

She shook her head. "Everybody's been looking for Neticia. Someone saw her getting on the bus this afternoon. She was carrying her suitcase."

"She hasn't come back?"

The woman shook her head. "I don't expect she will. Her things are gone from her room. She probably went back to her people. She's been unhappy because her friend died. This afternoon I heard the poor child crying."

"What time did she take the bus?"

"Six-thirty. That's the last bus into town."

"But she's from another island. How would she get there?"

"There are lots of people with boats. She could pay someone to take her. Or maybe she called her family and someone picked her up."

I mulled this new development over as I walked back to my room. At six-thirty that afternoon I had been in my room changing for the buffet. Leslie's mattress and the stack of books hadn't been disturbed then. The room had been searched *after* Neticia left the hotel. Which meant that Neticia wasn't the only one looking for *it*, whatever it was.

Back in my room, I latched both the screen and the wood door. The contents of my tapestry bag were still on my bed. I started putting them back absently: heavy parka and slacks, apartment keys.

Unlike Leslie, I'm not much for putting my initials on things. My mother is, though. She'd given me my keychain with *B.I.* etched in fancy script on a small wood disk. Resting back on my pillow, I let the keys dangle from my finger. Funny, how something as familiar as apartment keys can grow foreign to your touch in only a few days. I hadn't thought about my regular life for a few days, had I? I'd thought about my cat Moses, but except for the brief trauma of the book cover, it had been a while since I'd agonized about anything else in New York.

The keys swung hypnotically. I stared until they blurred. But . . . I blinked to bring the keys into focus. What was this?

There was an extra key on my chain. How could that be? Sitting up, I examined my keys carefully: building key, mailbox key, two keys to my apartment door (I live in Manhattan, you understand). What was this other, strange key? I balanced it on my fingers. As keys went, it amounted to nothing. A locker key, possibly, with a number stamped on it. G-9. The lock that went with this key wouldn't stop a New York City burglar for ten seconds.

The key to paradise. I closed my eyes for a moment, and again recreated the scene when Leslie had returned my overnighter. She had replaced my keys in my bag, and later she had said, "You might say I've got hold of the key to paradise."

It was as if a bright light had come on in my head. Leslie had gone somewhere and put something in a locker. She'd then hidden the key on my keychain.

Why hadn't the person who searched my bag taken this key? The answer was obvious to me. The searcher had spotted my initials on the keychain. Or maybe the searcher hadn't even gotten to the keychain. A look at my heavy parka and she, or he, would have realized the bag was mine, not Leslie's. Leslie had been in the islands for three years. What would she be doing with a down parka?

What Leslie had hidden in the locker I couldn't imagine. Neticia had known, but Neticia was gone.

It was as warm as usual that night, but I slept with the walkway windows closed and locked. Neticia hadn't frightened me, but this other, faceless searcher did. As I fell into a hot, restless sleep, a last vision floated through my mind: the beach shack, and a faceless man trying to smother me.

TWELVE

THE DEVIL EYE

The next morning there was a plain white envelope under my door. Opening it, I discovered that during the night the miracle of the paycheck had happened. It was a small, small miracle, but it was better than no miracle at all. In the envelope there was also a note. "Sorry I was short with you yesterday. Thank you for your hard work. Eleanor."

I called Mike from the extra phone behind the reception desk. As his phone rang and rang, I gazed out across the patio. The morning was beautiful, but it looked as if there could be rain later. Feathers of grey streaked the blue sky, and far offshore a bank of puffy clouds hovered over the water.

He picked up on the tenth ring. Yes, I was counting.

"Hello."

The second I heard his voice, I realized how glad I was he'd called.

"Hi. It's Bonnie. You phoned."

"Yes, I did," he said after a moment. "Just catching my breath. I was working on my boat. Do you have off tomorrow evening? Or have the Ledbetters come up with another costume extravaganza? Luau Night, maybe? You can wear a grass skirt."

"No. Much as I'd like to wear a grass skirt, our next

extravaganza isn't until Saturday night. We're doing Calypso on the Beach."

There was a chuckle from his end, but Calypso Night couldn't have sounded all that bad to Mike. His next words were, "Am I invited? I apologize for the way I stormed off on Sunday. Most of my dates don't end that way."

"Forget it. It was a rough situation."

"So what about tomorrow?" he asked. "You interested in getting together? I can't promise a repeat of the great time we had Sunday, but . . ."

"Let's hope not. Tomorrow I'm off after I've finished with Dancercize. I can take the five-thirty bus into town and meet you."

"Why take the bus when you can ride in luxury? I'll borrow my landlady's car. I'll pick you up and take you on a guided tour. Show you the island's hot spots, if I can find out what they are. Bring a bathing suit. Maybe we'll find a beach we can't resist."

"Better not let Colin or Eleanor hear you talking like that."

"Don't worry. While I'm at the resort I'll be a walking Flamingo Island Chamber of Commerce."

"Okay. Speaking of hot spots," I said, "can you think of any place on the island where you can rent lockers? The airport, maybe? Or the fishing camp?"

"Why? You got some valuables you want to lock up?"

"Sort of."

"I think you're out of luck. I'm not sure about the airport, but there's nothing at the fishing camp. Maybe the local bank has safety deposit boxes, but I doubt it. Don't you know that there's no theft on Flamingo Island? People don't need to lock things up."

"Right."

The key I had found was too junky to be a bank deposit box key. After we said goodbye, I called the local airport. No, they did not rent lockers.

When I'd hung up, I sat in the rattan chair for a second watching the activity at the registration desk. The same clerk who kept telling me about employee slowdowns was taking care of some new arrivals. She was speedy, cheerful and efficient. The miracle of the paycheck had touched her, too.

Early Bird Aerobics went smoothly with no police around to distract us. After the class I had breakfast, then changed into my old bathing suit. Earlier that morning, Eleanor had asked me to take over her water ballet class. She'd asked without hesitation, which meant that I'd lived down my earlier disgrace. At the same time, she'd mentioned expanding the activities program at Flamingo Cove, and hinted that if I were interested in joining the staff, there would be a place for me. It gave me something to think about. To live in a beautiful place with pleasant work and almost no expenses wouldn't be bad.

I wasn't nervous about leading water ballet until I saw Cindy standing beside the pool. When she jumped in, a ripple of anxiety swelled up out of somewhere and for a moment I watched her carefully. She went through the exercises like a regular, though—no tears, no suicide attempt. As she swam, I was again struck by how well she moved in the water. When class was over and we were drying off I said something about that to her.

A frown crossed her face. "It's the only sport I've ever been good at. I was always the skinniest kid on the beach, and one of the best swimmers. I never thought I'd get in trouble because of it."

"In trouble?" As if I didn't know what she was talking about.

Cindy glanced around at the other guests, then said softly, "Chief Richards asked me all these questions about Sonny and Leslie. It was so embarrassing I could have died, having to tell a stranger that I thought my husband was having an affair on our honeymoon."

I nodded sympathetically. "I can imagine."

"It was terrible for Sonny, too. He wasn't having an affair, you know. It all came out when the chief talked to us. Sonny admitted that he was trying to make me jealous." She fiddled with the strap on her bathing suit, not looking at me. "Sonny never touched Leslie. Never once went near her, except to joke around."

Amazing, wasn't it, how many men were suddenly eager to make it clear they had never touched Leslie, or at least hadn't touched her in a long time?

"Did he ever tell you where he spent that one night?" I asked, keeping my voice light.

"He fell asleep on the beach in a lounge chair, just like you said. The next night was the first time he ever saw Leslie. He started kidding around with her at the Casino. She was a big beautiful blonde, and since he'd told me he'd spent the night with a big beautiful blonde, well, she was convenient."

Poor Leslie, reduced to a convenience. A couple things about Sonny's story didn't ring true to me. Spending the night on the beach didn't explain how the buttons on Sonny's shirt had been ripped off, or why his chest had been scraped when he got back to the room the next morning. As for the big beautiful blonde, I know she's an old cliché, but for Sonny to describe the woman he would later meet struck me as a little *too* convenient.

"The trouble now is—"

A foursome of guests were gathering around a nearby table. Cindy moved a few feet away from them. I followed, eager to hear what she was going to say.

"The problem is *I* believed Sonny, and everyone around here knows it." She gave me a long look, then added, in a carefully polite tone, "Some of the people on the dive boat heard me say, 'I hope she drowns out there.' "

"I wasn't going to lie to the chief of police."

Cindy lifted her thin shoulders, then let them drop, a picture of dejection. "Well, you weren't the only one who heard me say things like that. Chief Richards asked me all these questions about what I did while we were underwater. He didn't come right out and say it, but he thinks I followed Leslie and threw that net over her. God, Bonnie! It was dark and scary down there. I spent most of the time swimming around under the strobe light.

I only swam away from the boat once. The worst problem is . . ."

She paused and gazed down at the water in the pool.

"What?"

"I don't think I'm supposed to talk about this."

"I'm working with the police," I said, bending the truth a little. "I'm their contact here. Maybe Chief Richards forgot to tell me something."

"Oh. Well, when the police searched our room, they found an underwater flashlight. It's one of the hotel's. I'm sure Chief Richards thinks I trapped Leslie under the net and stole her light so she couldn't signal anyone."

"Where *did* you get the flashlight?"

"On the night dive. It was in the sand off from the side of the boat. Toward the coral where the police say Leslie's body was. I found it when I swam over that way. It wasn't lit, and I thought probably somebody from another dive dropped it. I took it for a souvenir. But I didn't swim nearly as far as the coral, Bonnie. I didn't kill Leslie," she pleaded. "I didn't."

"Of course you didn't. What happens now?"

"We're not allowed to leave the island. We weren't going to leave until Sunday anyway, but now we can't." She glanced over my shoulder and waved.

I turned. Sonny was in the door of the Honeymoon Suite. Sleeping Beauty in red undershorts, stretching and yawning.

"This has got to be the crummiest honeymoon ever," Cindy said, "but at least one part of it has gotten better." With a jittery giggle, she trotted off.

It was just after noon. The clouds were gathering overhead, but the sun still found its way through. I had a few hours of free time and decided to grab a sandwich from the cafe and a towel from the beach shack. I could finally enjoy Flamingo Cove's beautiful beach.

I was on my way around the main building when the sound of a crying child stopped me. Glancing into the office, I saw Eleanor bent over her weeping daughter.

"I'll get you another one," she was saying to the crying girl. "Maybe a parakeet. Wouldn't you like that? We could keep him in a cage in the house."

"I don't want a stupid parakeet," Beth wailed.

I started to walk away. Too late. Eleanor glanced up and caught sight of me.

"Bonnie. Thank heavens! I need your help."

I stepped into the office, a reluctant helper if there ever was one.

"Could you stay with Beth for a while? She's terribly upset and I'm supposed to be in the cafe with our guests right now. I'll make the time up to you."

Eleanor looked exhausted. The puffiness around her eyes had receded, leaving smudged dark circles.

"Sure. I was going to go to the beach. Maybe Beth would like to go with me."

"Noooo!" the little girl howled. She clung to her mother's leg. Eleanor tried prying her off but the child clung tenaciously.

"Damn you! Let go!"

She had slapped her daughter across the face before I realized what was happening. I quickly grabbed Eleanor's arm, afraid of what she might do next. Beth let go of her mother's leg and fell back on the floor, surprised into silence. A red palmprint was clear across the little girl's cheek.

After a second Eleanor's eyes filled with tears. "I'm sorry, Beth. Mommy didn't mean to do that. This afternoon we'll do something special. Okay? Just the two of us."

The little girl rolled onto her stomach and shook her head. "I hate you!"

I let go of Eleanor's arm. She stared at her hand for a moment.

"I've never done that before, Bonnie. Never." She hurried out the door.

Beth was crying quietly now. "We could get a float if you want," I said as cheerfully as I could.

In response, the little girl turned over and lashed out with one of her feet. She got me right on the shin. It didn't hurt much—she was wearing sneakers—but it sure didn't help things, either.

"Okay, Beth. This is my time off and I'd like to spend it with you, but you've got to be as nice to me as I am nice to you. If you can't, I'm going to take you home and leave you with the housekeeper."

"You wouldn't dare," she said. "My mommy told you to stay with me, and my mommy's your boss."

"Get up. I'm taking you to the housekeeper. I want to go to the beach before it rains."

I pushed the screen door open and waited for her. I'm not sure what I would have done if Beth had held out. I wasn't about to wrestle with the kid. After a moment, though, she got to her feet.

"Well, I'll go to the beach with you, if you promise that after you'll get me . . ."

"You're pushing your luck, Beth. I'm promising nothing but a float from the beach shack."

So off we went to the beach, a sullen child and her reluctant babysitter.

The water was so still and warm that I felt as if I was drifting in a vat of unset green Jell-O. It was a good feeling. Beth was sprawled on her stomach across an orange and white striped float, arms dangling in the water. I drifted along beside her, my head resting on the warm plastic.

"Why did my mommy hit me, Bonnie? She never hit me before. Colin hit me, but my mommy never did."

"Your mom was upset. She loves you, but she's awfully busy these days, and . . . do you know what stress is?"

"Is that when your head gets too full of things?"

"Yes. I think your mom has stress right now."

"I guess so. She has stress 'cause Neticia left. I know that. She was crying about Neticia last night."

I turned my head so that I could look at Beth. "Was it late last night?"

143

"Uh huh." She narrowed her eyes. "Don't tell them I was listening. I'm not supposed to be up so late."

"How do you know your mom was crying about Neticia?" And not Leslie? That was the unspoken part of my question.

"Because she said so! She told Colin he scared Neticia and made her run away."

"What did Colin say about that?"

"He said he didn't do anything to Neticia."

He had never gone near her. Never once touched her. If "her" was Neticia rather than Leslie, what did that mean? And why would Colin want Neticia to leave?

"I'll bet you miss Neticia. I do." I meant it. Neticia was my only link with my dead roommate and the mysteries surrounding her.

"I miss her, I guess," the girl mused. "My mommy says she's going to get me another babysitter as soon as she can. Colin says Neticia was nosy and un . . . un . . . . I forget the word."

"Unhappy?"

"No, silly. I know that word. Untrusty."

"Untrustworthy?"

"That's it. Neticia was untrustworthy. Colin says my next babysitter is going to stay away from the woods. I hope they don't get me an old lady who wants to sit in air-conditioning all day. Yuck!" Beth pushed herself up on her elbows. "Maybe my mommy will let you be my babysitter," she said, her voice growing loud with excitement.

"I'm not a good babysitter. I'm untrustworthy too." I glanced up. Dark clouds roiled over us. "I think it's going to rain any second."

"So what? We're already wet."

"Rain is different. Let's go in." Without waiting for her permission, I tugged the float onto the sand.

"Help me get the air out of this thing."

"Neticia always did that by herself."

"I'm not Neticia."

Beth sighed one of her seven-year-old-girl sighs, but she

flopped down onto the float and started squeezing out the air. "Neticia wasn't untrustworthy. I'll tell you why she left if you promise not to tell anyone else."

"I promise."

"Lean down then. I can't say this out loud."

I gestured around the mostly empty beach. "Who would hear?"

She pinched her lips shut and shook her head. I didn't quite trust Beth. When I leaned toward her, I half expected her to sink her teeth into my earlobe.

"It was the devil eye," she whispered. "The devil eye killed our baby flamingo. Neticia said he killed Leslie, and she was afraid he was going to kill her, too."

Sitting back, I stared at the child. She squeezed out the last of the air and began folding the float.

"Tell me that again," I said.

"You know. The devil eye from the forest. After he killed Leslie, he killed our baby chick and twisted it's head all the way around on its neck. Poor little baby."

"Did you see it?"

She shook her head. "Neticia found it yesterday afternoon. She wouldn't let me look until she wrapped it in a scarf. She let me help her bury it. We made it a cross and everything. Neticia said that would scare the devil eye and he would be afraid to dig up the grave."

What a bizarre story. Why would the girls—either or both of them—make it up? There was no reason I could think of.

"Where did you and Neticia bury the chick?"

"At the back of the last building, near where its cage was." Her eyes brightened in anticipation. "I'll show you, if you want."

The cross was made of two wooden sticks, the longer no more than eight inches high. They'd been lashed together with string. I pulled the cross from the sandy soil and laid it carefully beside the grave.

"You're going to dig up the chick?" Beth whispered.

"Yes. Hand me the spoon."

She put the big kitchen ladle in my hand and I went to work on the loose dirt. The sun had disappeared completely, and under the cloud-filled sky the forest behind us looked shadowy and sinister. All the scene needed was some spooky organ music. As I dug, the first drops of rain fell on my arms.

"You better hurry."

It was a shallow grave. I'd dug only a couple inches when the ladle scraped across a dirty white cloth. I was pushing the dirt aside when I thought something stirred in the nearby forest. In spite of the heat a chill ran up my spine. It was only a flicker at the edge of my vision, though. When I looked up I saw nothing but the dense dark growth.

"What's the matter?" Beth whispered.

"Nothing. And I want you to forget all about devil eye," I whispered back. "There's no such thing."

I scraped off more soil, and saw an elaborate *L* embroidered on a corner of the cloth. Neticia had buried the chick in the scarf Leslie had given her. What did this mean? I momentarily wondered, and then I shook my head at my silliness. Was I nuts, searching for symbolism in a bird's grave?

"Close your eyes," I said to the little girl.

She pinched her eyes tight. I turned back a corner of the scarf, just enough to see that the girls hadn't made up the story. The poor little chick's thin neck had been twisted completely around. Its eyes stared up, a dull red in death.

"Do you see its eyes?" Beth asked. "The devil eye turned them red. Neticia said that was how she knew for sure he did it."

Bursting blood vessels when the chick's neck was twisted had probably turned its eyes red. I didn't tell Beth that, though. The devil eye seemed a kinder explanation than the human cruelty that had done this. Was Colin really responsible? If his wife accused him of driving Neticia away, she must have thought so. I turned to Beth.

"You said that Colin has hit you before. Did he hit you hard?"

Beth nodded. "Two times. When my mommy first got married

to him. But she said he better not do that any more and he didn't."

"Why did he hit you?"

"Once I wore his sunglasses and broke them." The little girl shrugged her shoulders. "I can't remember what else I did."

If I made too much out of this, Beth might mention my questions to her mother, and even to Colin. I didn't want that, so I dropped the subject. Still, what Beth had told me made me wonder about Colin. Pleasant, smiling Colin had hit his new stepdaughter in anger, hard enough to make Eleanor order him to stop. Could be the man's perfect self-control wasn't so perfect after all.

The sight of the mutilated chick sickened me. I pulled the scarf back into place and started scooping the soil over the grave. When I'd patted it into place, Beth put the cross back at the top of the grave.

The rain was coming harder now, and Beth and I ran for the main building. By the time we reached it there was a hard, steady downpour. The wind had risen, and waiters hurried back and forth, helping the guests move their lunches under cover. Beth and I had sandwiches on the terrace. Watching the wind whip up the palm trees and raise little whitecaps in the ocean helped dull the memory of the dead chick.

Tuesday night in the Flamingo Cove Casino. Vegas it wasn't, but there was action. The rain and wind had continued, forcing indoors the guests who usually spent their evenings by the pool or playing bridge on the patio.

"There's a sight to warm those Texans' cold hearts," Mrs. Hussy said. She tilted her head way down, until she looked as if she had ten chins, and stared hard at the action at the blackjack table.

"How much would you say the young fool has on that table in front of him?"

"At least five hundred, if I was going to guess." That came from one of the dinghies.

147

"At least," the other dinghy agreed. "Look at him; he's gone beady-eyed over those chips."

"Harumph! He always is beady-eyed. Closer to a thousand, if you ask me. And what do you suppose he's doing in here, anyway?"

He was Paul Tyndall, the ornithologist with the unfocused eye. Or beady eye, or maybe devil eye. It all depended on the eye of the beholder. To me, he looked a lot less threatening than he had the first time we met. His hair was combed and his beard neat. He was wearing wire-rimmed glasses, and looked like what he was—a graduate student. A blue-blooded graduate student, I should add. He had an air about him that I hadn't noticed in the forest. Part of it was the way he held himself: tall and straight and chin up. Part was the clothes he wore. They were similar to the clothes all students wear, but his khakis were cut to perfection and, I promise you, his work shirt had not come out of a bin in an East Village secondhand store. It was his shoes that really gave him away. The soft glow on his burnished leather loafers whispered "expensive."

"He comes from a very fine family," the pink-haired lady said knowingly.

"What do you mean by fine?" I asked.

"Rich! What else!" That was Mrs. Hussy.

"Not only rich. They're an old family, and . . ." A little line of consternation grew between her eyebrows. "And distinguished," she finally said. "I'm from Boston, and I often see the Tyndalls mentioned in the local papers for charitable work and that sort of thing."

"Charity begins at home," said Mrs. Hussy. "His family must have paid off his gambling debt here. Otherwise Colin wouldn't allow him at the blackjack table."

Tyndall was with an elderly man who was leaning on a cane, and a young woman.

"Who are the other people?" I asked quietly.

"The man is his professor. He heads the flamingo research project on all the out-islands. The young woman is the professor's

148

granddaughter *and*"—Mrs. Hussy gave me a significant look— "young Tyndall's fiancee. Handy for him." She drained the last of her rum drink. "When you're free, Bonnie, would you get me another of these?"

In unison, the dinghies thrust their glasses at me.

I was doing my substitute waitress stint, this time without the dubious benefit of a can-can outfit. As I wandered off toward the bar, one of Mrs. Hussy's friends said, "The fiancee is a biology professor. She's rather homely, isn't she?"

Mrs. Hussy agreed emphatically.

I wouldn't have called Tyndall's fiancee homely. Unadorned, maybe. She had a plain but pleasant face, and brown hair in a simple short cut. She was wearing a calf-length skirt and brown sandals. Among the tropical prints and pastels of the casino-goers, she was a bit drab—a sparrow among the flamingos.

As I waited for the ladies' rum drinks, I noticed the slightest frown forming on the young woman's face. The reason for the frown was apparent to me. She was standing at Tyndall's side, watching him play. If I'd been watching someone I was about to marry losing money the way Tyndall was, I would have been stonefaced.

I have my vices—some whoppers—but gambling isn't one of them. A nickel slot machine and two dollars worth of coins is my limit.

Paul Tyndall sat with one hand gripping the edge of the table. With his other hand he threw out chip after chip. But for that movement and the glitter in his eyes, he might have been dead.

I carried the drinks to Mrs. Hussy and her friends. They had lost interest in Tyndall's gambling and in his fiancee.

". . . jealousy, pure and simple," Mrs. Hussy was saying as I put her drink on the table.

"What's that?" I asked.

"We're talking about poor Leslie. This evening I was at the pool, and I heard someone say that she heard from a man in the restaurant that the autopsy turned up only a tiny amount of liquor. Not nearly enough to make Leslie drunk."

It was tenth-hand information, but it was probably accurate.

"That young woman in the honeymoon suite swims like a fish, I've been told," said one of the women. "The police had best keep their eye on her."

Mrs. Hussy nodded. "I'm sure they are. I heard that the young woman was found with . . ." She paused to give weight to her words. " . . . incriminating evidence."

"What kind?" her friend asked.

"It was incriminating. That's all I know."

They had to be talking about the flashlight. As I made the rounds of the casino, I again wondered whether Cindy could have pulled off Leslie's murder.

On top of calling off both her own name and Leslie's, Cindy also would have had to make sure nobody went back searching for Leslie before the ten minutes of air remaining in Leslie's tank ran out. So she confessed to the husband she was barely speaking to, and talked him into saying he had seen Leslie after the dive. It worked out that nobody missed Leslie until long after ten minutes had passed, but Sonny still covered for his wife on our trip back in the dinghy.

And what about Leslie's missing clothes? Had Cindy been watching when Leslie stowed them under the bench? Because on top of all the other scurrying around Cindy had to do, she had to carry Leslie's clothes off the boat, talk Sonny into carrying them off, or drop them overboard without anyone noticing.

Okay, all of this was possible, but it would have taken some real cool thinking. Could Cindy, the young woman who tried suicide in a crowded swimming pool, who made rash, public threats, have managed it? Just after trapping Leslie in that net? I couldn't imagine it.

I was collecting empty glasses from tables, trying to recreate that night on the boat in my head, when I glanced at the blackjack table.

Tyndall was losing big now. I don't know much about the game, but I know when a big stack of chips turns into a little one. His forehead was furrowed and he seemed to be breathing between clenched teeth. When the dealer scooped up the last of the chips, Tyndall put his hands on the table where the stack of chips had been, and slowly clenched them into tight fists.

The dealer glanced toward the far wall, catching Colin's eye. Within seconds my affable boss was there, all smiles, arm around Tyndall's shoulder. What an odd group it was that filed out of the casino: Colin smiling, Tyndall rigid with frustration, the fiancee's expression closed. Her grandfather relied heavily on the cane, and I watched the young woman help him through the door.

"The professor doesn't do field work any more," someone in Mrs. Hussy's group said. "Arthritis."

"Then pity the flamingos with no one but Mr. Tyndall looking after them," Mrs. Hussy said. "He has strange appetites for a birdwatcher."

Yes, he did. Was revenge one of them? Would he kill a flamingo chick out of spite, because two girls had taken it to raise?

I was glad to see the regular waitress come into the casino. The sick feeling I'd had when I looked at the dead chick had come back. On my way to my room a few minutes later, I hugged the building wall to avoid the rain. My path brought me close to the one that led to the chick's grave. As I passed there, I remembered that brief flash of movement I'd seen in the forest.

My room had a musty smell to it that night, but I again slept with the windows latched.

THIRTEEN

SPANISH MOUNTAIN

My date was a thief! That's right: Captain Mike. Not only was he a thief, but he was stealing a guest's camera. I stooped out of sight behind the potted palm that screened the door of the terrace ladies' room, and watched him slip the prim woman's camera into his pants pocket. How casually he pushed his chair back from the table and stood. When he had shaken hands with the man whose wife's camera he'd just stolen, Mike strolled to the men's room, cool and smooth as one of those icy rum drinks we'd just finished.

Almost from the moment he got to the resort, Mike had behaved curiously. I'd waited for him at the bottom of the stairs, expecting to leave right away. When he drove up though—and coincidentally it was at the same time that the prim woman and her husband walked by on their way to happy hour on the terrace—he had parked his landlady's old green car and suggested we take advantage of happy hour, too.

Sure, I'd said. Why not? But as we'd ordered our half-price Goombay Punches, he kept taking surreptitious little glances at the woman. There were so many little glances, in fact, that I'd begun wondering what he was doing with me. She and I couldn't have been more different.

What I hadn't noticed was that she had her fancy pocket camera with her. But Mike had. When you're a thief, you notice things like that. He had obviously been watching when she laid the camera on the chair beside her. He'd probably gone all feverish with excitement when she left her husband alone at the table and walked out of the restaurant.

"Excuse me for a second, Bonnie," Mike had said. "I'm going to go have a word with that man who was on the dive. What's his name?"

"I'm not sure. I'll meet you back here." I stood and walked toward the far end of the terrace as if going to the ladies' room. And from my hiding place behind the potted palm, I had just watched my date steal a guest's camera.

For a date with a thief, I had packed my sexy new bathing suit. I'd cashed a traveler's check that morning at the bar, and here I was going out with someone who would probably steal my wallet. I can really pick 'em.

Now what was I going to do about this?

I made up my mind on the way back to our table. I couldn't say anything while we were on the terrace—God forbid I should cause a scene at the resort—but I wasn't about to let Mike leave the resort with that camera in his pocket, either. I'd wait until we got to the car to confront him.

He came out of the men's room a moment later. I was surprised to see him pause, once again, and say a few more words to the unsuspecting husband. As he did this, he rested his arms over the back of the chair where the woman had been sitting. How arrogant he was, returning to the scene of the crime, chatting up the victim's husband!

"Nice guy," he said when he returned to our table. "You ready to get out of here?"

"I certainly am."

He reached out to take my arm. I pulled away and we left the restaurant and walked down the stairs in silence.

As soon as we got to the car I stopped dead and stared at him. He looked awfully cute that afternoon, I'll admit. The silly sailor hat was nowhere in sight, and the fair lines around his clear green eyes gave him a wholesome look that had nothing to do with the reality of what he was. A thief!

"You have to put it back," I said.

"I have to put *what* back?"

"You know what."

He opened the passenger door wide. "Can't imagine what you're talking about. Let's go see the sights."

"That woman's camera. You stole it."

He broke into a broad grin. Such nerve!

"You put it in your pants pocket."

In response, he raised both his arms. "Frisk me, then get in the car."

"You know I'm not going to frisk you or get in the car. Please put the camera back."

"The woman's camera is on a chair at the table where her husband is sitting." He nodded up the steps. "Want to go back up there and see for yourself?"

"Let's." I intended to call his bluff.

He had just closed the car door when the prim woman's husband walked out of the terrace cafe. Seeing us down by the road, he waved. The little camera hung from his wrist by a strap.

Mike swung the car door open again. "Satisfied?"

I slid into the passenger seat feeling like a world-class idiot.

"I'm sorry," I said when he got into the car. "I could have sworn you took that camera."

"It's no big deal."

No big deal? I'd just called him a thief and he didn't seem concerned. He turned the key in the ignition. The engine turned over, and over. Weaker and weaker.

"I was hoping I wouldn't have to deal with this today," he finally said.

Climbing back onto the road, he walked around to my side of the car. I opened my door as he fell to his knees by the rear wheel.

"You think prayer's going to help?"

"Prayer?" He picked up a rock from the road. "I've given up on prayer. I'm going to give the fuel pump a beating." He crouched until he was on his side half under the car. "When I yell 'okay' you turn the key."

A few thumps from the bottom of the car, a cry of "okay" and I turned the key. The old engine caught.

"Have you been to the top of Spanish Mountain yet?" Mike asked as he got back in. "It's the tallest point on the island. You can see smog over Nassau from there."

"No. This is a great car."

"Impressed you, didn't I? I call it the jolly green giant. Next time you get to beat the fuel pump, to make up for calling me a thief."

"I'm really sorry about that."

"Forget it."

I stared ahead for a moment. The afternoon sun beating through the palm trees cast intricate patterns across the dirt road. To our right was a magnificent sweep of beach, but I couldn't concentrate on the scenery.

"I can't forget it. I don't know how I made such a mistake. It's embarrassing."

He chuckled. "Yeah. It's a good thing you're pretty. Actually, I can't get too upset about being called a thief." For a moment his eyes left the road. "You see, Bonnie"—he smiled at me—"I *am* a thief."

"You mean there are two cameras? That man has his own?"

Mike shook his head. "No. There was only one camera at the table, and I didn't take it. I borrowed it."

"And took it to the men's room? What did you do that for? Don't try to tell me you planted a bugging device. You don't strike me as a government agent."

That made his smile broaden. "Anything but."

And then I got the most bizarre notion. It was crazy, so sick and all together preposterous that I started to giggle. "You didn't," I managed—but I couldn't go on. I turned away and looked out the window. We were beyond the sandy beach by then, passing

Rocky Point where rocks stretched like rough dark fingers into the water. I could hardly see, though. Tears of laughter were streaming from my eyes.

"I didn't what? What's so funny?"

"It's not funny. It's sick."

"Then why are you laughing?"

I couldn't look at him. "I don't know. Maybe I'm sick too." I stopped giggling long enough to gasp out my question: "Did you take some kind of obscene picture in the men's room?"

That did it. He roared with laughter, so hard that he had to pull the car to the side of the road. "God almighty! Where do you get these ideas? Can you imagine that woman's reaction when she got the film back if I did that? Yes, you can, can't you? That's why you're laughing. First I'm a secret lover, then a thief, and now I'm a pervert."

I composed myself with a deep breath before I faced him. "Then what did you do with the camera? You've got to tell me, because otherwise I'm going to go on thinking . . ."

"You're going to go on thinking that I went in the men's room and took dirty pictures of myself." He shook his head. "That is inspired. You have some imagination."

"Come on," I said. "What did you do with the camera?"

He reached into his shirt pocket. "You've got to swear you won't tell anyone about this."

By then I was so curious I would have sworn to anything. "I swear."

"I took this." He held his hand out toward me, palm up. In it was a film canister.

"Film? You took the film out of the camera?"

"That's right." He pulled back onto the road. "She got a shot of me with Leslie, the night of the dive. I don't like having my picture taken. There's no guaranteeing the woman didn't finish that roll of film and put in a new one, but when I saw her going to the restaurant with her camera I decided to chance it."

"Why are you so camera shy, Mike?"

"The fewer pictures of me that get around, the better.

157

Ordinarily it doesn't really matter much. In a case like this, though, with Leslie dead, you can't tell who's going to be looking at those pictures."

"You're hiding from someone? Or something?"

"You might say that. A lot of people down here are hiding from something. I have plenty of company."

"Well, I'm sorry to break the news, but the police confiscated the woman's film from the dive."

He shrugged. "Can't win 'em all."

The road followed the coast around the point, then swung inland through the forest. The turnoff for Spanish Mountain wasn't a road at all. Mike slowed the car at a curve where two dirt tire tracks lead off to the right.

"Hang on."

We bounced part way up the mountain. The road grew worse. The old green car hit bottom a few times and its sides were scraped mercilessly by the trees that lined the road.

"Your landlady's awfully generous," I said. "Even if it doesn't always start."

"She's worried I don't have a girlfriend. She thought you looked like a likely prospect."

"She knows me? I haven't met any locals but the police."

"She met you on the puddle jumper from Nassau. 'A pretty girl, all alone.'"

"Oh. The lady with the yellow bandana who wanted to fix me up with a 'sweetheart.'"

"That's me. A sweetheart."

The foliage was thinner now, but the ground had become increasingly rocky. It wasn't long before the tire tracks turned into one narrow path.

Mike switched off the engine. "We'll have to walk from here. It's not too much further."

The sun beat down on us as we walked the rest of the way. It was steep, but I climbed the distance easily. I could hear Mike puffing a little.

"You need to take one of my classes."

"Sure. Maybe I'll do Dancercize."

At the crest I stopped, stunned by the view. Since the rain, the air smelled rich and moist, and the island colors seemed even more intense. The turquoise water had a sheen over its surface, and the sand burned white under the sun.

I looked down. It was a steep drop. In a cove near the beach below, two men worked on a boat.

Mike came up behind me.

"They call it Spanish Mountain because this is where a small band of Spaniards who landed here in sixteen-something made their last stand against the English. When the Spanish realized they couldn't win, they cut straight down the side to the beach."

"So they got away?"

"Oh no. The ones who didn't fall to the rocks below were slaughtered by that cove where those two guys are." He put his hand on my shoulder and turned me around. "Over there you can see Woodestown, and there, that's north. See how the sky's smoggy. That's Nassau, less than fifty miles away."

I couldn't see any smog. The mention of Nassau, though, made my mind detour to something else: the locker key I had on my keychain.

"Would you go to Nassau if you wanted to spend the night somewhere glittery?"

"I suppose so. There's nothing glittery around here." His hand tightened on my shoulder. "What do you have in mind?"

"Just thinking."

"Okay. The clear area at the north edge of the forest is where the flamingos nest, where you had your run-in with Paul."

"I told you I met Paul. I didn't tell you we had a 'run-in.' How did you find out?"

"I saw him earlier today. I told him I was on my way to pick you up, and he said he'd chased you and those kids out of his woods."

"They're not his woods! He's very strange," I added.

"Strange? Maybe a little, but you've got to pity the poor guy. Comes from a wealthy family. Got used to having anything he wanted. Then suddenly he's cut off without a cent. He gets nothing but his tuition and enough to scrape by on."

I glanced at Mike over my shoulder. "Why is that?"

"Paul's father got tired of paying his gambling debts."

"Well, either daddy relented or the poor little rich boy found another source of income," I said. "You should have seen what he went through last night at the casino."

"Oh, yeah?" He shook his head. "It shouldn't surprise me. I've seen it before. Paul thinks he can beat the system by counting cards. He can't. The casinos use ten decks at their blackjack tables. Nobody beats the system."

Mike told me that one night he, Charlie and Paul had gone to Paradise Island. "What a bust! Paul wouldn't budge from the casino," he said, "and all Charlie wanted to do was sit in a bar and talk about Leslie."

"What did *you* want to do in Nassau?"

He shrugged. "Find girls, lose my troubles. See over on that next point? That's the fishing camp that Charlie works out of."

He had stopped pretending that he was merely steering me around with his hand. His fingers gently rubbed my skin.

I can't say I felt nothing. It was nice to have my skin, and my ego, massaged by an attractive man, even if the man was running from someone, or something.

"The fishing camp's a good place to hang out," he continued. "We can go there tonight. The food's terrific. And if you turn around and look west, you can see Pirate's Cay and . . ."

He paused.

"That's where we went snorkeling and found Leslie's body, isn't it?"

"I could get to really hate this place," he said. "Why don't we try to concentrate on good things."

Pulling me around, he kissed me. It was a good kiss. The kind of really good kiss that makes you feel as if a tidal wave has rolled through your insides. I pulled free, suddenly scared of what I could be getting into. "Let's go look for a beach."

I was on the path before he had recovered from the kiss. "What is it?" he asked as he hurried to catch up. "It can't be my kissing. I've been told I'm a great kisser." He clutched the top of his head. "I hope it's not my bald spot. If that's the case, I've got my hat in the car."

"It's not your bald spot."

"Is is because I steal things?"

I couldn't help smiling.

"Ah," he said. "That's it. Well, let me assure you I'm a good thief."

"A good thief?" Judging from his boat and the car he was driving, he wasn't all that good. "Do you mean you're good like Robin Hood?" I asked. "Steal from the rich and give to the poor?"

"No! Slow down and I'll tell you."

I stopped on the path and faced him.

"I stole from the rich and tried to keep it. I won't bore you with the details, but you're out with a man who's on the run from the Internal Revenue Service and a couple other bureaucracies I won't mention."

"At least you can joke about it."

"Let me tell you, Bonnie: I'm crying on the inside. I do a lot of that. Are you sorry you're out with a fugitive from justice?"

"No." I should have been, maybe, but he was funny. He made me laugh and I needed to laugh.

"Ah! You liked the kiss, didn't you."

"The kiss was fine. You're a good kisser."

"Phew. I was worried. I've lost my income and my home and my wife."

This was the first I'd heard of a wife, but I could sort of tell there had been one. Again he rubbed that bald spot. As he did, his glance flicked briefly past me, down the hill. "And my hair," he continued, his voice growing softer. "I wouldn't want to lose my kissing skill."

"Don't worry. You still . . ."

Pressing one finger to my lips, he leaned toward me. Closer. This time maybe I wouldn't back away. He drew my hair away from my ear, until I could feel his breath on my skin.

"There's a man down at the car. He has a machete. I don't know if he heard us, but he probably realizes we left the car to climb up here. Be quiet and maybe he'll go away."

My heart felt as if it had stopped beating. I let out my breath slowly. The men with machetes. Probably the men I'd seen in the boat on the beach. Men!

"There are two of them," I whispered.

"Yes, so I see," Mike said out loud. As he spoke, a little avalanche of stones spattered down from the trail above.

FOURTEEN

TWO MEN WITH MACHETES

The second man had circled around through the brush. He was lean, and wore ragged shorts and sneakers. From his place on the trail above, he looked about nine feet tall. His height, though, didn't scare me nearly as much as the machete in his hand did. The way the sunlight bounced off the blade, it looked sharp as a razor.

My legs started to tremble and I was afraid I might collapse. Mike slipped his arm around my waist. I was surprised when he spoke to the man. My mouth was so dry with fear I don't think I could have gotten a word out.

"Hello, my friend," he said. "What can I do for you?"

The man took a few steps toward us, and lifted the machete. "Walk down to the car slowly."

He followed us down the trail. The other man was in the car going through the glove compartment. He looked a little older than the man behind us. This second man's machete lay across the car's faded green hood.

"You got any money?" he called from the front seat.

Mike pulled his wallet from his back pocket and handed it through the open passenger door. The man took out the bills and searched through the rest of the wallet.

"Credit cards?"

"Not with me."

The man threw the wallet at Mike's feet, then looked at me.

I was carrying my day pack. Slipping it off my back, I dug through it for my wallet. The man behind me, growing impatient, snatched the pack from me and went through it quickly. When he had finished, my cash, my paycheck and my credit cards were in his pocket. My new bathing suit lay on the path.

"Give me the keys," he said to Mike.

Mike handed over the car keys without hesitation.

The older man had gotten out of the car. He was smaller than his companion, but the jagged pink scar across his chest made him look even more frightening. He walked casually around the car until he stood just a few feet from us. Reaching out, he took his machete from the hood, held it in front of him and ran the pad of his fingers over the blade.

I followed the machete with my eyes as he lowered it. When the machete reached his waist, I gasped. His belt was carved leather. Its big brass buckle was embossed with a silver *L*.

The man smiled at me. "Don't worry. You behave and you won't get hurt." He nodded up the hill. "Go back there and stay. Understand?"

"No problem," Mike said. Bending slowly, he picked my bathing suit from the dirt.

The man behind us moved close and held his machete near Mike's neck. "Don't come down until it's dark. Your car will be here."

The older man was already sliding into the driver's seat. "That's right. We're borrowing it to go visiting some lady friends." He smiled at Mike. "Mon, you do something to make your ladyfriend happy. She doesn't look so good."

As Mike followed me back up the hill, we heard the car start right up. It purred like a big old cat.

We stopped climbing at the place where the first man had found us. Mike collapsed onto the big rock. "Thank God the damned thing started. We'll wait until we don't hear the car anymore. . . ."

I found my voice. "We can't wait. Let's try to get down to the beach. We've got to make sure those men don't leave the island."

"How do you propose to do that?" He patted the rock. "Why don't you sit down next to me and I'll try to do what the man said. Make you happy." He held my bathing suit toward me. "Very . . . sexy. Maybe we can still get to that beach."

I snatched the suit from his hand and stuffed it into my pack. "The only way you'll make me happy right now is to stop those men from getting off Flamingo Island." Scrambling through the brush at the trail's edge, I looked down the side of Spanish Mountain. "It's not that steep. Let's get to their boat."

"Not that steep?" He said something about the Spaniards and rock slides, but I didn't pay attention. I stumbled down as far as I could, and when my legs could no longer hold me on the steep hill, I made my way sliding on my bottom, grasping onto the sparse foliage for support.

"Wait up," Mike said, sliding along behind me. "You are some strenuous date. You see, that's what I meant when I said I was a good thief. Your credit cards would be safe with me."

"My credit cards are safe with them too," I said. "That's not the problem. We have to stop them because that shorter man . . . he's wearing Leslie's belt. The one that's missing from the night of the dive."

Near the bottom of Spanish Mountain the ground leveled out some. We half ran, half slid the rest of the way down. My slacks were filthy when I reached the bottom. We were standing on the shore, catching our breath, when he heard the faint sound of an engine turning over and over.

Mike looked at me in alarm. "The driver must have eased off the gas. They'll never get it going. Which means they may be back here for their boat in a few minutes."

The boat was bobbing gently in the cove, completely concealed from anyone who wasn't looking for it. It was a sleek white beauty, equipped with an inboard motor. We hurried out and pulled ourselves on board.

"Wonder where they stole this little honey," Mike said. "I wouldn't mind having one like it."

"You're the thief. Can you start the motor?"

He shook his head. "Unfortunately, not with the time we've got. But I can take the spark plugs out of it."

He knew his way around a boat engine. Within seconds the spark plugs were in his hand. He pitched them off into the deeper water.

"Now what, Sherlock?"

"Are we closer to town, or the hotel?"

"The hotel, if we cut over to the road, but with that pair out there . . ."

We hurried to the shore and followed it toward town.

"Romantic, huh?" Mike said softly. "Just like I planned it. A candlelight dinner, lure you back to my place, ply you with liquor, put on soft music. . . ."

Chief Richards' brusque "Stay here" had the two of us glued to a couple iron-hard chairs outside his office. I stretched my legs across the police station's concrete floor and looked up at the clock over the secretary's desk. It had been almost an hour since the entire Flamingo Island Police Department—all four of them—had roared out to Spanish Mountain.

"It's been a long time," I said.

"Don't worry. Roscoe always gets his man."

I wasn't so sure. I was beginning to fear that the two men had gotten away when the big wood door that separated the police station from the other government offices banged open.

The two men who had robbed us came walking down the long corridor toward the cell. How unaffected they seemed. They shuffled along easily, as if they didn't have a care in the world, as if they hadn't noticed the handcuffs on their wrists and the four police escorting them. Spotting me, the shorter of the pair actually cocked an eyebrow my way, as if to say, "You're here too? What a coincidence."

Chief Richards had the two men stop in front of us. I was uncomfortable with everyone staring down at me. Mike must have felt the same. We both got to our feet.

"Are these the men who robbed you?" the chief asked.

"Yes."

He nodded toward the cell at the back of the hall. The two robbers started toward the cell so casually they might have been going to the Hilton for the night. As the second, shorter man, passed Mike, though, he shot him a nasty look and muttered something about motors.

Mike and I followed the chief into his office. He didn't sit in his splendid chair, or even bother to close the door. Opening a cabinet, he took out a thin plastic glove and drew it onto his hand. Then, opening a plastic bag he was carrying in his other hand, he pulled out the belt with the L on the buckle.

"Please be certain this is the belt your roommate left on the boat. Don't touch it."

I examined the belt. "If it isn't, it's an exact copy. Does that man's name begin with an L?"

The chief shook his head. "His name is Samuel Tyler." He reached into the sack again. This time he produced a maroon leather wallet. "You told me your roommate's wallet was in her pocket. Do you recognize this?"

I shook my head. "I never saw Leslie's wallet. Is there any identification in it?"

"Identification?" He glanced through the open door. "Our friend Samuel's driver's license is in it. There is also this." He showed us the flap on the change holder. An L was etched in the leather.

"These things don't look as if they've been in the water," I said. "That means they were carried off the dive boat."

"It would seem to."

"What about our money and credit cards?" Mike asked.

The chief shook his head. "The men may have ditched your

167

things in the water. When we got to them, they were trying to get the boat going."

He put the wallet and belt back in the bag. "The men claim they found these things at the fishing camp. A big black dog was playing with the belt. When they chased the dog, he led them to a pile of clothes. They found the wallet there."

I walked out of his office, my mind in turmoil. Charlie's dog. Charlie knew the reef, and he knew the beach shack. He'd visited Leslie there often. He could have seen those garbage bags stacked behind the door. I couldn't imagine Charlie O'Dell trying to kill me in the beach shack, but the evidence was pointing that way.

The policewoman was at the desk thumbing through a newspaper. "Today's paper is in from Nassau." She smiled at Mike. "You're a celebrity."

One of the prim woman's photos had made the third page, bottom right. There was Mike, one arm around Leslie's waist. My breath caught in my throat as I looked at the picture. Leslie's hair blew in the stiff wind, the strap from her bikini top slid off her shoulder. That belt with the big brass *L* on its buckle circled her waist. My eyes grew hot with tears.

"Let's get out of here," I said.

Mike was staring down at the picture. After a second he turned toward the police chief.

"Thanks a lot, pal. I really needed this."

Ignoring Mike, the chief said to the woman at the desk, "Get me Nassau."

I took Mike's hand and tugged at it. "Come on."

As we walked down the corridor past the cell and the two men who had robbed us, Chief Richards was saying to someone on the other end of the line, "We're going out to talk to Charlie O'Dell."

Our second date ended almost as early as our first. I was exhausted and Mike was both exhausted and distracted. At least this date ended better than our first one: pizza and beer, and an interesting invitation.

As long as you didn't look too closely, Barnacle Bill's was better on the inside than on the outside. Fishing nets were draped across the ceiling, partly obscuring the corrugated tin roof. Seashells, old life preservers, driftwood—the flotsam and jetsam of island life—hid the more serious cracks in the walls. A circular bar separated the wooden dancefloor from the dining area.

There were only a few other customers. Two men and a woman were at the bar talking to the chain-smoking bartender. Another couple was at a table. It was too early for the band, which was just as well. The low rock music from a radio behind the bar was about all the excitement I could take.

No sooner did we sit down at one of the rickety tables than Mike excused himself.

"Order us pizza and a pitcher of beer, will you? I have to make a couple phone calls. The pay phone's out back."

"How are we going to pay?"

"My credit's good here," he said.

He was gone long enough for me to finish a glass of beer and start another. He got back just as the bartender put our pizza in the middle of the table.

"Who did you call?"

He glanced up from his slice of pizza. "My landlady," he said after a minute. "Had to let her know the jolly green giant won't be coming home tonight. And my lawyer back in New York to let him know I'm a celebrity, and . . ." His shoulders sagged, and the last of his energy seemed to drift out of him like the smoke drifting toward the ceiling from the bartender's cigarette.

"Charlie didn't have anything to do with Leslie's death," he said after we hadn't spoken for a minute or two. "The way he felt about her, he couldn't have." He looked at me over the top of his glass. "I know what you're thinking. You're thinking that Charlie tried to strangle you in the beach shack. He didn't."

"He didn't know it was me. He mistook me for Leslie."

Mike shook his head. "I've seen Charlie put lobsters back in the ocean because they had 'nice eyes.' He adopted Beast when the poor animal was about to starve to death."

169

"Dogs and lobsters are not people. Leslie's things were found at the fishing camp," I added.

"The fishing camp is one of the most accessible places on the island. You can get there by car or boat easily. A determined hiker could get there from the hotel or town without winding himself."

After he had drained his glass, he nodded at the television over the bar. "On Christmas Eve I watched *A Christmas Carol* with Charlie. Right here. He cried at the part when Tiny Tim . . ."

"Oh, please! You win. Charlie's a sweetheart. I'm too frazzled to think about it any more."

We finished eating almost in silence. By the time Mike had signed the bill, I was conscious of nothing but my fatigue and the way my feet ached. As we left the bar Mike took my hand. He held it as we walked up the road, and I found myself wondering how I would have liked it if the evening had ended back at his place the way he'd planned.

"Just in time for the last bus," he said. "And so ends another romantic evening in the tropics."

From the rise where we stood, we could see the van making its way out of town toward us.

"It's ending better than the last one."

"You want to try for three? You're off tomorrow night?"

What was it one of the dinghies had said? Third time's charmed.

"Yes."

"I'm taking the big boat to Nassau for servicing. Why don't you come along? We'll have dinner and hit a few of the clubs."

The yellow headlights shined bright as the bus drew nearer.

"How will we get back?"

He shrugged. "Somebody with a boat's always willing to make the trip for a few bucks." Then he grinned. "Or maybe we won't come back all night. Maybe we'll end up somewhere besides the police station."

I knew the place he had in mind, but I wasn't ready to commit myself. "Can I let you know tomorrow?"

As the bus pulled up to the stop, Mike kissed me again. Then, with his hands on my shoulders, he stared me in the eye. "You're in the tropics, Bonnie. Paradise. Why not give yourself over to hedonism for one night?"

Hedonism. What a wonderfully nasty sound that word has. It set my imagination wild. For just one night, didn't I deserve to be a voluptuary? Shouldn't I reel from fleshpot to fleshpot, from one sensual indulgence to another?

I'd been in paradise for seven days. On the second day I'd been smothered with a garbage bag. One the fourth day I'd found my roommate's body. I'd been robbed by men with machetes on the seventh day. I'd watched two sunsets through the police station windows, sat with a weeping bride and dug up the grave of a flamingo chick.

Let someone else carry the tray of rum drinks. Let someone else prance around a stage in feathers. I wanted a purple headboard and a midnight pink bubblebath.

During the ride home, I slumped into a worn window seat and closed my eyes. Despite the bumpy road, despite the moonlit views of the sea, I dozed. I dreamed of the fleshpots of Nassau, and hedonism.

FIFTEEN

XANADU, THE PLEASURE DOME

Beth squirmed uncomfortably before the group assembled in the terrace restaurant. When her mother nodded, the child began to recite:

> *"In Xanadu did Kubla Khan*
> *A stately pleasure-dome decree:*
> *Where Alph, the sacred river, ran*
> *Through caverns measureless to man*
> *Down to a sunlit sea."*

Eleanor, Colin and the Texans burst into applause. A member of the local press snapped a picture of the little girl just as she tugged at the white lace collar of her dress. The rest of us tapped our fingers politely as Colin joined his stepdaughter in front of the stage where the reggae band usually played.

"Xanadu. The Pleasure Dome." Colin spoke slowly, as if savoring each delicious word.

"Eleanor and I, and our friends here"—a nod to the three

Texans who were standing at the side of the platform—
"considered dozens of names. For us, nothing says it better. I
think you'll agree when you've seen what we have planned. A
pleasure dome, for your pleasure."

With that, he pulled back the white sheet that had covered the
stage, revealing Flamingo Island, scaled in miniature.

The Texans led another round of applause. The three of them
wore Texas-sized smiles. Smiles as big as the Astrodome. Bigger,
even. Smiles as big as the Pleasure Dome.

Colin began by pointing to a black strip running along the
front of the display just behind the stretch of fake sand.

"I'll start with something all of us will be happy to see. We
expect the island government to approve funds to extend the
paved road all the way to Flamingo Cove. No more bouncing
through potholes." He nodded at the jitney driver and his helper,
who were at the back of the room.

"Bet you guys are glad about that."

The two men nodded back. I don't have to tell you that they
were smiling. All the employees, myself included, had on our
smiling public faces that morning.

"Here you will see our new entranceway. An arch of mature
palm trees will be planted so that our entrance is completely
shaded. . . ."

Colin was perfect for public relations. I admired his you-can-
trust-me-with-your-life-and-your-money smile. It was the smile
of the boy next door. I lapped up his accent, suitably cultivated
to let you know he was no fly-by-night operator, but never, never
snobbish. And I absolutely adored the way he took his little
stepdaughter's hand ever so gently in his big stepdaddy one.

I suppose his audience was as rapt as any group of people who
have come mainly for the sandwiches. Some political types were
there. They always smile.

"And here we have the mockup of the two-level pool and the
water slide. As you can see, the slide ends at the shallow section
of the lower pool, so that there won't be any danger to the little
ones. . . ."

Six nights before I'd cavorted in pink curtains and feathers in front of the platform that now held the Pleasure Dome. Fuchsia cellophane glass lit by blinking Christmas lights had skirted the platform on Monte Carlo Night. Grimy green outdoor carpeting had topped it. Now a decorous white cloth draped from the platform's sides, concealing lights, cellophane, and all other tawdry hints of Can-Can Reggae.

The half-moon beach of Flamingo Cove had been rendered in a larger scale than the rest of the island. There was the new and much expanded Flamingo Cove Hotel—or, rather, Xanadu, the Pleasure Dome—complete with a giant domed casino, four restaurants, a disco, a gymnasium with sauna. I didn't count floors, but I recall that two of my aerobics women exchanged lascivious grins as Colin caressed a domed tower with his hand and said it was the biggest structure on the out-islands. Buildings were everywhere—in the woods, on the beach, at the dock. They were all roofed with pink domes. Covered paths stretched tentacle-like between them. In the woods now shading the back of my room, Colin, the Texans, their architects—somebody— envisioned a hilly, green golf course. The disintegrating tennis court was to be replaced by six new ones. The beach shack would quadruple in size and serve liquor.

I peered down at a tiny figure in the fake sand. A waiter carried a tray of drinks from the shade of the pink-domed shack to a group of frolicking beach cuties. That, and the appearance of Eleanor and the Texas wife beside me, reminded me I was at work. With my tray of rum punch, I was almost purely decorative. Not as many people as you'd think go in for a Bahama Mama in the early afternoon.

"Drink?" I asked the Texas woman.

She turned me down.

Mrs. Hussy didn't hesitate a moment over the free drink tray.

"Having seen the Pleasure Dome, I need one." Drink firmly in hand, she nodded at the miniature island. "Didn't I tell you there would be jumbo jets?"

I peeked around a shoulder that partially blocked my view. On the far side of the platform there stood a miniature airport, complete with dime-sized radar and a tiny fleet of jumbo jets. If I had my bearings right, the control tower wasn't far from the marshy area where, with the help of my binoculars, I'd spotted the nesting flamingos.

"Next thing we know, they'll be roaring overhead night and day."

"Maybe not. There's a long way to go on this." I had heard that the island government was considering making that area a bird sanctuary. When I told Mrs. Hussy this, she rolled her eyes.

"You think a flock of birds is going to stop progress? You are naive, aren't you? That bunch . . ."

I followed her glance to the two Texas men. They were with Colin and some of the guests admiring the miniature resort.

"They would pave over the Philadelphia Zoo if there was money to be made. In any event, it's been decided that there aren't enough flamingos to worry about. There's an article in this week's island newspaper. It says that area is the only place on Flamingo Island suitable for the runways those big jets need."

Mrs. Hussy's blue-haired friend joined us. Her face was red and her lips were screwed into a fierce little knot. She snatched a drink from my tray. She'd always struck me as the least caustic of the three women, so I waited to hear what had her so upset.

"Disgraceful," she said when she'd taken a long swallow. "They mangled 'Kubla Khan.' You noticed, surely."

"Mrs. Hussy and I shook our heads.

"It's 'Down to a *sunless* sea.' I taught English for forty years. Retired only last year. I know Coleridge."

"Coleridge!" Mrs. Hussy drew back her formidable head. "I know about that one. Drugs!"

Her friend nodded. "The poem supposedly came to him in an opium vision. When he woke, the only lines he remembered were, 'A savage place! as holy and enchanted/ As e'er beneath a waning moon was haunted/ By woman wailing for her demon-lover!' "

"Demon lover." Mrs. Hussy repeated the words maliciously.

176

"They should have made the wretched little girl recite *that* part of it."

My attention was diverted by a trio that had appeared at the top of the steps: Sonny, Cindy, and the chief of police. The three walked to the deserted bar and talked quietly for a few minutes. Sonny had his arm around his wife's shoulder. He was smiling. She was almost smiling. I even saw Chief Richards give a bit of a smile. Good feelings reigned in the Pleasure Dome.

"Isn't it nice to see those youngsters looking so happy," the blue-haired lady said. "Always together now, after all that fuss at the beginning. It doesn't look as if they're in so much trouble any more, does it? Everything seems to be working out nicely."

Mrs. Hussy sniffed. "I give that marriage a year."

If that. The moment Chief Richards left the couple to join the political types at the side of the terrace, Sonny the affectionate and attentive husband was off like a shot. He rushed the drink tray, leaving Cindy alone at the bar.

"Hey, Bon . . ."

I backed away. He held up his hand.

"Oops! Sorry, Bonnie," he said, shaking a finger in my face. "I got it right this time. Whatcha got here?"

Okay. So he was trying. I would try, too. Nodding politely at my tray, I began: "This is a coconut daiquiri, and that's a . . ."

He snatched a drink without waiting for the rest of my spiel. Within seconds he was making the rounds.

I followed him around the crowded patio, picking up snatches of conversation.

". . . that dive leader. Charlie, from the fishing camp . . . wanted for questioning in Leslie's death. I mean, nobody's saying the guy did it, but he didn't seem wrapped too tight to me. Trouble is, he's disappeared. They got a manhunt going. The chief's here to warn . . ."

"Miss Indermill? May I have a word with you?"

Chief Richards looked a lot less happy with me than he had looked with Sonny and Cindy. I felt every eye at the gathering on me as I followed the chief to the bar.

"What did you and your friend Mike do after you left my office yesterday evening?" he asked, not wasting one breath on pleasantries.

I told the chief that we had had dinner, and where.

"After dinner, I took the bus . . ."

"I'm more interested in what you did before dinner than after."

"We didn't do anything. We went straight from Government House to Barnacle Bill's."

"You walked?"

"Yes."

"And Mike did not stop on the way to make a phone call?"

"Well, no, but . . ." I was shaking my head in denial, but a terrible thought had occurred to me. "When we got to Barnacle Bill's, he called his landlady to tell her about the car, and he called his lawyer . . ."

"Were you with him when he made those calls? Are you sure he made only those two?"

"No, but that's what he told me."

The chief studied me with his eyes. "When do you see him again?"

"Tonight, if I decide to go to Nassau."

"Nassau? He must be taking the big boat."

I nodded.

"People come to these islands for many reasons, Miss Indermill," he said quietly. "Most come for the sun and the water. A few of them come because they are trying to outrun something. Your friend Mike is one of those people. I'm afraid he hasn't learned that you cannot outrun your problems."

Chief Richards left me shaken. As soon as I could do it without looking as if I was trying to outrun something, I put my tray down and hurried from the terrace. As I rushed across the open walkway, I glanced over my shoulder. Chief Richards was staring down from the railing. I smiled weakly and made myself walk slowly until I was out of his sight in the reception area.

Pulling the receptionist's extra phone as far from her desk as I could, I huddled over it and dialed Mike's number. Like the chief, I wasted no time with niceties.

"You warned Charlie O'Dell that the police were coming," I said with my voice low so that the woman at the desk couldn't overhear.

"What? Interfere with a police investigation? A pillar of the community like me?"

"Yes, you! You put me in a terrible position. I was just questioned by Chief Richards."

"Roscoe came to Flamingo Cove to question you?"

For the first time, there was concern in his voice.

"Not just for that. He came out to ask around about Charlie, and to talk to Sonny and Cindy."

"Busy guy."

"He came for the reception, too. Colin and Eleanor have just unveiled Xanadu, the Pleasure Dome."

"I know. There was an article in the paper. Your employers have gone crazy for sure."

"Not as crazy as you have, warning Charlie . . ."

"Calm down. Roscoe can't prove a thing. We still on for Nassau tonight?"

"I never said . . ."

"Do you know where the pier is? At the top of Main Street. Have the bus let you off after the bridge and follow the dirt road right. I'd like to get going around six but I'll wait if you can't get here that early. I'll wait until seven in case you catch the last bus. Bring your dancing shoes," he added.

My hand was so sweaty that when I first tried replacing the receiver I dropped it. The clerk at the desk looked at me, then lowered her eyes. What did that mean? Had she overheard anything? And who was that man with the broom? He wasn't the usual porter. What if Chief Richards had someone watching me? I looked back at the phone. Maybe it was tapped, and . . .

Tapped? On Flamingo Island? Snap out of it, Bonnie!

As I passed the clerk on my way back to the terrace, I called a cheerful "hello" to her.

179

"Having fun on the terrace?" she asked. "I wish I was there."

"Want to carry my tray of drinks around?"

She laughed. "I don't want to be there that bad."

The man with the broom got my biggest smile. He smiled back. His face wrinkled up like a raisin. My would-be undercover cop looked about eighty.

The crowd at the reception was thinning out. Walking up the steps, I passed Colin and Chief Richards on their way down. The chief didn't glance my way.

Eleanor met me at the top of the steps. She had my tray in her hands. "Where were you?" she whispered, shoving the thing at me.

"Ladies' room."

She nodded toward the room behind the palm tree. "What's wrong with that one? Never mind. Make one more round with the tray. After that the bar opens and they can pay for their drinks. This is getting expensive."

This tray carrying was getting to me. I scowled as I took it from her. "And smile," she snapped.

Seconds later she and the Texans left the restaurant. Most of the remaining guests weren't far behind. Only a few diehard drinkers and a handful of diehard gossips remained.

Sonny held center stage, literally. He stood right in front of the Pleasure Dome, rum drink in hand. This was not Sonny the loudmouth braggart, or Sonny the frightened bridegroom. Charlie's troubles and a couple rum punches had turned Sonny into the voice of sodden deliberation.

" . . . didn't trust that guy for a second. Dumb, bringing liquor on the dive boat. Way I see it, he had this planned. Get Leslie drunk, then once they're underwater, he leads her away from the group and throws the net over her. Traps the poor girl down there."

"But why?" somebody asked.

"Jealousy," he said knowingly. "Had to be. Leslie was hot." He shot a quick glance at Cindy. She was alone at one of the tables, sipping a drink. "I mean," Sonny continued, "she was bad news.

Even when I was single, I wouldn't have messed with someone like her." He drained his glass. "Where's that girl with the drinks?"

It took every bit of control I could muster to walk up to Sonny with my tray. I did not smile.

"First time I ran into Leslie I said to myself, 'That girl is asking for trouble.' I mean, come on. She's got on those tight clothes and that blonde hair's hanging down to you-know-where. . . ."

"Right," someone said.

But it wasn't right. I plopped my tray smack in the center of the Pleasure Dome's proposed golf course, sending a couple tiny plastic golfers to golfer heaven.

"No, Sonny. Don't you remember? The first time you saw Leslie was on Monte Carlo Night. She had her hair up."

"Yeah, yeah," he said with a disparaging wave of his hand. "Sure. And she's wearing the feathers and bustin' out of that outfit. But I'm talking in general. You know what I mean. Like the way she came on to guys. Take a guy like Charlie, not wrapped too tight to begin with, and a girl who don't watch herself can end up in deep doo-doo."

Having made that delicate point, the deep thinker fell quiet. His audience wandered away.

Cindy called to her husband from the table, "Want to go to the beach?"

He waved his now-empty glass toward me. As I took it from his hand, I said softly, "You met Leslie before Monte Carlo Night. You 'ran into' her the night you didn't come back. That's when you saw her with her hair down."

He glanced toward Cindy. She was standing now. She took a few steps toward us.

"Get out of here with that stuff," he whispered. "You nuts? You want to make trouble with me and my wife, just when we're getting things straightened out?"

"No, but I will if you don't tell me the truth. I'll be in my room after four. If you don't want to talk there, I'll come visit you in your room."

"What are you two whispering about?" Cindy asked.

"Nothing."

"Deep doo-doo."

Four o'clock came and went. Sonny didn't. It was almost four-thirty. My threat didn't seem to have worked. Maybe he was telling the truth. Maybe he had just been "talking in general."

My tapestry overnighter was on the bed before me, still unopened. I was no closer to Nassau's fleshpots than I was to Leslie's secret lover and the thing she had hidden. Twice I'd held the clasp in my fingers. Twice I'd let it drop. No sensible, respectable woman would do what I was about to do: head off for what was sure to be a one night stand with a fugitive from the I.R.S. who helped a suspected murderer escape. But . . . oh, could he ever kiss!

I had hold of the clasp for the third time when Sonny tapped at my door.

"Come in."

He swaggered into the room, chin first. As soon as the door was closed, he crossed his arms over his chest.

"Okay. So I'm here. What do you want out of my life, anyway?"

"That first afternoon you got to Flamingo Cove you met Leslie somewhere. I want to know where, and I want to know what you did."

"You want to know a lot, don't you?"

He was staring down at the tapestry bag. I flipped the clasp. "You recognize this? Leslie was carrying it that afternoon. I don't think you're the man she spent the night with, but you know more than you've told the police. Or Cindy."

"You're wrong about that," he said belligerently. "The police know everything. Hey! Cindy told me you're working with the cops. How come you don't know about that night?"

"Roscoe must have forgotten to mention it to me."

"Well, it's no big deal!"

"Okay." I stood up. "Let's go find Cindy."

182

He backed into the door, blocking it. "Gimme a break, Bonnie. It's like this: I told Chief Richards what happened, but I don't want Cindy finding out. Not unless she has to. Cindy's not just my wife, you know. She's my bread and butter. She gets pissed off some day and tells her old man I picked up a woman on our wedding night, where does that leave me?"

"I won't say anything to Cindy, as long as you tell me the truth. If you don't . . ."

His hands fell to his side. "You girls don't know what it's like being a guy. You got to understand. A guy can't just lay there the way you girls can."

"I understand that, Sonny. It must be rough."

"Are you putting me on?"

I shook my head. The last of his fight seemed to leave him. He slumped into the door.

"I had a real hard time with Cindy that afternoon. Drank too much champagne. Anyway, I went out to get some air and get my head together. So I borrow one of the motor scooters and I'm riding around when there's Leslie, standing on the side of the road with that." He nodded at my bag. "When she smiles at me and puts out her thumb, it's like something out of the best dream I ever had. I mean, a guy feels like everything's going to hell, and here's this gorgeous sexy blonde coming on to him. What's he supposed to do?"

"You picked Leslie up on the motorbike. Where did you go then?"

"Almost all the way into town. You know where that bridge is? She had me let her off right after that. Where the turnoff for the fishing camp is. "

"Leslie went to the fishing camp?"

"No. She took the road toward town. At least I thought that's what she was doing. But after I turn the bike around, I look back and she's cut off on a path. I think it goes to the pier." He shrugged. "By that time the champagne's really hit. I can't be bothered with her. I try to get back and make things up with Cindy, but I'm having a hard time keeping the bike on the road.

Last thing I remember from that night is landing on my face in a ditch."

He started chuckling. I was no longer his enemy. I was a buddy. "So there I am the next morning, scratched up, shirt all ripped to hell, motorbike covered with mud. I'm thinking, 'Shit! What am I going to tell Cindy?' I slip the guy who rents the motorbikes twenty bucks so he'll clean the thing up and keep quiet about it. And then I get to the room and I hear Cindy telling you that I couldn't . . ."

He was unable to say it. He backed through the screen door and stepped onto the walkway. "A guy's got his pride, you know. I couldn't let you go off thinking I was . . . that way. Everything's fine with Cindy now. Couple times a day, no sweat."

As usual, I'd heard more than enough about life in the Honeymoon Suite. "See you later, Sonny."

When the door had slammed behind him, I sat for a few moments staring down at the tapestry bag. Leslie had gone to the pier on a Thursday afternoon. What do you do at the pier? You get on a boat. The boat Leslie got on had taken her to a place where hotels glittered and sported purple headboards. The mailboat from Nassau alternated days. Beth took it to Flamingo Island on Fridays. That meant that on Thursday afternoons it went to Nassau.

Nassau. That sure narrowed things down. Between downtown Nassau, Cable Beach and nearby Paradise Island, there were probably dozens of hotels that could boast some degree of glitter.

The question no longer was *whether* I would go with Mike. It was how soon could I get to the pier. It was almost five o'clock. I had just enough time to pack and catch the five-thirty bus.

On my way to the bus stop, I passed the pool. Happy Hour was there that afternoon, and it was in full swing. The vegetables and dip on the table looked fresh. The bartender held a glass toward me. I shook my head.

Sonny was next to the punch bowl with Colin and Eleanor. As I approached, I heard my name mentioned.

"Here she is. Girl detective. Bonnie, I was telling them you're trying to get a jump on Roscoe."

I stared pointedly at Cindy. She was across the pool, dangling her feet in the deep end and talking with some new guests. Sonny couldn't have understood why I didn't want my questions broadcast, but he managed to grasp that he better shut up.

"I mean"—he gave a dumb shrug—"I just mentioned that you asked me a couple questions. Bonnie's working with the cops, you know," he told the Ledbetters.

"I'm taking off for the night," I said to Eleanor. "I'll be back in the morning."

Colin had already been diverted by some guests. Eleanor fell into step beside me as I walked to the road.

"Where are you off to?"

There was no point in trying to keep my destination quiet. As Mike said, there were few secrets on Flamingo Island.

"Nassau."

She nodded. "Mike?"

"Yes."

She gave a noncommittal "em." We crossed the dirt road and stood under the palm trees. A ball of dust rose down the road. The bus was coming.

"I hope . . ." she began. The bus bounced into view. I stared at Eleanor, waiting for her to finish. She looked away.

"Just take care of yourself," she finally said.

I climbed aboard the bus, wondering if she had been warning me away from Mike, or from Leslie's trail, or simply saying "so long and watch out for those fleshpots." Whatever her meaning, it wasn't going to stop me. The fleshpots of Nassau were waiting, and I had the key to paradise.

SIXTEEN

MOONLIGHT CRUISE

By six P.M. I was walking down the dirt road to the pier, tapestry overnighter in my hand, locker key in my pocket. The bus ride had given me time to think about what I was doing. To be honest, I felt that my chances of finding whatever Leslie had hidden, or discovering the identity of her "special mate," were almost nonexistent. To be a little more honest, responsibility and reason had lost the battle against self-indulgence. If I get painfully honest about it, maybe the battle was lost on Spanish Mountain with that first kiss. I'm not sure that amount of honesty is healthy, though. Take away all our little self-deceptions, and what do we have left?

On the other hand, it's not so good to walk around with your head in the clouds, either. The way the evening turned out demonstrated that.

Chief Richards and two of his men were leaving the dive boat when I got there. We passed on the wooden pier.

"Good evening," I said.

The chief nodded curtly at me. I crossed the gangplank. Mike was standing at the railing.

"What did they want?"

Even as I spoke, part of the problem rammed into the back of my knees. Beast! He paced the deck, whining nervously. Every few seconds he leapt so that his front paws rested on the railing. From there he stared anxiously into the distance.

Mike waited until the three policemen had gotten into their car and were driving away from the pier before he said, "He's looking for Charlie. I wonder how he found out I was going off island tonight."

"I told him. It sort of came out when we were talking."

He widened his eyes in mock wonder. "You volunteered the information? Please tell me he beat it out of you. It will make me feel better."

"He used a rubber hose on me."

"I guess Roscoe doesn't trust me."

"Imagine that. What's with the dog?"

"You know what a pain in the neck Beast is," Mike said with a shrug. "Who's going to take care of him if I don't?"

We climbed up to the bridge, leaving Beast alone on deck. I watched Mike manipulate the various levers and wheels as he backed the big boat out of its mooring. The floor vibrated when the engine changed direction and we started moving forward. The boat hugged the pier for a few minutes, then Mike steered us alongside the row of old buildings that lined the deepwater harbor.

"Aren't you cutting it awfully close?"

"I'm trying to impress you with my piloting skill. Look out there." He pointed across the water to a little stretch of land. "That cay is what makes this harbor so secure. It's a natural breakwater."

"But the harbor's not deep enough for the cruise ships, is it?"

"No," he said. "Cruise ships can anchor offshore and have their passengers ferried in, but there has to be something to attract tourists. Flamingo Island doesn't have much."

I grinned. "Not until the Pleasure Dome is finished."

He started steering away from land. After a few minutes, when the village was a blur of pastel houses against the horizon and there were no other boats in the area, he offered me the wheel.

"Why don't you take this for a minute. I'll go below and put on water for coffee. We have a long ride ahead of us."

I stared at the wheel, surprised.

"I'm better at boiling water than boat steering. I'll go below."

Taking my hand, he placed it firmly on the wheel. "There's nothing to it. See the compass there? You just hold on to the wheel and keep us going north. I'll be back in a minute. If you're interested"—he reached onto a shelf beneath the wheel and pulled out a rolled sheet of paper—"here's a navigation chart. You can chart us a course to Nassau. If you see any other boats, scream."

He clattered down the steps before I could reply. Sliding into the pilot's seat, I gripped the wheel firmly in both hands. After a few seconds, when I felt secure, I turned it a couple inches to the right. The needle on the compass moved slightly. This was okay. I unrolled the chart and took a look. What a wonderful, intricate thing it was: depths, shallows and reefs, and uninhabited islands. I turned the wheel maybe four inches to the left. The boat moved slowly, gently under my touch, and my imagination took a big jump.

Wouldn't working on a boat be a great job! There's always something to do on a boat. Do they take apprentice pilots? Maybe they have hostesses on some boats. I can hostess like nobody's business. Or guides. I can stand on the deck and point out the sights to tourists. "On your right is famous Paradise Island. Once known as Hog Island, Paradise Island was the private enclave of millionaire Huntington Hartford. . . ."

If I get a few things wrong, they'll never know. They're tourists. They've had a couple rum drinks. They're easy.

Between these fantasies, and my power over this fifty-foot giant of a boat, I almost let the yelp from down below pass by me. But a second, louder yelp followed.

"Mike? What are you doing to Beast?"

No answer.

Keeping a fingertip on the wheel, I stretched to peer over the edge of the bridge. The main deck under me was empty.

"Mike?"

"Coming," he called from the cabin.

A moment later he climbed back onto the bridge and took the wheel.

"What was wrong with Beast?"

"I don't know." He put an arm around my shoulder. "You're doing a great job here, Bonnie. Maybe I'll let you steer all the way."

As he spoke, another yelp came from down below. It was a real hellhound cry that made the hair on the back of my neck stand up.

"Something's wrong with that dog." As I spoke, an awful suspicion took hold of me. "Is Charlie O'Dell on board?"

"Bonnie, you saw the police searching the boat."

"I'm going below. If I find Charlie down there, you can take me back to shore."

"When you come up, bring me a cup of coffee. Cream, no sugar." He turned back to the wheel.

I stood at the top of the ladder staring at him. He looked ahead for a moment, then glanced at a dial and consulted the chart. If he was smuggling a fugitive off Flamingo Island, could he be so cool? Probably. He was a fugitive himself, with the I.R.S. breathing down his neck, and he had already helped Charlie avoid the police.

Even knowing this, it wasn't until my feet hit the lower deck that a twinge of apprehension hit me. It was growing late and below the bridge there was a shadowy stretch where the light from the setting sun didn't reach. Beyond that was the cabin. A tube of light shone from the fixture over the stove, and a red ring glowed under the kettle.

I walked to the railing and peered over. It was a tropical postcard night, the deep blue sky streaked with red and yellow. Mike had upped the boat's speed, and its nose threw clouds of salt water against the sides. I felt the boat veer. A fine spray washed over the deck.

"Sorry about that," he called down from the bridge. "We

weren't headed straight north. You didn't steer us off course, did you?"

He knew I had. "Maybe a little," I shouted back.

The kettle's thin whistle broke through above the sound of the engines. I took a couple steps forward into the cabin and peered carefully around it.

Beast was sprawled in front of the door that led below to the bunk room. Rousing himself, he gave a few halfhearted wags of his tail. I wasn't what he wanted, though, and he soon collapsed on the floor again, head plopped on paws.

The kettle's whistle was going full out now, and the boiling water had the pot banging around on the stove. The coffee and cups were in the cabinet over the sink, and the milk in the neat little refrigerator under it. I spooned coffee into both cups. As I stirred the milk into Mike's, I watched Beast. If it wasn't for his chest slowly moving up and down, the dog could have been a big ratty stuffed toy.

"A little depressed, hum?"

His head shifted slightly. He sniffed at the narrow gap under the bunk-room door. Putting aside the spoon, I crossed the floor and crouched beside him.

"Feeling rejected, Beast? It's no wonder, the way you smell."

When I patted his head, he responded by wedging his nose further into the crevice. I smelled a dank breeze from under the door. Stretching my free hand to the door knob, I watched the dog's reaction. His eyes followed my hand. I grasped the knob. The dog's tail began thumping wildly. Charlie was in that room. I would have bet what was left of my money on it.

"Poor doggie," I said softly. "I've got to go now." Still holding the knob, I got to my feet. The boat must have hit a big wave at that instant. The floor of the cabin dropped from under my feet and I was thrown into the door. As I tried to balance myself, I accidentally turned the knob. The door opened in just a crack. Beast, seeing his chance, blundered into the opening. The door opened wide and Beast and I stumbled into the bunkroom at the same time.

The room was dim, lit only by a small high window. Charlie was crouched against the wall. Even though I had figured he was there, I gasped with fright.

Charlie gasped too, and cowered even lower. When he saw that I was alone, he rolled his eyes toward the ceiling and said, "It's my girl Bonnie. Thought it was the cops."

Taking Beast's head in his two hands, he caressed the dog's muzzle. "You know what the cops are saying, Bonnie? They're saying I might have killed Leslie."

I stared down at Charlie's rough hands. They *were* rough. I could remember the feel of his skin from the time we had shaken hands on the plane. The man in the shack hadn't had that rough skin, had he? I recalled his hands on my throat as strong, but not rough.

"I wouldn't have hurt a hair on that girl's head," Charlie was saying as I backed from the cabin. "I loved her," I heard him say as I closed the door.

When I'd taken a few deep breaths, I collected the coffee and left the cabin.

"You're a fool," I said to Mike as soon as my feet hit the bridge. "You're smuggling a criminal. Please take me back now."

His eyes were locked on the horizon. "I can't. I gave Charlie my word I would get him off Flamingo Island. And he's not a criminal. He's wanted for questioning."

I handed Mike his coffee. "If he's innocent, why doesn't he let himself be questioned? Sonny and Cindy aren't running away."

"If it comes to it, Sonny and Cindy can probably afford a good lawyer. And they're kids," he added. "Life hasn't ground them to a pulp yet."

"Doesn't it matter to you that Charlie may have tried to kill me in the beach shack?"

He shook his head. "Bonnie, if I thought there was the slightest chance that was true, he would not be on this boat."

I leaned on the rail next to him. We didn't speak for a long time, and during that time I admitted to myself that it wasn't Charlie I feared. I was almost as sure as Mike was that Charlie

192

hadn't been the man in the shack. What I feared was getting further on Chief Richards' bad side.

"I'm sorry you're upset by this," Mike finally said, "but Nassau is the only place around here big enough for Charlie to get lost in. Poor guy's been hiding in the woods. Taking him along with me seemed"—he shrugged—"logical."

Obstructing a police investigation in a country where he was a guest was anything but logical, but there was no arguing with Mike. The deed was done. I turned away from him and stared out over the water. The sun was already below the horizon, but the remaining red light shimmered over the waves. A gorgeous night for a moonlight cruise.

Charlie had known Leslie a lot longer and better than I had. He might be able to shed some light on what she had been up to. If I was going to be an accomplice in transporting a fugitive, I might as well get something out of it. After a few minutes, I looked back at Mike.

"Too bad Charlie's not enjoying this ride. You think he'd want to come up and talk?"

His eyebrow rose in surprise. "Sure. Charlie will talk to anybody but the cops."

It was a while before Charlie's grizzled head poked up over the ladder. He looked around the bridge cautiously, as if expecting Chief Richards to spring from under a bench. I could hear Beast's claws scratching against the ladder as the dog tried to haul himself up behind his master.

"There's no one around," I told Charlie. "I don't even see any other boats out there."

He climbed onto the bridge, a cup of coffee in one hand. Mike followed him and took the wheel from me.

"Feels good up here in the air. Thanks for springing me from the hole." He scraped his fingers through his hair. "I tried to get myself cleaned up before I showed my face up here in polite society, but I don't even have a toothbrush."

I shook my head. "That's okay. I'm not polite society."

193

Charlie collapsed onto a bench and stared out over the water. The night and day hiding in the woods had taken a heavy toll on the man. Charlie had never looked particularly debonair; now, with his dirty clothes and the gray circles around his red eyes, he looked positively disreputable.

What could I say to a man who was being hunted by the police for questioning in the death of the woman who had dumped him?

I sat down at the other end of the bench. "This is a bad mess. I wish I could help."

For a minute I didn't think he was going to answer me. He swirled the paper cup of coffee and we both watched steam rise from the hot liquid.

"That it is, Bonnie. A terrible bad mess." He looked up at me. "There's a fellow I know, runs a big fishing boat between Nassau and San Juan. If I can get hold of him I can catch a ride. But thanks for offering."

Helping Charlie get away wasn't the kind of help I had in mind.

"What I mean is, if I knew who Leslie had been going out with, maybe I could help tie up some loose ends."

He gave a sad smile. "She wouldn't tell me. For a while I thought it was my friend there"—a nod toward Mike—"but he gave me his word he wasn't the guy. Mike's word is good, you know."

I nodded. "How did you and Leslie meet? She never told me."

"It was at the fishing camp. She was having dinner with the Ledbetters and some other people from the hotel. I thought she had a thing going with Colin, the way she was hanging on to him. I got to know her better, though." He shrugged. "That was just Leslie's way. She didn't mean anything by it."

"Leslie told me things, Charlie. I think she was trying to . . ." I searched for the right way to put it. ". . . manipulate her new boyfriend. That may have gotten her in trouble."

My choice of words brought a rueful smile to Charlie's face. "Manipulate," he said. "She could manipulate a man all right,

194

without half trying. Twisted me right around her little finger."
Holding out his hand, he wiggled his pinky. "Got me so I didn't
know whether I was coming or going."

"When she told you she had this new boyfriend . . ."

"I cried like a baby," he said softly. "You wouldn't think a guy
like me would to that, but I did."

"Did she tell you anything about him? Where he lived? What
kind of work he did?"

Charlie leaned back on the bench and stared off into the
distance. "She said he was closer to her own age. And
more . . . refined. That's the word she used. I guess I wasn't
good enough for her."

"How old are you?"

"Forty-two. Leslie was only twenty-five. Guess I can't blame
her for wanting someone younger. She wouldn't find anyone who
loved her more, though." He looked at me with sad eyes. "You
were her roommate, Bonnie. Did she ever say anything about us?
I mean, how good we were together?"

I didn't recall Leslie saying much of anything about Charlie,
but I nodded.

"What did she say? I know how you girls talk about things. You
don't have to tell me the personal stuff, but . . ."

"She talked about some of the things you did, and how you
had such nice times."

"Oh, didn't we though! How can the police think I'd have
anything to do with killing her? Roscoe Richards questioned me
already. Right after you and Mike found her body. I told him that
there were at least half-a-dozen people around me the whole time
we were underwater."

"Then why are you running? The police could get some of
those divers to back you up."

"Roscoe doesn't like me much. You've seen that cell in
Government House? Christmas Eve after I left Barnacle Bill's,
the bastard got me on a drunk and disorderly and threw me in
there. Christmas Eve! I don't want to go back."

"Hey, you two," Mike called. "Take a look. You can see

Nassau. Charlie, you better get below until we're sure it's clear."

The city glimmered in the distance, a vast carnival of lights.

"Over there's Paradise Island," Charlie said, pointing to a cluster of tall buildings.

The key to paradise. Did it open something on Paradise Island?

"Is that where you'd stay, if you wanted to go somewhere really special?"

"Maybe. Or Cable Beach. Maybe if I'd taken Leslie places like that, things would have been different." As he stood, he gave me a sly look. "You and Mike staying over?"

"I don't know." Sticking my hand into my pants pocket, I pulled out that mysterious key. "Leslie hid this, Charlie. She called it 'the key to paradise.' Do you have any idea what it would unlock?"

" 'The key to paradise.' " He took the key from me. A small smile grew to his lips. "Leslie had a nice way with words. This looks like it might open a locker. You might try some of the hotels. Or private clubs. There are some of those around. A couple golf clubs, and tennis . . ."

Leslie had gone to a club with Beth and Neticia. I searched my memory for the name. "The Paradise Water Club? Did Leslie mention that to you?"

"That the place she went with Beth Ledbetter and the kid's babysitter? Yeah. She liked that a lot. It has class." Charlie sighed wearily. "That was my problem. I didn't have enough class."

He handed the key to me. A second later he had disappeared down the ladder.

I went back to the front of the bridge. Without looking at me, Mike said, "You understand why I'm helping Charlie? The guy's beaten." He was intent on getting the big boat around a breakwater and into the harbor.

As I watched him do this, I found myself feeling almost as sad for him as I did for Charlie. Charlie was more beaten than Mike, sure. He'd been running from one island to another longer. He'd spent more nights in dank jail cells. More young girls had found other men. But give Mike a couple years and where would he be? The reality of where his life was going wasn't very pleasant.

"I understand. You see a lot of yourself in Charlie, don't you?"

He tilted his head. "Are you kidding? He's a wreck."

We rode into the harbor in silence. Mike was a master at maneuvering the big boat. There were a lot of things he was a master at. On the plus side were making me laugh, patience when I was upset, boat piloting, kissing. On the minus side there was his tangled-up life. Giving myself over to hedonism had sounded great from a distance. Nassau had been far away, physically and in time. Now, though, with the city spread out in front of me, I wasn't sure. As I helped Mike tie the boat lines to the dock, I wondered how I was going to handle that evening. After dinner and a couple drinks, and dancing, who could say what might happen?

Charlie had come out of the bunk room with a duffel bag over his shoulder. He and Mike spent a few seconds looking out over the Nassau pier. The sky was dark by then, but the pier was well-lit and very busy. Lights from boats and restaurants dotted the area. Tourists strolled past, stopping to bargain with the native women who sold straw hats. Under a street light near the end of the pier, two men worked on a section of paved road, while several others were busy scraping paint off an old sailboat.

"Seems okay to me," Mike said after looking around the pier. He and Charlie shook hands. Mike winked at me. "Let's go dancing."

Mike and I were first off. When we got to the concrete pier, he took my hand and began leading me toward the busy street.

"Don't turn around. Charlie's going to slip away . . ." He paused. What he said next made no sense at all.

"If things get desperate, see Red at the bar at the Acropolis Hotel on Conch Street. He'll put you up."

Everything happened very quickly. The two men working on the road stepped directly in front of us, so threateningly that for a second I thought we were about to be robbed. A woman who had been selling straw hats was suddenly at my side. And—good grief!—she looked exactly like the Flamingo Island policewoman who had borrowed Leslie's books. I could hardly believe it: She *was* the same woman. The sharp screech of a whistle erupted behind us. I glanced over my shoulder as the three men who had been scraping the sailboat surrounded Charlie. One of the men in front of us pulled something from his jacket pocket. It glinted under the street light. It was a badge.

"Bahamas Police," he said in his wonderful island English.

SEVENTEEN

A NIGHT ON THE TOWN

I walked out of the Nassau police station at nine that evening. Mike and Charlie had convinced the police I wasn't involved in smuggling Charlie off Flamingo Island. The young policewoman put in a good word for me, too. As far as I was concerned Leslie's nurse romance was worth a thousand times its inflated price.

By that point I was so undone that dancing and whatever might follow it were the last things on my mind, so it was probably just as well that I walked out of the police station alone. Charlie was held for obvious reasons, and Mike for less serious but just as obvious ones. As for Beast, I saw him being taken away by the local humane society truck as I walked toward Nassau's main thoroughfare, Bay Street.

I faced Nassau unencumbered by just about everything. The boat was under police guard. My date was in the jail, and so was my overnight bag. The police had promised to drop it at my hotel by noon the next day. I'm sure they intended to search it thoroughly before they did that. My remaining traveler's check and what cash I had amounted to barely sixty dollars. It would take twenty to get me to Flamingo Cove on the next afternoon's mailboat, which meant I had about forty dollars to spend a high-season night in Nassau. Things had gotten desperate.

Following directions I'd gotten from a police clerk, I turned right at Bay Street. The luxury hotels of Paradise Island lay that way, only I wasn't headed for luxury that night. I was headed for Red and the Acropolis Hotel twelve blocks to the east. I was headed there with some apprehension. The police clerk's eyebrows had all but disappeared into her hairline when I'd told her where my bag should be delivered.

For the first few blocks, good stores lined Bay Street. There were clothing and jewelry shops, and places that sold nothing but perfume. I bought an ice cream cone from a street vendor, but decided to wait for the Acropolis for a real meal. Surely there would be a cafe. A Greek diner would be nice. I could go for a nice, greasy burger.

I continued up Bay Street, strolling past clusters of vacationers and nodding to a young woman shopkeeper standing in the doorway of her still-open shop. My spirits were pretty good. Mike had said, "really desperate," but this wasn't territory for the desperate. Not yet.

I walked on, across one intersection and another, until I wasn't passing so many tourists, until the few shopkeepers standing in doorways wore the wary expressions of guards. Their merchandise was poorer, and so were their few customers. Buildings were shabby, and the streets littered.

I crossed another intersection. The tourists had disappeared. So had native women. A group of boys loitered around a couple of rusting bicycles. As I passed a T-shirt shop, a ragged young man fell into step beside me.

"I hope you are enjoying my beautiful island, pretty lady."

I quickened my pace. He quickened his.

"Is there something I can help you find?"

He may have been perfectly harmless, but I doubt it. When you live and work in New York City, you develop a sixth sense about street hustlers.

"No," I snapped.

The young man followed me as I hurried across another street. My heart started beating faster. Open stores were further apart now, and there were shops that had obviously been boarded up for a long time. Music blared from an alley. I could hear laughter, but the alley was full of shadows and I didn't dare turn that way.

"What's your hurry? I can show you a nice . . ."

Conch Street! The intersection was deserted. I paused long enough to look both ways. Toward the right there was a big abandoned building. Beyond that were the hills of East Nassau. To the left Conch Street was not much more than an alley. It led to the water. In the middle of that block, one tiny beacon of yellow light shone over a door.

Stepping off the curb, I stared up. The faded sign hung flush with the wall above a second floor window. ACROPOLIS HOTEL.

There was no door on Bay Street so I headed down the alley toward the light. The young man followed a few paces, then stopped.

The door was at ground level. I knew, without taking one step inside, that the Acropolis was a true dive. In my wild youth I traveled fourth class through southern Europe. I know a dive when I see one.

I stood in the open door for a moment, seriously wondering if I would be better off on a park bench. Footsteps retreated behind me. The young man was leaving. I looked back to Bay Street. A long shadow moved against the wall of the building across the alley. My young man, or another one? It didn't matter. I could not spend the night on a park bench.

I stepped through the door. The rock music I'd heard from Bay Street filled the narrow reception area. Across the chipped linoleum floor stood an unmanned reception desk. There was a half-shut door behind it. Next to that was a steep wooden stairway, palm prints running up the wall beside it. A phone hung on the far wall, the painted surface around it covered with scrawled numbers. There was a hall leading off that same wall. The music was coming from that direction.

"Hello?"

When no one answered, I stepped around the desk and tapped on the open door.

"Comin'."

A tall black woman in a housecoat pushed through the door. As she eyed me suspiciously, a barrage of voices exploded on the upper floor. There was high-pitched laughter. A glass broke.

The woman looked up briefly, then positioned herself so that she barred the staircase with her ample hip.

Did she expect I'd make a dash to join the fun up there? Fat chance! I had a pretty good idea about the Acropolis' usual clientele. I didn't think I looked like one of them, but I hadn't looked in a mirror since my long visit with the local police. Maybe I was a little ragged by then.

"What do you want?"

"I'm here to see Red."

She nodded toward the hall. "Tending the bar."

The hall was narrow, and very dim. I felt the woman's suspicious glare on my back until I had followed it around a corner. The music was growing louder, and I could hear voices. I held my breath as I passed a filthy open restroom. Beyond that were two other doors. I pushed through one and found myself looking at a back alley filled with garbage. As I stood there, something shuffled down near my feet.

All things considered, I'd held up well until then. That shuffling noise did it. My stomach flipped. I slammed the door shut, unnerved. The whole evening had been awful. Crazy thoughts began rattling around in my head. Maybe Leslie's ideas weren't so nutty. What if there really were white slave rings? And what if a white slaver decided I wasn't up to snuff? Somebody would find my body in an alley, my throat slit.

I thought about Mike. Was this where he'd planned to take me? My eyes grew damp and this pinched feeling started in my throat. If I stood there much longer I'd end up doing some serious crying.

Pulling myself together, I tried the door at the hall's end. It swung open easily on well-worn hinges. A blast of music, a faceful of cigarette smoke and stale alcohol. I was in the right place.

It was a big room, and it was packed with a mixed crowd. Most were men, but there were a few women. Some stood, some sat around tables. A few couples danced. This wasn't a place where I'd meet friends for wine spritzers, but as I glanced around, my feeling of looming danger began evaporating.

A tall and skeletal white man was behind the bar. The light over the bar glanced off the bones of his face. In contrast to his red hair, his pale skin looked ghostly.

"You're Red?"

"Not on my birth certificate," he responded, "but that's what everyone calls me."

When I introduced myself as a friend of Mike's, the man's bony features managed to twist into a creepy smirk. He stepped from behind the bar.

"How is Mike? Is he going to meet you here?"

"Not really. The thing is . . ."

I told him why I was there, leaving out the more awful parts of the story. I thought that even my censored version was awful, but Red treated it like business as usual. I suppose in his circle it was.

"So Charlie and Mike are both in jail. I already knew about Leslie. It made the Nassau paper." Red reached for my hand and patted it softly. "With Mike locked up, I guess you won't be needing a room with a double bed tonight."

I pulled my hand free. "Just a place to sleep."

He had already signaled another man to take his place behind the bar. As he led me back into the hall he was chuckling. "I'm kidding, Bonnie. All the rooms at the Acropolis have double beds."

We passed the open toilet. At the reception desk Red stepped into the room where the woman was. I heard them speaking softly. A moment later he was back.

"There's a room empty at the back. It's small," he added, starting up the stairs.

"It will be fine. Is there a phone in it?"

203

"The only public phone's the one on the wall. You know Leslie well?" he asked over his shoulder. "Damned shame what happened to her. She was a fine piece of work."

"I'd only known her for a few days. Did *you* know her well?"

"Not was well as I would have liked to. She and Charlie stayed here a couple times, but that was a while back."

The Acropolis' second floor had the same cracked linoleum as the first. The walls were even dirtier. The loud voices I'd heard earlier came from a room near the stairway.

I was glad when we continued up another flight. Near the middle of the third floor hall, Red stuck his key in a lock and opened the door to a tiny box of a room.

"Hadn't seen Leslie for a couple months when she came in last week."

I was so distressed by the room that what he'd said almost went by me. It was a little box, but that was hardly the worst of it. I have friends in Manhattan who live in boxes and pay handsomely for them. But this box was in a class of its own. In addition to the same cracked yellow floor and dirty walls, it boasted an unspeakably filthy wall-mounted sink in one corner, complete with a rusted coffee can under it to catch the drip. There was no dresser, not even a shelf. Two nails had been pounded into the back of the door. A wire coat hanger swung from one of them. The *pièce de résistance*, though, was the double bed that sagged desperately, not in the middle but on the side away from the wall. What on earth kind of action had that bed seen?

Red had pulled up the shade on the one narrow window. "She'd been over on Paradise Island. If you look out here, you can see it."

I forced my eyes away from the bed.

He was smiling at me. The bare bulb overhead glanced off the angles of his face. I was suddenly very uncomfortable.

"I'm sorry. You were saying something about Leslie."

"Step over here. You can see Paradise Island. Leslie had been there . . ."

I walked to the window. Across a few rooftops, beyond a stretch of water, twinkled the bright lights of Paradise Island's luxury hotels. If I was on the right track, Leslie had hidden something in a locker on Paradise Island. Why had she left Paradise Island then? If she and her friend had wanted a luxury hotel, there were more than enough of them there. But she had ended up at the Acropolis. I looked at the sink, appalled. Where, exactly, had she and her friend enjoyed their bubblebath romp?

"Bathtub's down the hall," Red said, as if reading my mind. "Be sure to lock it when you're in there."

"Was Leslie alone?"

"She was when she stopped by. I doubt if she was later, thought. The way she was dressed with those little beads in her hair . . ."

"You mean she only dropped by here? She didn't stay?"

"No. There were a dozen guys in the bar willing to put her up for the night, but she only hung around a few minutes."

This puzzled me. Leslie had said she was pressed for time that night, yet she had taken the time to stop by the Acropolis.

"I wonder why she stopped here?"

"That's no mystery," Red said with an oily smile. "She wanted to borrow ten dollars. It was after seven o'clock. Leslie had forgotten that the buses stop running at seven. She needed cab fare."

So Leslie had visited Paradise Island, but she hadn't stayed there.

"Could she get a cab to Cable Beach for ten dollars?"

"Easy."

"Did you loan her the ten?"

Red nodded. "You bet I did! There was always the chance she might decide to pay it back, one way or another."

I was well out of Red's path, but when he walked away from the window he managed to push my knees into the bed. I grasped the iron frame to steady myself.

"Sorry about that. You had dinner?"

"Not much of one. Does the bar serve food?"

He shook his head. "No, but I could get you something. You like Chinese? I can get a kid to pick it up for you."

I didn't want any favors from Red. If there was a place nearby, I was prepared to go myself.

"Where?"

"Center of town. But I'll find a kid. In this neighborhood all you've got to do is open the door and wave a few bucks. You'll get a dozen guys willing to do anything." His eyes actually twinkled. "Been thinking about getting one of them to kill my mother-in-law."

With that, he managed to kill my appetite. The ice cream cone would do until breakfast.

"No thanks."

"Okay," he said with a shrug. "It's your stomach."

He pressed the room key into my hand and let his fingers rest against my palm long enough so that I would get the message.

"If you get lonely tonight come down to the bar," he said on his way out of the room. "I'll buy you a drink."

I said I might, but I knew I wouldn't.

When I was sure he had gone, I went back to the lobby and borrowed a phone book from the desk. The woman reluctantly changed a five dollar bill for me.

I called the Paradise Water Club first. "Yes," a cheerful female voice said. "We have lockers."

How easy that was! I was feeling optimistic when I started calling hotels at Cable Beach. That optimism faded quickly. The first desk clerk I got laughed when I asked about purple room decor. He hung up without answering. Another simply hung up without answering or laughing. At the end of twenty minutes, I was out of change and had found only two hotels that admitted to purple print. Not one of the hotels I called was willing to check their records to see if Leslie had been registered there the week before. I'd have to win them over with my smile in the morning.

It was a horrible night, one I thought would never end. When I managed to battle the mattress into an uncomfortable truce, the party downstairs was still going strong enough for the riotous howls to carry up the stairs. Several times the rhythmic squeaking of bedsprings in the room next-door woke me. Once there was a volcanic eruption of angry curses in the hall. And some time in the blackest part of the night the crowd from the Acropolis Bar spilled into the street. For a few minutes it sounded as if the whole bunch of them were mixing it up in a huge brawl. I couldn't see the street from my window, but finally there were sirens. A blue light circled above the rooftops. A police raid! I thought. I'll end up in the jail yet.

The street grew quiet finally, and I got back in bed. I didn't fall asleep as much as crumble into senselessness.

EIGHTEEN

THE FLESHPOTS

The morning sky was filled with monster towers, in shades of pink so loud they thundered. The moment I laid eyes on them, I felt sure I had found Leslie's hotel.

I called out "Bus stop," the standard cry when you want the bus to stop on New Providence Island. My voice joined a chorus of voices from women in maids uniforms. You don't find many tourists riding the New Providence bus system at nine A.M.

I followed a group of chatting maids across the road and up a long circular drive to the hotel's entrance.

It had to be the right place. "Dazzling," Leslie had said, and this hotel was exactly the kind of place that would have dazzled her. Leslie loved fantasy, and this pink extravaganza stretching into the sky and across the horizon seemed designed to help you forget the real world. This was a place to let your imagination go crazy.

I had no plan, except possibly meandering up to an idle desk clerk and inquiring about Leslie. And if the clerk wouldn't help, I'd do what I'd seen done in countless movies: wait until he was diverted and peek a look at the guest registry myself. With any luck, I'd see not only Leslie's name, but the name of the man she stayed with.

At Flamingo Cove I might have managed that, but one step into this hotel and I knew that a peek at the registry was impossible. The reception area was huge. It was manned by a team of bustling clerks who stood behind a wide counter. There wasn't a registration book in sight.

Faced by milling tourists, ringing phones, trolleys of luggage being moved with Manhattan-like speed, I almost lost my nerve. I felt grubby and out of place. I'd had to make do with the clothes I'd worn the day before, and soap for toothpaste.

Finally, I got into one of the shorter lines and waited. When my turn came, I said that I was looking for my sister. "She registered last Thursday night. I don't know if she's still here."

I gave the clerk Leslie's full name. He took a quick look at a computer screen.

"We had no one by that name Thursday."

I took a wild guess. "Maybe she registered under her husband's name. Ledbetter."

He looked again, then shook his head. "No Ledbetter. Perhaps your sister is at one of the other Cable Beach hotels."

I thanked the man. Pushing past the crowd around the desk, I found a quiet corner and tried to collect my thoughts. I had the wrong place, but which was the right one? How many more hotels would I have to visit? And for what? It was stupid. Here I was in an unfamiliar city looking for an unknown man who probably had nothing to do with Leslie's death anyway. And even if he had, that was police business, not mine.

My eyes were gritty with fatigue. On top of that, my head ached and my stomach had begun to make rumbling noises. I hadn't eaten since the ice-cream cone the night before. Food. Before I could think, I had to eat.

On the far side of the lobby there was a map. Not a map of the area. A map of the hotel. That's how big the place was. It dwarfed even the Ledbetters' planned Pleasure Dome.

A quick look showed me a dozen restaurants. The hotel might not provide me the name of Leslie's lover, but it could provide me breakfast. I chose a place called the Manhattan Deli. Homesick, I suppose.

I must have walked half a mile, through tree-lined arbors and glass walls supported by soaring purple pillars. As I passed sunken pools and fountains spraying high into the air, the hotel was coming to life. Guests moved through the maze of corridors and stairways searching for food.

I spotted the deli finally, its neon sign calling to me through the morning light.

On the last landscaped patio that stood between me and my target, I passed tables loaded with food. A chef in a tall hat was cooking pancakes on an open grill. There were trays of eggs and bacon and ham, and huge baskets of pastry and bowls of sliced fruit.

"Is breakfast for all guests?" I asked him.

"It's for the International Farm Equipment Dealers Convention."

He flipped a pancake. It spun through the air, golden brown and perfect. God, it was beautiful! I stared hungrily. The chef didn't seem inclined to flip one my way, though, so finally I continued to the deli. En route, what looked like the entire population of a midwestern town in the U.S. passed me, heading to their patio breakfast.

At the restaurant's entrance was a big bulletin board. The right portion of it was taken up by the deli's menu. Expensive. I'd either have to skimp now, or skip lunch.

The scent of the farm equipment breakfast filled the air. Their menus for the day were posted, so I took a quick look. Wow! There was going to be some extra poundage on the return flight. Their schedule for the day was on the board, too, so I studied that. An afternoon tour of a rum factory, then a glass-bottomed boat.

I could hear the tinkling of their silver. What fun, to be part of a group that comes to a place like this.

My eyes wandered further on the bulletin board. There was a schedule of conventions posted for the month. Next week it was

211

podiatrists, and civil engineers. Last week the Western Association of Ornithologists had been there.

I shook my head, amazed. You think office temps ever have conventions in the Bahamas? The only place we ever meet is at discount stores. What do you have to know to get a job selling tractors?

I must have been so hungry that my mind was going. I had walked through the deli door before I realized what I'd just read.

"Ornithologists?" I said out loud.

A hostess tilted her head quizzically—"Breakfast?"—but I was already on my way back to the bulletin.

Ornithologists. I'd read it right. They had met at the hotel the week before, from Tuesday until Friday. Leslie had been in Nassau Thursday night. Friday at around noon, Paul Tyndall had driven into his camp site wearing that silly T-shirt. "Ornithologists do it with fantastic birds."

Fantastic birds is right! Paul Tyndall had done it with Leslie.

How had they met? At the Flamingo Cove casino, maybe. He gravitated to the blackjack table, she gravitated to the crowds and noise. She might have been pressed into waitress duty. Their eyes would have locked over a tray of Goombay Punch. Perhaps he was having a bad night. From all reports, Paul had more bad nights than good ones at the blackjack table.

I never thought I'd end up quoting Sonny, but as he said, "A guy feels like everything's going to hell, and here's this gorgeous sexy blonde coming on to him. What's he supposed to do?" The difference was, Sonny talked about it and didn't do it. Paul had done it and didn't talk about it.

Why hadn't I ever considered Paul? As I ate breakfast— pancakes, bacon, and a side of homefries (the cholesterol special)—I answered that question for myself. It was easy. Paul hadn't been on the night dive.

I didn't know if Paul dived or not, but even if he did, and if he had been diving solo at the reef that night, he couldn't have known that Leslie was wearing a bright blue wetsuit. He would have to spot her from her long hair, and at night that wouldn't be easy. Besides, he couldn't have returned to the dive boat to answer when I called her name. Too many people would have recognized him.

I left the hotel full of food but empty of ideas. I'd found Leslie's secret lover, but it didn't mean much. As Mrs. Hussy had said, Paul Tyndall had curious appetites. Leslie had been one of them. In a heated moment he may have mentioned marriage, and talked about getting rid of that unpleasant "other involvement," his fiancee. Leslie must have been smitten. She hadn't recognized that talk for what it was—hot air in a hot climate.

I was almost ready to forget about my trip to Paradise Island and spend my remaining time in Nassau on a walking tour. The thing Leslie had hidden was probably as meaningless as Paul's identity. Most likely, Neticia had taken it from his camp. I'd heard Paul accuse her of stealing the first time I ran into him. Neticia had searched my room for this thing she'd taken not because it had value, but because she was afraid the devil eye might twist her neck if she didn't return it.

But who had searched my room the last time? Paul Tyndall? If he wanted this thing and it belonged to him, why not simply ask me if I'd seen it around?

That question nagged me during the ride back to Nassau, so much so that when the bus I was on swung a wide arc around Nassau and circled back not far from Paradise Island, I got out and caught a cab at the foot of the bridge.

My driver followed Casino Drive toward the eastern end of the island, past towering hotels and casinos. This seemed a world away from the bustling city just over the short bridge. The landscape here was manicured, the sidewalks well kept and the gutters clean. Car and taxi horns didn't blare. There were no buses. Bicyclists toured the gently curving roads.

As the cab wound around a lush golf course, I ran a comb through my hair and put on some lipstick. No point in looking any worse than necessary. When we reached the green-hedged perimeter of the Paradise Water Club, I asked my driver to wait.

I walked up the shrub-lined path to the club knowing there was

213

a good chance I'd never get hold of whatever Leslie had hidden. This visit to the club was going to be the end of the trail for me, though. Leslie's life had been a tangle of daydreams and schemes long before I came along. Untangling it was not my job.

Getting into the club was simple enough. At the gate, the world's politest guard asked my name.

I used Eleanor's maiden name, and showed him the locker key. "I'm picking up something my parents forgot. They're members. The Simmonds."

His eyes flicked over my face, and for a second I was afraid he knew Eleanor Ledbetter. He only nodded, though, and gave me a smile that made my heart warm. Eleanor's parents must have been generous at Christmas.

I couldn't very well ask him directions, so it took me a few minutes to get my bearings. I walked among well-groomed trees and shrubs, drawn by the shade and flowers. A bit farther and I found myself in a wonderful, Versailles-like garden. Above me rose a series of lush landscaped terraces. I glimpsed an elegant outdoor restaurant, where the waiters wore white coats and the sunlight glanced off fine crystal. A formal reception was in progress. Two women who looked as if they'd pillaged Madison Avenue's designer dress shops passed me on their way in. One of them was chattering excitedly about "Viscount Linley."

Beyond that, I passed a beautiful pool, complete with the water slide Beth was so taken with.

In little more than twelve hours, I'd seen the seediest hotel in the area, and the flashiest. Now I was walking through a club that reeked of money. Of the three places, only the Acropolis would fit even the broadest definition of a "fleshpot." The fleshpots of Nassau weren't nearly as fleshy as Mrs. Hussy had promised.

I got to the beach finally. Same old turquoise water, same spun-gold sand. You see enough of it, you get blasé. I was ready to find the locker and be done with this.

A long wooden building set back away from the water looked promising. As I approached, a few other people entered in

214

bathing suits, and someone left in street clothes. A white-uniformed woman sat in a chair inside the door.

Leslie's mind hadn't worked like mine, or, for that matter, most other peoples'. If this was the place where Leslie had hidden something, I couldn't guess how she had gained access to one of these lockers. It was a private club. Wouldn't members be assigned lockers?

The matron didn't glance my way when I passed through the entrance hall. I followed signs reading "women" into a big combination shower and dressing room. Against one wall was a bank of steel lockers.

The dressing area was empty. Showers were running, and women's voices rose over the splashing water. I dug the locker key with the G-9 on it from my pocket and hurriedly examined the lockers.

M. All the numbers began with M. How could this be? I'd been so sure I was right. M-9, maybe? Were keys coded differently than locks? The water in one of the shower stalls stopped. I was working my key in the M-9 locker when a tall woman wearing a towel strolled into the dressing area. She startled me and I jumped.

"You have the wrong locker," she said, not very nicely. "That one is mine."

Pulling out my key, I examined it closely. "Oh. I see. This opens G-9."

"Are you a member? I don't recall seeing you here."

From the woman's tone, not to mention the way she narrowed her eyes at me, she was about one breath away from calling the security guards. Pulling back my shoulders, I said haughtily, "I'm with Viscount Linley's party."

"Oh? Well, you had better check with the matron about that key."

I left the women's locker nodding as if I intended to do just that. I didn't. I'd been wrong, and I'd wasted enough time.

Up the hall, past the woman in the white uniform. . . .

What I saw stopped me. Behind her desk was another bank of lockers. I squinted, but couldn't make out the numbers.

"Are these the G lockers?"

"Guest lockers. That's right."

I handed her my key, hardly believing my good luck. My euphoria didn't last long. She turned as if to open the locker, then hesitated and glanced back at me.

"You're not the lady who took this locker last week."

"That's my sister."

"Oh. She phoned that night—it was Thursday, I think—to say she'd been called away. She said she would collect these things herself when she got back to Nassau."

"She can't get here after all. I told her I'd pick them up."

Satisfied, the woman put the key in the lock. It turned easily. "Was your sister mad that I wouldn't open the locker for her maid?"

"Her maid? She didn't mention that to me."

The woman reached into the locker. "That girl yesterday, she didn't have the key. The rules"—the woman nodded at a sign on the wall behind her—"say if you lose the key, you pay the seven dollar replacement. The girl didn't have the money."

"The maid was a young girl? Very thin."

The matron nodded. "Tiny thing, and so shy."

I intended to act unfazed no matter what came out of that locker. Well, there wasn't much danger of getting worked up over the booty the matron put in my eager hands. I could feel my expression drooping as I stared at it. I'm afraid that diamond ring I'd envisioned was pretty firmly fixed in my mind.

"Is there something wrong?" the woman asked.

"Oh, no. It's fine."

I left the locker room carrying two small black and white composition tablets—the kind you can buy in any stationery store.

During the ride back I thumbed through the books. Paul Tyndall's name and the address of the fishing camp was written inside each cover. After that were pages of flamingo counts, broken down by male and female, egg counts, miscellaneous sightings.

How sad, I thought, as my cabbie crossed the bridge into Nassau. Leslie, hoping to manipulate Paul Tyndall into marrying her, had gotten Neticia to steal some of his dissertation notes. And poor Neticia, so afraid of Tyndall's devil eye that she was trying to recover the notes. The entire business was beyond sad. It was pathetic.

In the harsh noon light the Acropolis wasn't nearly as frightening as it had seemed the night before. It was still every bit as seedy, though. The same woman was at the reception desk. She handed me my overnighter and I thanked her. I was about to leave when she stopped me.

"A man called you."

"Oh? Did he leave his name?"

She shook her head. "No. He asked if you'd gone but I told him you were coming back for your bag."

It had to be Mike. Maybe he'd gotten bail and was on his way to the Acropolis! I wasn't sure how I felt about Mike, and I didn't want to deal with him right then. I'd planned to walk to the pier. Instead, I hurriedly shoved the notebooks into my tapestry bag, rushed from the hotel, and flagged another cab.

"Look at that crazy boy on that bicycle. Going to get himself killed."

My cab driver lady shifted her eyes away from the rear view mirror. "Will you be needing a guide while you're on vacation, Miss? I know every spot. The whole island, one end to the other. Best shopping . . ."

I told her that I was only there long enough to catch a boat. She quickly lost interest.

"That boy will be killed for sure, riding that way. Then what does his poor mamma have? Dead child. They don't think, these boys."

The traffic on Bay Street barely moved. Where there weren't cars, there was construction. Tourists and natives crossed at random as bicyclists zipped between and around them. It was getting close to the time when the mailboat left. After inching along a few blocks, I decided I could do the remaining few blocks on foot. I had the driver pull over and let me out.

Fearing that I might run into Mike, I decided to avoid Bay Street. I turned down a side street so that I could reach the wide walkway that parallels the harbor and runs into the dock.

It was midafternoon now, and the sun beat relentlessly on the sidewalk. My bag wasn't very heavy, but it weighed enough so that when I was within a couple blocks of the dock, I stopped to switch hands. My bag was on the sidewalk when, behind me, there was a scraping noise. I turned as a kid on a rusty bike raced at me. He was going so fast that I was sure he'd run me down. Grabbing my overnighter, I jumped off the sidewalk into the door of a restaurant. The bag was clutched against my body when the kid got to me.

His hand darted out. I flinched, thinking he meant to hit me. With one swift movement he got hold of my bag's handle. I reacted by grasping the bag closer. The bike wobbled. I braced myself to receive its weight, and the kid's too. He put his feet out to steady himself. With one fierce tug, I pulled the handle from his hand. He reached again, but suddenly a man appeared in the restaurant door. The man never turned to see the bicyclist, but within seconds the boy had pedaled out of sight around the corner.

It had all happened so quickly that I never got a good look at the kid. He was a blur, a threat speeding toward me. My fear had been purely physical. Now, though, as I leaned into the restaurant's cool glass door, a new fear filled me.

My driver had spotted a reckless boy on a bike. The boy had followed my cab, and then he had followed me. He had been watching me since I left the Acropolis with my bag.

Why? Why pick me out of the mass of tourists? I didn't look particularly affluent. My bag looked a lot more affluent than I did, but was that enough? Had my new carry-on tempted this kid enough to make him follow my cab and wait until he could get me alone?

I stood there for a few minutes, wondering what I should do. Call the police, and endure another episode with them? Since I'd gotten to the islands there had been police and more police. And what would the police say this time? They couldn't blame it on the men with machetes. They would probably tell me that robberies weren't unusual in Nassau, that tourists carrying expensive luggage occasionally get relieved of it. If I tried to convince them that this attempted robbery might be related to the scuba diving death of an Australian woman . . .

No police, I decided. I hadn't lost anything. Actually, if I overlooked the fact that I was out one night of hedonism, I was leaving Nassau better off than I'd arrived there. I knew the identity of Leslie's secret lover, and I had the black and white notebooks.

I walked on to the dock, looking over my shoulder every few seconds. I'd been thinking of returning Paul Tyndall's notes to him, but the kid on the bike had changed my mind for me. I finally get the thing Leslie has hidden, and within minutes someone tries to rob me. I couldn't be sure that kid had been paid to follow me and steal my bag, but if he hadn't been, it sure was some whopping coincidence! Somewhere in Paul Tyndall's notes might be the answer to Leslie's death.

NINETEEN

CALYPSO ON THE BEACH

The questions that plagued me in my dreams were the ones that had plagued me the afternoon before. In the morning I floated in and out of sleep, trying to adjust my eyes to the advancing light and trying, half awake, to make a connection between my dead roommate and the two books of notes. Something came to me and drifted away. My mind was like the floor of the forest: shadowy, with thick vines creeping across it. The thought came back, tickling at the edge of my understanding.

There was no flash of clarity. Awareness grew slowly, as the morning light grew in my room.

A man who tries to beat the odds at the blackjack table runs up a debt there instead. His wealthy family has bailed him out for years, but now the family cuts off his money. The hotel's owner forbids him in the casino. After a time, though, the gambler is back.

I got up, dressed, and went to the reception area before the sun was completely over the forest. The hotel was silent. Taking one of Flamingo Island's weekly newspapers, I carried it back to my room.

. . . but according to ornithologist Paul Tyndall,
who is conducting research on Flamingo Island for

221

the second year in a row, the flamingos have not returned in the numbers anticipated by earlier studies. At present there are less than seven hundred birds nesting here, several hundred fewer than Tyndall counted last year. In the absence of a viable flock, approval for the new airport is expected. It will boast an 8,500-foot runway, capable of accommodating wide-bodied jets. Travel time from Miami will be cut to less than an hour. At least one major air carrier has expressed interest in New York City departures. . . .

Putting aside the paper, I flipped through Tyndall's notes. In some ways the two tablets appeared to be duplicates. Each had, at its start, the same date. Then, at the top of pages, came subsequent dates. Under these were columns—number of birds sighted, sex of the birds, approximate age. Some entries noted the return of birds Tyndall had banded the prior year, while others mentioned birds that had migrated to Flamingo Island from other places. The entries had begun when he arrived on Flamingo Island about four months earlier, and covered about ten weeks of research.

It was the differences in the two books, rather than the similarities, that interested me. One book was filled with diligent records of flamingo sightings. The second book began diligently, but soon Tyndall's record keeping became sloppy. In that second book, Tyndall seemed to have run out of enthusiasm after a few weeks on the island. There were no entries for days at a time, and when there were entries, they were sloppy, sometimes barely legible.

Oh, yes—there was one other difference in the books. In the better-kept book, the numbers were far smaller—fewer birds sighted, fewer returning birds. In this better-kept book, the figures matched the figures in the newspaper article. Studying the two books, I became convinced that this second book was fraudulent.

Paul Tyndall had sold out the flamingos. And Leslie had gotten hold of the evidence and tried to blackmail him with it. "I can be awfully persuasive," she had bragged, and I'd thought she meant she could persuade with sex appeal. I'd thought wrong. She'd meant she could persuade with these two books.

Who had he sold out to? Neticia might have known, but even if I found her, she was too frightened of the devil eye to say anything. It could be the Ledbetters, or the Texans, or both, or one of those happy politicians at the Pleasure Dome's unveiling. Corruption in government is not unknown. Or it could be someone involved with the airport, or the airlines. There were lots of possibilities. But only two of those possibilities had been on the night dive: the Ledbetters and the Texans. Ted the Texan and his wife had dived, but they didn't know the reef. Colin did. Smooth, smiling Colin.

Never trust someone who smiles all the time.

Before I left my room for the day, I tore the pages from the two books. They separated easily from the cardboard covers. I tucked the covers under my mattress. As for the pages themselves—I was crafty there.

Eleanor shaded her eyes with her hand and looked over our handiwork on the beach.

"I can't think of anything else. Can you?"

I gazed out over the tables and chairs we'd set up, the pink paper tablecloths we'd anchored with dishes and cutlery, the stacks of pale pink napkins, the baskets of fruit.

"There's always something else."

The faintest smile crossed her face.

"I suppose you're right."

She hadn't smiled much that day. Neither had I. I'd been recruited straight from Early Bird Aerobics. It was now late afternoon and I hadn't stopped since. The handymen were hauling kindling for a bonfire while Colin and the chief set up a portable grill. Calypso on the Beach was shaping up as a major production.

223

"Where is the band going to be?" I asked.

As Eleanor stared across the stretch of sand that lay between where we stood and the beach shack, Colin walked over and put his arm around his wife's shoulder. She immediately took a step away, and his arm fell to his side. A breach had come between the Ledbetters. From what I could tell, it was affecting their marriage, but not their business partnership.

"There for the band," Eleanor said. "What do you think, Colin?"

"Okay with me." He looked down the beach. "We don't have to worry if people wander off. With those two thieves locked up here and Charlie in jail in Nassau, our crime wave is over. I let the extra security men go yesterday morning," he added.

Eleanor glanced at me. "I guess Mike won't be here."

"It doesn't look like it."

I waited until Colin had wandered off before saying anything more on that subject.

"How did you find out Mike and Charlie had been arrested?" I asked Eleanor.

"Roscoe Richards called Thursday night. He knows how worried we've been about security. I hope you managed to enjoy yourself in Nassau," she added. "What did you do?"

Maybe her question indicated nothing more than casual interest, but it put me on edge. "Do?" I asked warily.

"Yes. How did you pass your time, with Mike in jail?"

"Well, the evening was shot. I fell asleep as soon as my head hit the pillow."

She didn't ask where I'd stayed, but I suspected she knew. And if she did, she wouldn't believe I'd spend the next morning luxuriating in my hotel room.

"In the morning I wandered around town looking in shops. There are some wonderful ones on Bay Street."

She had busied herself rearranging a basket of fruit. Without looking up, she said, "You must have gone to the straw market."

Was there a straw market, or was this one of those trick

224

questions? I responded "Em," and hoped that that covered both possibilities.

"Do you really think Charlie had anything to do with Leslie's death?" I asked, changing the subject. "It seems so out of character."

Eleanor looked at me from the corner of her eye. "We all do things that aren't in character. These days I seem to be doing quite a lot of them."

It was my turn to give her one of those corner-of-the-eye glances. She looked away.

"I've been feeling a bit guilty about you," she said. "You're leaving us tomorrow."

"That's right," I said, wondering what there was about my leaving that would make Eleanor feel guilty.

"I had mentioned the possibility of your taking a permanent job, but I don't feel that your experience . . . That is, the program we plan is quite broad. Please don't misunderstand, Bonnie. It's not your work. You've been . . . you've done a fine job. But we've got Marilyn for the classes and . . . em . . ."

She was stumbling for words, afraid to look at me. Talk about out of character! I'd never seriously considered staying at Flamingo Cove, but I took advantage of Eleanor's embarrassment.

"Frankly, I'm a little hurt. How was this decision made?"

"How? Well, Colin and I talked things over. You see, we want to hire a person with a more administrative background. Someone who has run a health club or something of that sort. After all, merely leading dance routines . . ."

She started firing off defenses. After a few, I tuned her out.

"Colin and I talked things over." That was what I grabbed onto. Three days before, Eleanor had wanted me. Now Colin and Eleanor didn't. Maybe she was telling the truth about this administrative person, but I doubted it. She and Colin knew I'd been asking questions about Leslie, and they knew I'd gone to Nassau. Colin had caught me searching the beach shack. He might have seen me dig up the chick's grave. There had been that flash of white, and my feeling that someone was watching from the forest. What the Ledbetters wanted wasn't an administrator. It was me, out of their hair.

". . . you can hand out cold drinks this evening until everyone feels comfortable getting their own. Once you're through with that, please circulate. Draw people out. . . ."

Eleanor was all business again. I stayed on the beach for another half hour or so, barely speaking to her. She may have thought I was quietly sulking because she hadn't offered me a job. What was actually going on in my head was something else entirely.

The aftermath of Leslie's murder—the part on the dive boat—the Ledbetters could have managed. Eleanor had met Colin as soon as he stepped on deck. I hadn't watched them after that, but how much of a problem would it have been for Colin to tell his wife that he had accomplished what he'd set out to do. Eleanor would tuck herself out of sight and wait until I called Leslie's name. Once she'd answered "here" or "yes" or simply one of the "ems" that had been coming at me from all over the boat, Eleanor could reappear. Since she had helped Leslie get into the blue wetsuit, she knew where Leslie had left her clothes. Having no equipment to deal with herself, it wouldn't have been difficult for Eleanor to grab Leslie's things from under the bench. Early the following morning, Colin could have jogged to the fishing camp and planted Leslie's things there.

It was basically the same scenario I'd worked out for Sonny and Cindy, with one big difference. Colin. He had dived at the reef frequently. He would have known about the net on the ocean floor.

I saw one problem with this: Leslie was a good swimmer, but a nervous diver. How could Colin entice her away from the group? Would she follow Colin off if she was blackmailing him? No way. Not after what had happened to me in the beach shack the night before. Leslie would have been watching her back, like the spies in the thrillers did.

My mind was wrestling with this when I heard my name called. The woman from the reception desk was across the road.

"You have a call. Urgent."

Eleanor glanced at me, one eyebrow raised.

I shrugged. "I can't imagine who."

"I'm a free man."

"Mike. How did you get out?"

"I squeezed through a window. Didn't want to miss Calypso on the Beach."

My confidence in Mike's judgment was at such a low point that I almost believed him.

"You didn't! What about Charlie?"

"Charlie was too fat to get through the bars. He's still locked up. And you're right. I didn't break out. I made bail. So? Am I still invited, or do you hate me?"

Did I? No. Mike was hard to hate. I wasn't sure I wanted to see him that night, though. When I told him that, there was a pause at his end. When he finally spoke, his voice was flat. "You think I'm a jerk. I can't blame you, but I'm a reasonably normal guy. I've just taken a few wrong turns. You should give me a chance to defend myself in person. Even Roscoe's going to do that."

"Roscoe didn't spend the night in the Acropolis Hotel."

"Come on, Bonnie. The Acropolis is a dump, but hell! I only had five seconds to think of a place where you could go. It wasn't all that bad, was it? It's got lots of local color."

This was more like the Mike I knew—cajoling, charming. "It was awful. Is that where you had planned for us to go if we stayed over?"

"What? Never. I planned to take you back to the boat. The bunk room's not half bad if you leave the porthole open."

"The boat would have been better than the Acropolis," I said. "I stayed away from there as much as I could. I'm sorry I didn't return your call, but I was in a hurry and you didn't leave a number. Were you out of jail by then?"

"What are you talking about?"

"You called the Acropolis yesterday, didn't you? To find out if I was still there?"

227

"No. Until this morning I was enjoying the hospitality of the Nassau police. The only person I called was my lawyer."

If Mike hadn't called me, who had?

Colin and Eleanor had known I was alone in Nassau. They wouldn't have had much trouble finding out where I was staying. If Chief Richards didn't know, the Nassau police did.

"I'm wondering about something, Mike. Could a boat like Colin's make it to Nassau and back quickly?"

"Faster than a speeding bullet."

"And that neighborhood around the Acropolis . . . it's well known? I mean, would people who have lived here a while know that a lot of rough types hang around there?"

He laughed. "Anybody who reads the police report in the local papers would know that. Why?"

That was all I needed to convince me that the kid on the bike hadn't been a random thief. My charming employer had paid him to steal my bag.

I stared out across the beach. The sun was lower on the horizon now. The night loomed in the lengthening shadows of the palm trees.

"Bonnie? You still there?"

"Yes. I've changed my mind. Why don't you come tonight. I'll go back to your place after the party."

He must have been stunned into silence. "That's the best offer I've had in a long time," he said after a moment.

It wasn't quite as good as he thought. I hadn't sorted out my feelings about Mike, but I knew that I didn't want to spend the night at Flamingo Cove.

The sunset was a gold and red extravaganza, and when that was done the moon began to peek through the palm trees. By dark, the entire staff and virtually everybody staying at the hotel had wandered down the steps to the beach. I recognized some of the political types who had been at the reception, too, and a few people from the fishing camp who had been on the night dive. I spotted Beth sitting alone by the water. She was dressed in a

228

makeshift sarong and had put a couple of pink feathers in her hair.

The menu was fish and more fish, and most of the fish was conch. There was conch chowder, conch salad, conch fritters.

I was handing out cold drinks from an aluminum barrel filled with ice and bottles when Paul Tyndall and his fiancee pulled up in a jeep. She went off to a table but he stood by his jeep for a moment, looking around the beach. When he began coming toward me, I tensed. He and the Ledbetters couldn't be sure that I'd found the notebooks, but I was suddenly aware of how outnumbered I was.

"Hi, Bonnie," he said genially. "I hear my buddy Mike had a problem in Nassau."

"A little one."

"Everything will work out. Mike's gotten through some tight spots before. Got a couple cold beers in that bucket?"

The normality of this exchange made my tension seem foolish, but it didn't make it go away.

As I dug the beers out of the cooler, Tyndall's fiancee strolled over. "Mike's a decent guy," Tyndall was saying. "What he needs is a good woman to put him on the straight and narrow."

His fiancee agreed. "Don't you all."

She was smiling up at him as they strolled away. No, she wasn't a sexy blonde, but she had a sweet smile, a decent education and a respectable job. Just as I could understand how Tyndall had gotten involved with Leslie, I understood why he had wanted their romance to be their secret.

The band had carried their instruments onto the beach. As they began tuning up, Beth tugged at my sleeve.

"Did you see my mommy?"

"She's around. Why don't you go look for her."

"I don't want to. The devil eye is here."

Good point. There was that to worry about. I gave the little girl's sarong an approving nod.

"You look pretty tonight."

"Thank you. I get to stay up as late as I want. Mommy said

that's 'cause of the party, but it's not. It's 'cause there's no one to babysit me." She dug a bare toe in the sand. "I don't get to do anything fun since Neticia left."

"I'm sorry to hear that."

She tilted her head and said in a small, appealing voice, "Colin says you found the parasailing harness. Tomorrow will you do it with me?"

"No, Beth."

"How come?"

"I'm leaving tomorrow. Besides, parasailing would scare me."

"Please. We can do it first thing in the morning. Colin can pull us with his boat."

"Maybe Colin doesn't want to pull us. I've never seen him use his boat."

"He does use it! A lot!"

"When is the last time he took it out?"

Beth shrugged. "I don't know if he did today, but I know he did yesterday. Please, Bonnie. He'll pull us. I know parasailing's not scary."

I had no intention of finding out. "Take a look at the fire," I said, trying to divert the child.

One of the handymen had started the bonfire. Paul Tyndall, his fiancee and some of the guests were watching the first yellow flames leap from the kindling. There was surprised laughter as wayward sparks flew into the dark sky. A quickening breeze ruffled the palms. Down the beach, the band began playing. The plunking steel drum seemed to beat in slow rhythm with the tide.

"Beautiful night for a beach party."

Colin, Eleanor and Frenchie had stopped to dig some drinks from the ice.

Colin's resort-owner facade had been honed to a new perfection. He wore white slacks and jacket, and an open-necked blue shirt. He was barefoot, and he'd rolled his pants legs up a couple times. He looked as if he'd stepped out of a magazine spread promoting laid-back elegance on the beach. Seeing Eleanor next to this thing of beauty was almost a shock. Her face was drawn and her skin seemed to have a parched quality. She looked as if she had aged ten years in the ten days I'd known her.

"You having fun, Beth?" Colin asked his stepdaughter.

The little girl shook her head. "No. Only Bonnie will talk to me, and she won't go parasailing. She's scared. I wish Leslie wasn't dead. Leslie wouldn't be scared."

Beth had a child's simple honesty. She didn't realize she had wandered into choppy waters. For a moment nobody said a word. Colin picked up the little girl and, to her delight, lifted her onto his back. She wrapped her arms around his neck.

Frenchie nodded solemnly. "No, Leslie wasn't afraid of anything."

"Oh, yes she was!" Beth said. "Colin and I know one thing Leslie was scared of, more than anything else. Want to know what?"

Eleanor and Frenchie were already wandering toward the bonfire. Colin started after them.

"Sharks!" the little girl shouted. "Leslie was more afraid of sharks than anything. Don't you remember, Colin?"

He stopped. "No. I didn't know that."

Beth gave his shoulder a slap. "You did too! Remember? Leslie told us about how when she was a little girl she went to the beach and saw a shark eat a man alive. She said how the man was screaming and the water all turned red 'cause he was bleeding and his leg was eaten. Don't you remember?"

Eleanor and Frenchie were a few feet ahead of Colin. Frenchie kept moving but Eleanor stood still as death. Colin stared at her back, then turned toward me. His eyes caught mine. He only held my gaze for an instant, but in that instant the missing piece of the puzzle fell into place. I knew how Colin had gotten Leslie away from the group on the night dive.

And in the same instant when our eyes met, things became much more dangerous for me. Before that moment I had been a snoopy temporary employee, soon to be gone. Now I was a real threat. I'd been in the dinghy when someone mentioned seeing Colin give the underwater hand signal for a shark sighting.

I had to play dumb, to pretend that Beth's words hadn't taken me back to the night in the dinghy. I dug through the iced drinks for a soda.

"Guess I'll have one myself."

"Once the dancing starts you won't have time," Colin said. Hoisting Beth further up his back, he caught up with his wife. "We better check on the grill. The last time we used it . . ."

What a sweet family picture they made as they walked off through the sand: Colin and Eleanor side by side, little Beth on Colin's back, legs dangling.

I waited until they had gone, then wandered out to the road. Where was Mike? Probably trying to start his landlady's car. When I looked back at the beach, I couldn't make out faces. There was a throng of people backlit by the bonfire. The party was growing noisy. The music was louder, and so were the voices of the guests. Before long I'd have to get out there and socialize. If I wanted to call the police, I had to do it right then.

The hotel's entrance was a few hundred feet away. I walked up the beach and crossed the road under the cover of some palm trees. Light from the hotel fell onto the parking lot, lighting the Flamingo Cove jitney parked at the bottom of the steps. Hurrying across the lot, I crept behind the jitney and took the steps two at a time.

The casino was closed until later that evening. Yellow garden lights lit the shrubs along its wall. The back of the building abutted the pool area. As I trotted toward the reception desk, I saw two scuba tanks on their sides in the bushes, ready for the next day's resort course.

The reception area was deserted. One thin light burned behind the desk. I didn't have time to look for a phone book. I sank into the receptionist's chair and picked up the receiver. I had just begun dialing the operator when I heard a bare foot sliding over the floor.

"Who are you calling, Bonnie?" Colin asked.

My mind searched frantically for an answer. It was a moment

before one came. "Mike," I said. "He can make it tonight after all."

A step brought Colin behind me. Before I could move, his hands were on the back of my neck. They didn't close around my throat, but they rested so close that I felt my chest tightening with fear.

"Mike? I thought he was in jail. Please put the phone down."

When I had cradled the receiver, Colin took his hands away. Pulling another chair close, he sat down.

"I'm hoping we can work this out in a way that is not unpleasant for either of us, Bonnie."

I shook my head. "I don't know what you're talking about."

"I'm afraid you do." He reached inside his jacket to an inner pocket. Blood rushed to my head when I saw the black and white notebook cover in his hand.

"You didn't do a very good job of hiding these, but I give you credit. I couldn't find the pages anywhere. Are they still in your room?"

"No."

He stared straight into my eyes. "Why don't we go up there and take a look. After we find them, we'll have a talk about your future."

I was afraid that the future Colin had planned for me would last about as long as it took him to find the missing pages. I hunkered further down in the chair.

"You're frightened?" he asked with an air of surprise. "You needn't be. I like you. You're smart. The way things are going, there will be a lot of opportunities at Flamingo Cove for someone with a good head on her shoulders."

I'll never know if he really meant that. Probably not. I knew too much. Still, there was a second when I almost believed him. I wouldn't have gone along with him, but I remember thinking, "Maybe I can pretend to cooperate. . . ."

Colin smiled then, that same little-boy smile that had swayed so many angry employees, so many guests. The smile that had swayed Leslie. My stomach clenched into a knot and I thought I might faint. I put my head in my hands.

"We don't have much time, Bonnie. Come along now."

Taking my wrists, he tried to pull me from the chair. I raised my head and slumped deeper in the chair, a dead weight. Beyond Colin, I could see the pool, still water glistening in the moonlight. Just past that, around the casino wall, were the steps. If anybody came up the road, I could call to them. What about Mike? He would be there soon. If he didn't find me on the beach, he'd look for me. Mike didn't know where my room was, though. I had to stay down here. I had to stall.

"Why should I believe you? You killed Leslie. You and Eleanor planned it."

Colin's smile held steady. "Eleanor knew nothing. You're trying to buy time, Bonnie. We can talk on our way to your room."

He tugged at my arm again. "Actually, what happened on the night dive was a spur of the moment thing. After the episode in the beach shack, I couldn't imagine getting Leslie alone, but . . . there she was, swimming just out of reach of the strobe. I saw an opportunity, and took it."

"You gave the hand signal for a shark."

"Aren't you bright?" he said with a self-satisfied nod of his head. "The poor girl was so frightened that she dropped her flashlight and swam away. As I followed her, I flicked it off.

"My wife's a trooper, Bonnie. When I told her what had happened, she did what she had to do. And now you're going to do what you have to do. Let's go find those papers."

In a struggle I had no chance, but I was in good shape. In a race, I might make it to the beach. I stirred in my chair as if about to rise. Bracing my feet against the floor then, I leaped past Colin and jerked my hand free of his. In my rush I threw him off balance. He slammed into the reception desk. The phone crashed to the floor.

He recovered quickly. He was running by the time I reached the open door. I'd never make it to the steps. As I ran, I screamed, "Help me!" The party was going full swing by then. The music and laughter drowned out my voice.

Changing direction, I raced around the pool, hoping to put it between us. He was too fast. As I dashed past the diving board, I could hear his feet slapping against the concrete behind me. The steps were in sight, but Colin's hand closed around my wrist before I reached them. He flung me toward the casino wall and I stumbled into the bushes. He pushed in after me.

There was nowhere I could go. The wall was in back of me and Colin in front. Bushes on either side scraped into my arms and legs. My head was pounding. I collapsed against the wall, gasping. Colin was winded, too. His chest heaved beneath the white jacket.

The man actually managed another smile. "How is it going to look if the two of us get back to the party looking as if we've been rolling in the bushes?"

It would look a lot better than me not getting back to the party at all. I glanced desperately toward the stairs. Colin's grip on my wrist tightened. He had started dragging me from the bushes when something cool rubbed against my leg. I glanced down and saw one of the scuba tanks resting inches from my feet. Compressed air, and explosive. I gave the tank a gentle shove with my foot to hide it from the yellow light.

"Believe me, Bonnie. I won't hurt you. I didn't hurt Neticia, did I?"

He hadn't, but only because it was easy to frighten her away. I shook my head, and forced myself to smile. "No, you didn't. I'm just so upset by all this."

He let my wrist drop and backed from the bushes. "That's a good girl."

I took a step toward Colin, then pretended to stumble. Falling onto one knee, I grabbed the scuba tank on either end. It was heavy, but not so heavy that I couldn't handle it. I took a deep breath. When I rose, I had the thing cradled against my chest.

I stepped onto the concrete. Colin was a few feet away. His eyes flickered over the tank. I acted as if my arms were giving. He

235

took a step back. Keeping the tank between us, I moved toward the stairs.

Colin had begun having trouble keeping that smile on his face, but his voice remained calm. "An explosion will hurt you as much as it hurts me. Actually"—he shrugged—"Frenchie's over cautious. The impact isn't going to be great enough to make the tank explode. Put it down, Bonnie."

The tank was my only defense. I didn't want to drop it, but it was so heavy that I might not have a chance. The muscles in my arms were beginning to throb. I was almost at the steps when Colin darted at me. In an instant, he had slammed the tank into my body with his. Half-stunned by the impact, I tried to spin out of his grasp. Panicky, I staggered the last few feet to the steps. He stayed with me. At the top of the steps we wrestled over the tank.

My legs and arms were quaking now. I couldn't hold the tank any more. My elbows gave and it dropped between us.

There was an awful sickening crunch, and a split-second later a loud clang as the tank hit the concrete.

Colin's face was only inches from mine. He blinked, and tears gathered in his eyes. His mouth opened wide. He screamed.

"Aaaagh!"

The tank had dropped on Colin's bare foot. He fell to the ground. As he groped wildly at his foot, he shoved the tank away. It rolled along the top step, and dropped over the edge, banging hard against the concrete. On the second step it teetered at the brink, up an inch, back an inch. Then it dropped.

Just before I hit the ground, I saw car headlights coming around the curve from Rocky Point.

The tank rang against one step, and then another. It picked up speed, and each ring was louder until finally the night air seemed to vibrate with the sound. A moment came when there was no sound at all. The band had stopped playing. The guests had stopped their frolicking. Even the surf seemed to have quieted. I caught a glimpse of Colin writhing on the ground. I put my hands over my ears. There was another enormous ring.

And then the explosion came, blasting through the night like a volley of cannon fire. The ground trembled under me. The night sky was filled with a streak of white light.

I lay still until everything was quiet again. My ears were ringing when I got to my feet. The steps were a shambles of broken concrete. I scrambled down them and ran past the jitney. I didn't stop to study the damage, but it had taken the worst of the explosion. The side nearer the steps was collapsed in on the seats. The bad brakes were the least of the jitney's problems now.

What a beautiful sight Mike's landlady's old green car was as it rolled slowly into the parking lot. Jerking open the passenger door, I jumped in.

Mike had his hand on the ignition key. He stared at me, eyes wide.

"What the hell was that?"

"A diversion. Don't turn off the engine. We have to go to the police station."

"You mean before we even *try* another date?"

"Yes."

Throwing the car into reverse, he backed out of the lot. "Okay. It seems to be inevitable, doesn't it?"

TWENTY

A WEEK LATER

Yesterday, Colin Ledbetter was formally charged with Leslie's murder. He languishes in the Nassau jail, his foot in a cast. I wonder if he's still smiling.

It has taken a while for the bits and pieces surrounding Leslie's death to begin falling into place. Neticia is partly to blame. She was located at her home on Andros Island with no trouble, but I understand that getting her cooperation has been an uphill battle. I haven't seen a transcript of her statement, but Chief Richards tells me it is full of references to the devil eye.

Neticia has confessed to some of the things I'd heard her accused of: listening behind doors, snooping and stealing.

Upset by the devil eye's visit to the Ledbetters' home, Neticia listened behind the door and overheard Tyndall agreeing to falsify his records. Neticia later snooped through Tyndall's campsite. When she found both his accurate and false records, she took them.

To Neticia's dismay, her friend Leslie was friendly with the devil eye. Neticia told Leslie about the fraud, hoping her friend would see the light about this bad man.

Leslie saw the light, all right! With her eye on the prize—

Tyndall himself—she took the notes and tried using them as "persuasion."

Neticia doesn't know much about what happened next. She thinks she does. She thinks the devil eye killed Leslie for any number of perfectly understandable reasons, and then killed the flamingo chick to punish Neticia for stealing.

"Why didn't he kill you, then?" Chief Richards asked her.

"Because I was careful not to look in his eyes."

I expect that this part of her statement won't be of much use to the prosecution.

Neticia isn't aware that Leslie, having failed to persuade Tyndall, turned to Colin. It is not yet clear what Leslie asked of Colin. Colin's lawyer has advised him to admit to nothing. I suspect, though, that money was involved.

On the advice of *her* attorney, Eleanor Ledbetter isn't talking, either. Surely she will be charged with complicity, but for now she is free. She has taken Beth and gone to stay with her parents in Nassau.

Paul Tyndall has said that he knew nothing about Leslie's murder, or about the attack on me in the beach shack. I tend to believe him. Tyndall has a lawyer, too. His father came through, and one of Nassau's best defense attorneys has been retained. But Tyndall, who doesn't strike me as being nearly as intelligent as Leslie thought, admitted to falsifying his records and entering into a deal with Colin so that his debt at the casino would be forgiven. Those admissions were made before the attorney had been retained, though, and Tyndall now claims he made them under duress.

Charlie and Beast have returned to Flamingo Island. Charlie's taking the fishing parties out again, but when I saw him a couple of days ago, he said something about "hanging up" his mask and tank. I think his scuba instructing days are over.

The Flamingo Cove Hotel stands empty now. I went back there the morning after the explosion, accompanied by two policemen. The lobby was piled high with luggage. The Texans, who claim to have known nothing about anything, had already saddled up and ridden away, via private plane. I've heard that departing guests kept Flamingo Island's tiny taxi fleet busy all day. When I arrived at the hotel, the prim couple was just getting into one. She took a picture of me before they pulled away.

I met Mrs. Hussy and her two friends as they helped each other down the ruined stairway.

"Didn't I tell you all this tarting up would come to no good," Mrs. Hussy said.

The ladies were off to one of the French islands.

"We've been told it's quiet."

"And the food is better. No more suffering with that infernal conch."

Sonny and Cindy were at the desk with their luggage. As I passed, he shouted at me.

"Yo, Bonnie. You heard what's going on around here? With Colin and all. He's in the island clinic. Got a cop guarding him. I never trusted that guy. Too good to be true. You know what I mean?"

As Cindy listened to her husband, I saw something new in her face—an almost imperceptible tightening of her lips, a fleeting roll of her eyes. Annoyance. I wish them happiness, but who can say that they'll find it with each other?

My police escort and I passed the place where the dead chick is buried. The sight of that flimsy little cross made me shiver.

Once in my room, I gathered my things. I'd hidden Tyndall's records in Leslie's books. The falsified report was folded into the dog-eared pages of A *Heartbeat from Bliss*. The accurate pages were tucked between the pulsing purple covers of a romance about a pirate and an indentured servant. The pirate has a patch over one eye. The servant wears her blond hair flowing loose. After I turned Tyndall's reports over to the police, I pocketed that one. It might be good.

Maybe I'll have a chance to read it on the plane. Chief Richards got my ticket extended for a week, but tomorrow I must fly back to New York. For now . . .

I've been staying with Mike.

241

Yes, to almost anything you might be thinking. If I overlook my repeated visits with Chief Richards, these last days have been leisurely and sweet. I'll be returning to the Bahamas to testify, and will probably see Mike then. I don't hold much hope for us, though. This morning he started talking about the good life in Venezuela, and tried to tell me I could get by on my high school Spanish. I had to fight an almost overpowering urge to call the airline and confirm my flight to New York.

I must do something about my job situation. Deep inside, I am convinced that there is nothing in the want ads for me. But I'm not giving up. I can't. I'm too young for Social Security and too old to be adopted. As soon as I get back, I'm going to press my interview suit and polish my sensible pumps. For tonight, I'm an island girl, on island time.